ARLO BLACKWOOD, WYNNE COOPER, RACHEL
EMBER, ZELENA HOPE, CHU PARTRIDGE,
ELYSIA SONG, AND KATE VITTY

Not So Grimm: New Takes on Old Tales

Chestnut

Press

Contents

1

The Golden One and the Miller's Son by Wynne Cooper

O nce upon a time there lived a golden-haired boy with a bright mind and a not-so-bright future. He had the misfortune of being born a miller's son instead of a wealthy merchant's or a prince. Their town was small, poor, and unexceptional. There was little room for dreams in such a town, when there was flour to be made and fields to be sown. Instead of keeping his eyes firmly on the ground, the miller's son looked to the sky and dreamed.

His father noticed. Big dreams had a way of going wrong, of spinning away instead of closer, and he did not want such a fate for his only son. He boasted of his son's talents to all who would hear him, of his son's handiness at the mill. His strong hands and kind heart.

And, when he spoke to the king, he said to him: It is not only flour my son can make from grain, but gold!

For his son had a good brain on him too. He could sell the flour better than the miller ever could. It was a priceless gift, a good, kind son who would take care of him in his old age and earn enough to see them through the winters even when the miller began to grow old. It was all he needed in this world that was never quite kind enough.

Alas, the king only heard one word.

Gold.

The miller's son was brought to the king's mill and shown to the heaps of grain that would one day feed the inhabitants of the castle. He bid the miller's son to make gold of it by sunrise, lest he no longer keep his head. Escape was futile. The doors were locked and guarded from the outside and the windows were too small.

Tears did him little good. Neither did operating the mill. He was a good son and a good worker, but he could not make gold from grain, not without money changing hands the usual way. The miller's son wished his father had not been so free with his words. He wished he had quit his dreaming and told his father he would stay by his side until the end. And finally, he wished with all his might that he could grind grain into gold.

It was a foolish wish. But there was power in the number three and there was power in desperate hopes, the kind that are whispered on bruised and bent knees as night falls outside.

It was then that the Golden One appeared to the miller's son.

The miller boasted of his son's golden tongue, but it could not compare to the promises of the Golden One, who bargained with kings and queens and peasants alike, taking all that he could from desperate men and women.

It was to the miller's son that the Golden One spoke his words: What will you give me if I grind this grain into gold?

And the miller's son gave him his ring, for it was the most valuable object he owned. His clothes were dirty and plain, but this ring had once been his grandfather's, and he kept it around his neck on a cord. This was the first thing that the Golden One would take from him.

* * *

Caleb crossed the forest with the look of a man who had certainly seen worse days, but perhaps not recently. His clothing was plain but hardy and his fingers curled around the map that he worked to decipher ever since he learned of its existence. Only three days ago, it had led him to the small, quiet town on the edge of the forest, and now it led him into the forest itself. His footsteps were sure and his spirits were high.

This would be the day, Caleb swore to himself.

If not, then today, he would be drained by mosquitoes until there was no blood left in his body.

Caleb slapped one more off his arm, sighing at the red mark that remained. He would have preferred dealing with vampires. At least they would take heed of a wooden stake and a muscled arm that knew what to do with one.

Squinting down at his map, Caleb followed the trail first with his eyes, then with his feet. Both led him to a house deep in the woods. It was of sturdy wooden make with a small garden in front, encircled by a wealth of purple flowers.

Caleb's heartbeat was loud in his ears as he approached the door and knocked. His words, now practiced for so long, held his tongue down like stones. What did he have to offer this man, truly? A hand, a sword, some small manner of income. Would it be enough?

The door opened. Behind it stood a man Caleb had not seen in a decade.

The Golden One hadn't changed. His name came not from his hair, but from the wealth he tricked and bargained out of so many people—but it could have, for it was golden under the summer's light. His eyes were sharper than Caleb's sword. Even now, surprised as he must be to see Caleb once more.

"I have come to renegotiate our bargain," Caleb said to him. His words came out all strange, like he was speaking from a far distance. He could barely believe that he had found this man again after so long. "If you are agreeable, I will—"

"You can have her," scoffed the Golden One.

Caleb hadn't moved. He was wrong-footed all the same. "What?"

Glancing behind himself, the Golden One reached for something—some-one—and shoved a girl out the door and in Caleb's direction. Caleb kept her from falling, though she did not seem perturbed by the Golden One's handling. She looked back at the closing door and yelled, "You're not getting rid of me, Dad!"

"Yes, I am," called the Golden One from inside the house. "I'll finally have some peace and quiet."

The girl gave a loud harrumph at this.

When she looked at Caleb, her gaze was as shrewd as her father's, though her eyes and hair were much darker, and she could not boast of the same height. She was a slight thing and perhaps only eight or so. Her voice was

3

firm. "I am not going anywhere with you."

"Of course not," Caleb replied. This was not what he came to bargain for. Well, not exactly.

With a nod, the girl picked up a basket sitting by the door and began to walk. She didn't turn around as she said, "If you want, you can go somewhere with me."

It was not her company that Caleb sought. But with one last look toward the closed door of the cottage, he decided that hers was the only company that he would receive at the moment. And she did seem like rather adorable company. Caleb followed her onto the forest path that somehow made itself available to them in a way it hadn't before.

"It annoys him when I call him Dad," she said by way of explanation, which was no explanation at all. As they walked along the path, Caleb noted that she did not seem to be in low spirits, nor worried about her so-called father attempting to give her up. "I'm Mabel. Who are you?"

"Caleb."

She shook her head. "No, not your name. Who are you?"

Caleb sighed. "Doesn't he tell you names?"

"Did he get your name?"

Memories threatened a resurgence. Bad ones, worse ones, and... maybe one or two that weren't so bad. "He did."

She shrugged. "He never gave it to me. He never gave me my name, either. He told me I had to choose it myself. It's because—"

"—names have power," Caleb finished, smiling despite himself. "He told me that, too. I'm the miller's son."

Thankfully, she didn't ask him which miller. Perhaps the Golden One was not in the habit of bargaining with many miller's sons. They had so little to offer him. Caleb still could barely believe that he had met the Golden One himself. It was like a book of stories had opened itself for him, with Caleb's own name on the page.

Or rather, the miller's son. It seemed that Caleb's name hadn't made it into the Golden One's own book of tales.

"He made grain into gold for you!" said Mabel, remembering him quickly.

"Because an evil king said that if you didn't, he would kill you. But my father saved you."

"For a price," Caleb agreed.

Mabel nodded. "There's always a price."

She said the words with the ease of someone who has never been made to pay a price. With a painful swallow, Caleb wondered if it had been her parents who paid the price instead. The man of cruel tales and mothers' warnings seemed like the type to take her as his right. But when Caleb looked at her, he reminded himself that she was cheerful, curious, and healthy. There was no sullenness to her, nor bruises. If she was someone's price, then she was a very treasured price indeed.

"Did you marry the king?" she asked eagerly. "That's what they do in all the stories. The Golden One saves someone and then they marry princes and dukes and kings. I don't see why anyone would want to marry a king—they're very old, you know—but maybe he had a princess for you to marry as a thank you for the gold."

Caleb huffed, shaking his head. He rarely spoke of his time inside the king's mill. He never knew where to start. It was a strange tale, horrible and not, ancient history compared to the present. Ten years was a very long time. Boys became men, and millers' sons became handy with swords and careful with words.

Leaving the forest brought Caleb out of his thoughts. "It took me days to find your home. I was nearly bled dry by the bugs. I'm up to my knees in mud. And you can get out of the forest in less than an hour?"

"It's magic," she replied. She had an air of smugness that was either inherited or learned. Caleb remembered it on the Golden One, when the man appeared in the king's mill with all sorts of teases and promises. "You didn't answer my question."

"You're a sharp one."

Mabel grinned at him. She was missing a tooth. "Thank you."

"I didn't marry the king," Caleb said to her. "He held me captive, remember? He ordered me to do the impossible, driven mad by his greed, and I was only a peasant. My life meant very little to him. I would never have married

5

him."

Mabel led him out of the forest. Together, they walked the path to the village that Caleb had spent one night in. "But it was your gold. Didn't you want to keep it?"

"It was your father's gold."

"He made it, but you bargained for it."

"Then, it was the king's, since it was made from his grain." Caleb sighed, thinking of those mountains of gold as high as his head, and of the man who invited him to climb the top of one, both laughing and helping Caleb when he fell. In that moment, Caleb felt powerful and rich, but one could not keep both his head and his gold on the king's land. Something had to give. Caleb enjoyed his continued life very much. His head may have led him into trouble on occasion, but he preferred it to be attached to his shoulders. "I wanted it. Of course I wanted it. But I wanted to leave more than I wanted gold or power or marriage." He looked her way and held her steady gaze. "Isn't there something you want more than gold?"

"Dad says there isn't anything more important than gold. That's why they call him the Golden One."

Caleb hummed and stayed silent.

With a disgruntled sound, Mabel said, "I want to study magic more than I want gold. But I still want some gold. A room filled with gold, but not a lake filled with gold."

"Very sensible," Caleb said to her, hiding a smile.

Mabel looked at him like she could tell what he was doing, but soon they were both distracted by the sounds and sights of the village. In contrast to their walk through the forest, she walked close to him. Their arms brushed on occasion and her expression gained a pinched look. Caleb's fingers twitched. He wanted to comfort her, to hold her hand. She was a strange child and she was the Golden One's, but she was still just a child.

Caleb stood beside her as she bought eggs and meat and bread with golden coins. Mabel was not treated unkindly, but there was a distance between her and the villagers. It prodded at Caleb's heart, which was all too soft already.

"They don't like me much," Mabel admitted. "They think I'm strange."

"It doesn't matter what they think." Ignoring all of the reasons not to, Caleb held his hand out to her and smiled when she took it. He picked up the basket with his other hand, ignoring her momentary protest. "Let me carry it for you?"

She was silent for a moment. "Fine. But you have to tell me a story on the walk home."

"My stories are too long for the walk. I have a tendency to ramble."

"We'll walk slowly," she replied. Her walk was lighter out of the village than toward it. Caleb's was, too.

* * *

You must know that the Golden One was not a kind man. He always asked for too much. His words were simple and his tone was light, but he was unkind in his bargains. He danced on the blade of cruelty, him and his magical hands. On the first night, he took the ring from the miller's son and placed it in his pocket. He did not ask for more that night.

Magic was not without its own price. The Golden One labored all night to turn grain into gold, working tirelessly as the miller's son sorted the gold from the grain and brought him more. Thrice, the miller's son brought him water, and each time they spoke of everything and nothing. There was a certain recklessness on the eve of one's possible death. His tongue loosened by worry and tiredness, the miller's son spoke of everything he wished to do if he made it out of the king's mill with his life. He would travel the world. He would learn the way of the sword. And he would embrace his father, because despite everything, the miller's son was a kind son. He was not as dutiful as he wished, nor did he want to work in the mill forever, but he forgave his father almost instantly for the situation.

The Golden One called him a fool for it. With a sigh, the miller's son agreed, looking down at the gold bar in his hand. It was surprisingly heavy. He had never seen so much wealth in one place and knew he never would again.

In the morning, the Golden One vanished, and the king returned. He rejoiced to find that his grain had become gold, embracing the miller's son and inviting him to dine with him. It was not a request.

The miller's son feasted at the same table as the king.

The next night, he found himself locked inside the mill once more. All the gold had been removed, replaced with grain for him to toil over. There was more grain than there had been last night. The king would not listen to his pleas.

This time, the miller's son did not cry. He sat down on top of a pile of grain, since there was nowhere else to sit, and he waited.

The Golden One appeared in all his splendid glory and his cruelty, for he would not help the miller's son escape from the king. He would only ask his question: What will you give me if I grind this grain into gold?

The miller's son had nothing material left to give. He sought something immaterial: I will give you a secret, one that I have held all my life.

With a smile, the Golden One accepted this bargain. Words had power, but secrets had more. There was magic in a secret held for so long, especially one that rested against the heart of the miller's son, one that had him so troubled to share. As the Golden One worked harder than he had the night before, turning even more grain into gold, he listened to the story the miller's son told of the princess who escaped from her father's castle and hid in the village mill until the guards stopped searching for her. Only the miller's son had helped her, listening to her stories of the cruel king and ignoring the gold offered for her to be brought back to the castle. It was treason and, as the Golden One told him, it was terribly stupid.

The miller's son only shook his head and said: It worked.

Not even his father knew of the precious cargo the village mill once held. The princess could not part with the small amount of gold she escaped with, for she would need it for her own journey, but the miller's son said her thanks were enough.

The Golden One continued to work his magic. When asked if it was payment enough, this secret, the Golden One said: for tonight, yes.

It was on the third night that the Golden One asked for his customary price, that of the firstborn of the miller's son, should he have children in the future.

* * *

Mabel's hand was small within his own. She listened with rapt attention as Caleb told her of his travels to find the Golden One. It took him a year, but finally he made it here. A little poorer, with one more scar, and with more stories than he wanted to tell, but he found him again. Caleb couldn't regret his decision, no matter how this story ended. He didn't regret making his bargain and he didn't regret the time spent tracking down the Golden One.

It was human nature to want more. As a boy, Caleb wanted to travel. As a man, who had put his father and his wanderlust to rest, Caleb wanted to settle down.

Caleb looked at the cottage with new eyes as he and Mabel approached it, basket laden with goods and spirits lighter with stories. It was this that he wanted, if he looked within his heart: a place to rest his head, a partner to love, and a son or daughter to hold. When he made his bargain, he hadn't been old enough to appreciate that he might want children one day. That the thought of giving away his firstborn would leave him with grief and terror.

Mabel opened the door without knocking. When Caleb hesitated on the porch, she said, "Come on. You can tell Dad your stories, too." She tugged him inside and Caleb went willingly. "We're home!"

She abandoned him with his basket and with her father, who peered at him from the sitting area, to speed out into the woods again, yelling something about catching a glitterfly.

"So you've decided to return her to me," said the Golden One.

Maybe it was Mabel's influence or the effect of the stories that Caleb told of the past, which brought a glow to it and let the terror fade, but the Golden One looked less intimidating than he had earlier. For all that he was handsome and tricky and magical, he was still only a man.

"She's yours," Caleb said, shaking his head. "I wouldn't take her from you."

"Like I took her from her parents?" the Golden One stepped closer, peering into the basket. "Too many eggs. We'll never eat them all."

Still, he took the basket, and Caleb followed him into the kitchen out of a lack of anything else to do. "Did you steal her, really? Is this what you do with firstborns?"

"Give them away to the first person who comes knocking?"

"Love them," Caleb said, sitting down at the kitchen table. "Care for them. Let them run amok and catch glitterflies."

It was forward of him. Much more so than he ever had been with the Golden One, all those years ago. But Caleb had been young and scared. Now, he was older and he was cautious, but even in his short time in Mabel's presence, he could see love. She was so very loved, growing up without fear or shame.

The Golden One looked away. There was color in his cheeks. Caleb delighted in the fact that his words had put it there. When the Golden One looked at him again, it was to needle him. "But you still don't trust me with your firstborn."

"I want to raise my child. It's not such a terrible thing to ask."

Before Caleb's very eyes, the teapot boiled its own water and a teacup landed in front of him. The Golden One glared at the devices, and said to them, "Stop that. He's not staying."

The teapot whistled in response. Two sugars flew into Caleb's cup, just how he liked it.

With a roll of his eyes, the Golden One settled into the chair next to Caleb and another teacup joined them. "Not all people are so overjoyed at the thought of parenthood. Mabel's parents offered her in their bargain to me when she was small. She was unwanted. There is great magic in the potential of the bargain of firstborns, but I rarely collect on it. I have no need of children."

"One is enough?" Caleb asked, failing to suppress the amusement he felt.

"I could hardly let go of a bargain. Even a loud, silly one."

Caleb glanced down into his cup. "Does that mean you won't renegotiate with me?"

When he looked up again, he found the Golden One's gaze had never left him. It was something very special, to be looked at by a man such as this. Caleb had seen him at his cruelest, bargaining with a poor peasant boy in over his head, and now he thought he saw him at his kindest. There was love and kindness woven into the very wood of this house. The Golden One's eyes were warm when he spoke of Mabel. The tales of him never told of this.

"What do you have to offer me?" asked the Golden One, leaning forward. "Ten years is a long time. I hardly have the time for bargains anymore. It will have to be something special to tempt me into my old ways."

All year, Caleb had practiced his words. He intended to give the Golden One his time or his sword or his aid. Perhaps the Golden One would send him on a quest or he would make him labor in the fields. Now, Caleb realized that the Golden One had no need of anything Caleb had. His hard edges had been worn away. Perhaps they came back occasionally, for the right price or situation, but he was no longer the man who appeared in the king's mill.

"I—I still have nothing to offer you," Caleb said, feeling as though no time had passed, and he was a teen again. "I can't ask you to be the man you were."

They were so close that Caleb saw every minute shift of the Golden One's expression. Finally, a small smile made its way onto the Golden One's lips. "You haven't changed."

"I have," Caleb began to argue.

He only stopped because he was being kissed. It was hard to argue with the Golden One's lips on his own. Caleb needed no encouragement to kiss him back, to knock his teacup to the side and reach for the man next to him. The very first time he thought about this, he had been sitting on a pile of gold. It had been the first, but not the last.

When the Golden One pulled away, his words echoed with magic. "For the price of a kiss, you may keep your firstborn."

"What about the price of two kisses?" Caleb asked, and instead of finding out, he simply kissed him again.

It was reckless and just a little bit perfect. When the Golden One asked him to stay, Caleb agreed, though he did not promise it. Maybe one day he would.

* * *

On the third night, the Golden One turned grain to gold once again, after receiving the promise of the firstborn of the miller's son. This time, the promise left the miller's son sullen and angry. It was one thing to give away his ring and his secret, but another thing entirely to promise a child to a man such as this.

And still he did, for he wanted to live.

With a laugh, the Golden One asked him if this unknown, unborn child was more important than the favors the king would give to the miller's son in return for the gold. He said to the miller's son: He will marry you and you will feast every day. Will that not make you happy?

The miller's son shook his head. Again, he reminded the Golden One of his dreams of travel and adventure.

The Golden One did nothing for free. He made untold bargains, swindled royalty and geniuses, and enjoyed his reputation. The miller's son had nothing more to give him. Nothing that would prevent the king from marrying him, for one could *not say no to a king such as this, who would not listen to a miller's son with golden hands.*

Once his work was done, the Golden One bid the miller's son farewell.

But instead of vanishing, the Golden One opened the door, which had been locked moments ago. The guards were nowhere to be found. The miller's son followed him from the mill, relief and joy in his expression.

Within moments, the Golden One vanished.

The miller's son escaped the king and lived happily ever after, as any story will tell you. In some versions of the tale, he married a princess or sailed the seas. But in one version, he knocked on the door of a cottage in the woods, and he found his happiness there, waiting for him to claim it.

2

Breath of Roses by Rachel Ember

When their mother fell in battle and Ruby and Scarlet were brought to Grandmother's tower, Ruby was three and Scarlet was five. Every night after that, for years, Ruby crept from her chamber to Scarlet's, where Scarlet would pull back the blankets without entirely waking up and Ruby would crawl in beside her.

However, as they grew older, Scarlet became closer to Grandmother, spending more and more time at her side. Ruby never grew comfortable in Grandmother's forbidding presence, so she spent most of *her* time alone in her own chamber with her ink and paints. Eventually, she slept there too.

Ruby was eighteen now, and the war drew ever closer to the walls of the tower. It had been many years since she'd gone to Scarlet for comfort, but when the pulse of some distant explosion reverberated through the tower with enough force that her bed trembled, she untangled herself from her sheets and slid to the floor, half-awake and frightened, moving almost without thought.

Before she knew it she was down the corridor and at Scarlet's door. Though the years had carved rifts between them, Ruby felt better as soon as she passed through Scarlet's door and inhaled the minty smell of her sister's favorite soap. The dark, quiet chamber was almost identical to Ruby's. The ceiling tapered to a point two dozen feet overheard, with a single high window. A circular bed sat in the center of the space. The only real difference between

Ruby's chamber and this one was that Scarlet's shelves were filled with tidy rows of books instead of Ruby's random trinkets, brushes, and messy pots of paint and ink.

On the bed, nested in pillows, sat Scarlet. The sisters looked alike in many ways. They were both pale-skinned and as lean as boys. Scarlet's hair, though, was a lighter shade of red than Ruby's, and to Grandmother's chagrin, she kept it very long in the new fashion. It fell all the way to her shoulders in soft waves, whereas Ruby's was darker and cut close to her head. Not because Ruby was traditional, but because long hair annoyed her. The extra length suited Scarlet. Ruby paused to admire how ethereal her sister looked, her face as silver as the starlight in the high window, framed by hair as bright as flame.

Scarlet must have caught sight of Ruby in the corner of her eye, or maybe she'd heard the quiet rush of the door closing. With no outward expression of surprise or turn of her head, she patted the place on the cushions beside her.

Ruby crawled across the bed to Scarlet, thrusting her cold feet beneath the blankets. Scarlet took her hand for the first time in years.

"Can they really do it?" Ruby whispered. "The anarchists?" It was hard to believe anyone or anything could overpower the Queen of the Red Vine, but so many of the blood were already gone. The anarchists were clever; with their tools of glinting metal and fire, they had done what the kings had said was impossible, and brought the war so close to the tower that Ruby could practically hear the warriors' shouts.

Scarlet lay back, pulling Ruby with her, so that Ruby's cheek rested on Scarlet's collarbone. The ridge of bone was uncomfortably sharp, but her sister's body was warm in the cold chamber, so she didn't move away. Scarlet's voice rumbled in her chest when she answered. "I do not know."

"What does Grandmother say?"

Scarlet huffed, not quite laughing. "Grandmother speaks in riddles and old stories. She does not tell me what she expects." She paused and added more quietly, "But she is not at ease. That much is clear."

Ruby didn't expect Grandmother to pour her heart out to anyone, not even Scarlet, but it was still strange to hear Scarlet speak of Grandmother in this way—with frustration. They'd always seemed to be of one mind, at least for the past few years.

Through the high window, Ruby could see a shard of starry darkness. Usually she took comfort from the sky's bright tranquility. Not tonight, though.

When Scarlet's breathing turned even and her eyes closed, Ruby burrowed against Scarlet's shoulder and closed her eyes, too. But sleep still didn't come...not for hours. Hours which she spent adrift between the placidity of the stars above the tower and the tumultuousness of the war below it.

* * *

The next morning, the tower was cold and dark. Ruby and Scarlet dressed in their warmest clothes in silence, then went to the greenhouse.

The greenhouse was a tall, columnar chamber just like the other portions of the tower, but larger. Its only window was its ceiling—a single, pentagonal skylight some fraction of the size of the floor, because like the other chambers in the tower, the greenhouse walls sloped as they ascended to a narrow apex.

On the long bench in the middle of the chamber, the greenhouse's only furnishing, sat Grandmother. She wore one of the identical plain, long dresses she wore daily, the velvet a green so dark that it looked black in the dim light. Climbing the bench to either side of Grandmother and spread on the floor beneath her feet were the last of the unpruned vines, delicate fingers of brilliant green interspersing with the withered old growth. Some of the dormant vines were as thick as Ruby's waist. These husks were the majority of what plastered the walls and carpeted the corners.

Grandmother relished every chance she got to tell Ruby and Scarlet old lore of the vine. She always told the same three stories. Yet she never told them quite the same way. Ruby had come to think of each story as a rose in full bloom, and each variation on the telling as a single, vibrant petal.

She liked the image, even though she couldn't remember the last time she'd seen a rose; the vine had long been fighting for its life against the anarchists and couldn't spare the effort to bloom. Though, until recently, the war had been waged far from the tower, to the extent that Ruby could almost forget it was happening at all, the solemn utility of the vine had always been a reminder.

Scarlet left Ruby's side and walked the periphery of the chamber, trailing her fingertips over the ridges of vine running vertically up the walls, the starlight lighting the crown of her head like a silver circlet. Ruby put her hands in her pockets, curled into fists to protect them from the chill. In times of peace, the vine would fill the tower with warmth and perfume, but those days were as distant as the days of roses.

"What's this?" Scarlet asked, getting Ruby's attention. Scarlet leaned against her knees to peer into a wooden pail resting on the floor, partially shrouded by a patch of leafy vine.

"Moonsalt," Grandmother answered, still seated on her bench. Ruby joined Scarlet, bending over the pail herself. The substance inside looked like a million miniature crystals; it seemed to give off its own soft light.

Someone knocked at the greenhouse doorway. Grandmother left her bench to answer. Ruby only saw the outline of a person in the shadowed corridor outside the chamber, but she knew it must be a warrior, here to make a report. They came at least once a day.

When Grandmother returned, Ruby burned with curiosity, but didn't bother asking Grandmother what the warrior had told her. She knew Grandmother wouldn't answer.

Scarlet was combing her fingers through the moonsalt. Ruby stole a glance at Grandmother, almost expecting Scarlet to be scolded for touching. But when Grandmother only watched them, her expression as stony and unrevealing as always, Ruby dipped her own fingers into the pail. She shuddered; it was so cold that she felt the faintest burn in her skin. She pulled her hand back and rubbed her tingling fingers against her palm.

The quiet in the greenhouse bothered Ruby more than the cold. She'd often wondered what Grandmother and Scarlet spoke of in their hours here, together. She hadn't thought Grandmother was spilling secrets and strategies, but neither had she expected the heavy silence.

Picking up on her sister's unease, Scarlet caught Ruby's eye and smiled.

"Grandmother," Scarlet asked, "will you tell a story?"

Ruby's eyes widened. Surely, in the middle of the bloodiest war in five hundred years, Grandmother would not even dignify that question with an answer.

Then again, Scarlet knew Grandmother best.

Adjusting her skirts around her knees and resting her hand absently on a coil of withered vine, Grandmother cleared her throat and began to spin a new petal on an old rose.

"The Queen of the Red Vine was first a princess, adrift for a thousand years, fated to sleep until a worthy king's son should find her."

"Is there such a thing as a worthy king's son?" Scarlet arched an eyebrow, a line of red-gold that was perfectly drawn against her pale brow. She was clever; even Grandmother thought so. But Grandmother disliked interruptions, so the look she cast upon Scarlet was not amused.

Ruby knew the story well, yet she was still curious. How would Grandmother tell it today?

"When the fire of the vine had almost burned out, and with it all hope, the last breath of the fallen queen sent a contingent of travelers to the princess's vessel—including the king's son who was fated to wake her..."

* * *

The day Theo seizes his royal inheritance begins early. He wants to inventory the ship's systems while the rest of the crew is still asleep and won't bother him. The *Destrier* is operating with a skeleton crew, just its Captain, navigator, two swabs for muscle, and one swab for maintenance duty—Theo.

The Destrier crew, like most pirates, are a superstitious lot; they take their cycles very seriously. Barring an emergency, when the clock (which tracks station time no matter how far they are from Aurora) tells them they should be in their cots—roughly, from the twenty-second hour mark until the seventh—in their cots they stay.

But Theo isn't a real pirate. He doesn't believe in bad luck and he prefers to be alone. So, he moves carefully through the corridors just before the fourth mark, pulling the instrument cart behind him and flinching when its wobbly left rear wheel emits a squeal.

He's surprised anyone can sleep at all. Not because he's going past crew quarters while pulling a cart that occasionally makes a sound like fingernails on glass, but because, any minute now, the ship's autopilot will bring them to the prize they've crossed half a galaxy to find.

Another less-than-relaxing fact is that they're perilously low on fuel and oxygen since setting off from Aurora station. The smallest setback could seal a grim fate. Aurora pirates can't just mosey into any way station they please and resupply, which is why they always keep sufficient stores to get them all the way home. They've pushed their range to its limits this time. At their current rate, unless they have to flee an interloper—not uncommon for pirate crews—they'll run out of oxygen before they run out of fuel. An exciting gamble. Theo can't wait to find out how they'll all die.

He shouldn't even be there. If *Destrier* hadn't lost half her crew in her last voyage, he wouldn't be. It was only desperation that had made the old man conscript Theo from janitor duty on Aurora, bringing him on for maintenance duty on the *Destrier*. Theo has never imagined himself on any crew, but that he's wound up *here*, aboard *Silv's* ship, is the cruelest of ironies.

Silv is the irritatingly blond, young, and handsome captain of the *Destrier*. Young for a Captain, that is; he's close to Theo's age, around twenty-three. Theo hates Silv, and his list of reasons why is long and varied. It includes Silv being vain, spoiled, and leveraging his good looks to influence women, and the fact that Theo harbors an overwhelming desire to see Silv naked, along with a persistent fantasy of kissing his stupid, constant smile.

But he isn't thinking about Silv right now. He's blissfully alone for at least a couple more hours, and he finds the tedium of running system maintenance pleasantly hypnotic. This is the closest Theo ever gets to relaxation, and he's determined to savor it.

Unfortunately, luck—which he *doesn't* believe in—isn't with him. When he enters the bridge, he does a double-take. The bridge isn't clear.

Silv is here.

Theo can't even slink back the way he came before he's noticed because the squeaky wheel on the cart turns to the fatal angle as it rolls behind him. If the near-silent *whoosh* of the opening hatch didn't alert Silv to his presence, the sharp wail of metal on metal has.

The tall, muscular man spins on his heel and has his hand on his fire baton within a half-second. By then, Theo has hastily released the cart and raised his hands.

"It's only me," Theo says.

Somehow, he's avoided speaking to Silv before now. There are plenty of things he's muttered under his breath in Silv's direction, sure, but they don't count if he never meant them to be overheard, right? So, these are practically their first words.

Not that Theo cares.

"Sorry," Silv says, frowning. His eyes are narrowed, and he wears a vacant sort of expression. Is he drunk? Theo's gaze skirts the bridge again, half-expecting to see a bottle somewhere. The consoles are clear, though he has to narrow his eyes to see. The bridge is dark except for the illumination beyond the viewscreen. They're very near the gaseous red planet the old man's pings sent them toward—or, more specifically, its moon.

In fact, the view from the bridge is incredible at the moment. So incredible, Theo ignores Silv with his fire baton dangling from his hand, and his possible drunkenness, in favor of stepping nearer the pane of clearide.

The red planet's moon all but fills the viewscreen, framed by the cusp of the planet beyond like it wears a fiery halo. The moon is nothing special, just a pitted white rock. But what it has managed to attract to its feeble gravitational field is nothing short of extraordinary.

An imperial pod hangs in the space between the *Destrier* and the moon. It looms several times the size of the *Destrier*, egg-shaped, dark as a void, blotting out the pearly moon behind it like a tear in canvas. It's by far the largest pod Theo has ever seen. It's also larger than anything he's heard described in the veterans' exaggerated reminiscences.

And its size isn't the only thing unique about it. The pod's skin is dark with vitality, not the leached pale green they usually see. It's very much alive.

Theo shudders, the hair on his arms standing on end. He blinks and looks back at Silv, and their eyes meet. Theo understands the faraway, drunk look on Silv's face from before. Now, Theo probably wears the same one.

"What *is* it?" Theo asks, though he knows. He knows.

Silv grimaces and folds his arms so that his jumpsuit pulls taught over his biceps, molded to every muscle. The collar and first four buttons are unfastened, the fabric gaping apart. Theo has often privately mused that if Silv squeezed into a suit that was even a half-size smaller than the painted-on numbers he usually wears, his voice would rise an octave.

But his deep voice is intact when he murmurs, "No telling."

Theo tries to remain outwardly calm while his heart leaps and hammers. The old man's voice rings in his ears, reminding him of a promise that he never imagined he'd have to make good on.

Because what are the odds that, in the vastness of the universe, the imperial spore of the Red Vine would be found at all?

Let alone in his lifetime?

Let alone *by him*?

"Okay there, swab?" Silv's voice interrupts his thoughts—threaded with what sounds like sincere concern, but it grates anyway. That he'd think Theo was anything but okay. That he'd refer to Theo in the same casual way he does the other crew members. Why these things bother Theo so much, he can't say, but for whatever reason he grits his teeth, his momentary despair overridden by irritation.

"I'm fine," he mutters. "You mustering the crew, then? Or just letting them get their beauty sleep while we burn some more fuel idling here and staring?"

Theo has not excelled at subservience in the best of times, and his meager skill has apparently dissolved now that he's simultaneously being confronted with his destiny *and* the need to actually speak to Silv.

To Theo's mystification, Silv doesn't seem at all bothered by Theo's insolence. Instead, Silv is grinning, his deep blue eyes bright and fixed on Theo in delighted surprise. While Theo glares back, Silv rolls his shoulders and deliberately angles his body away from the viewscreen, toward the hatch.

"Good point, swab. You run your little tests in here. I'll get out of your hair and rouse them."

Theo's *little tests* include the delicate diagnostics and recalibrations that keep the ship environment habitable—in other words, they're the reason why the entire crew is alive. Silv *knows* this, presumably, so Theo assumes he's deliberately making light of the significance of Theo's work.

"Thanks," Theo bites out, scowling when Silv's smile widens further and a dimple blooms in either cheek. Maddening. The kissing fantasy has never been stronger during waking hours, but it's neck-and-neck with the punching fantasy.

Theo hunches his shoulders, returns to his cart, and hauls it clear of the hatchway. He feels a childish rush of satisfaction when the wheel squeals yet again. Sure, it cuts into Theo's ears like a knife, but Silv winces too.

"Get suited up when you're done and meet us in the belly" is Silv's parting order. When the hatch has closed behind him Theo wilts against the cart, burying his face in his hands.

The only thing propping him up had been the rigid exterior he always maintains in Silv's presence, and now that Silv is gone, all of his trepidation redoubles and guts him.

You are a king's son. The old man's words echo in his head.

"But I was raised a stowaway, a station rat. I'm nothing now but a janitor." He knows he's talking to himself, but the words rush out anyway.

None of that matters. You are the blood of the vine. And when we find her, it will be you who wakes her.

After forcing a few deep breaths, Theo tears free of his thoughts to focus on the system calibrations. It's delicate work, and mistakes can be catastrophic. But it's a challenge to give the familiar, tedious work the undivided attention it deserves when he knows that as soon as he finishes, he will be putting on a space-ready jumpsuit to breach an imperial spore.

There is a chance, however small, that Theo is wrong about what they've found. It's possible that the monstrosity just beyond the viewscreen is just an oversized, oddly power-packed pod like so many others the old man's gang of pirates has found and harvested over the past few decades. Maybe it's not the fabled imperial spore that so many—the new order and the dwindling numbers of vine loyalists alike—believe to be their ultimate downfall or only salvation.

But Theo knows he isn't the only one who thinks it's more than that. He saw the expression on Silv's face, after all.

He shakes his head hard as if the external movement can banish the internal thoughts. "*Fuck*," he mutters. He's been completely tuned out through the entire sweep of the arsenal console. He'll have to start over. He consciously clears his mind as his hands slide across the keyed sensors, leading with his thumbs. A formally-trained technician would initiate commands more from the ring finger, but when Theo began teaching himself, that position always strained his wrists. From the time he was five or six, he observed a range of technicians from the station air vents, then dropped from the ceiling after-hours to emulate what he'd seen them do. He'd set off a lot of alarms and had several close calls with capture before he got the hang of it.

Now, his run-through of the tactile controls completed, he holds his hands clear of the sensors and stares unblinking at the screen until the retinal scan activates. Then he goes through all the standard commands he just performed tactilely, this time with eye movements. It's an intuitive method, but he still has to go slowly; there are limits to the skills gleaned through an air-vent apprenticeship.

When he finishes, he checks the read-out on the instrument cart and sees a row of green lights: all is well. After powering the instrument down, he grabs the cart and starts back across the bridge, the squeaky wheel rattling along.

For a moment it's just another morning, like all the mornings on this voyage so far. Tripping over that thought, Theo pauses in the hatchway and looks over his shoulder.

The silent panorama is still there in the rectangle of transparent ship's skin. His fleeting hope that he hallucinated the last half-hour vanishes.

With a sigh, he pushes the cart out into the corridor and back to the maintenance closet where it's kept secured in a hollow part of the wall, then heads to his quarters to change into his ready suit.

Standard-issue jumpsuits never fit Theo right. He plucks at the baggy fabric around his hips with a frown as he emerges from his quarters, helmet dangling from his other hand. He almost collides with the other three members of Silv's understaffed, overextended crew.

"You," Mika says tersely by way of greeting, giving him a once-over, eyes narrowed behind her spiky black bangs. "You're coming with?"

The question seems rhetorical since she can't miss Theo's suit, so he doesn't bother answering.

"Better get going." Chels is already wearing her helmet; the speaker on the back emits her voice with a slight distortion.

She nudges Mika forward with a sidelong glance and nod of greeting for Theo, which he returns. Theo exchanges the same gesture with Pilar, the navigator, then silently falls into step behind them. Pilar coiled the braid of her unusually long hair at the nape of her neck. It reminds him of a shiny, sleeping serpent.

Shorter hair is more common around Aurora—easier to care for and out of the way. Other than Pilar, Theo can count on one hand the number of people he's seen with hair long enough to braid or tie back, though that looks more manageable than Silv's golden hair, which is somewhere in the middle. It can be tucked behind his ears, but it seems to flop constantly over his eyes. Impractical, if frustratingly cute.

Silv is waiting for them in the *Destrier's* belly. "All ready?" he asks, sweeping them with a look. His gaze snags on Theo and he frowns. "Tech, is that jumpsuit going to inhibit you? It looks two sizes too big."

Theo can't stop himself, making a point of looking Silv over from his jumpsuit-encased boots, up the visible line of his calf, and over the bulge of muscle in his thighs and chest. "Maybe I should borrow yours. It looks about right."

Pilar and Mika snicker.

"Ohhh," Chels says, grinning at them. She positions her helmet and flips the seal under her chin, so that her voice is tinny through the external speaker as she singsongs, "You got *burned*, Cap."

Silv's cheeks are a warm pale pink, the faintest blush. Instead of smug, the sight of it inexplicably makes Theo even surlier.

Pilar is the only one without a ready suit. She steps back out of the belly with a salute.

"Have a good walk," she calls in farewell.

When everyone has double-checked their rigs, Pilar's voice comes through the comm inside Theo's helmet, tickling his ear. *"All set, unit?"*

They each signal affirmatively, and she initiates depressurization in preparation for releasing the exterior hatch. There's a low whistling noise, the only noticeable sign that their lives now depend on the integrity of the ready suits.

"*Here we go,*" Silv says. He may as well be whispering straight into Theo's ears, and it makes him shudder.

They engage thrusters when the belly depressurization is complete. Then, the hatch lowers. Theo's thrusters counteract the vacuum enough that he doesn't get sucked out of the hatch, but the powerful force still whips his suit against his body, filling him with a moment of stomach-flipping doubt. Had he been too distracted to secure the suit and helmet properly...?

But all is well. He's alive, in a controlled glide out of the belly and into the chasm beyond, while the primary tether at his back unspools from the suit, a tiny thread of filament.

Theo turns his head, taking in the surrounding emptiness, this dark shard of the universe where their small breathing bodies have latched onto a strange anomaly orbiting a moon, orbiting a planet blazing poison red, orbiting a dim star. It wouldn't surprise him to wake up this moment and realize he was dreaming all along.

Within a minute or two, they're a dozen yards from the pod. This close, Theo thinks it isn't a pod at all, just a wall of terrible darkness, its surface a pebbled skin. It isn't black, Theo realizes as they drift to within several feet of the slightly-curving surface. It's a very, very dark green.

"*Testing tether engagement,*" says Chels. Theo isn't surprised she volunteered. Boldness is Chels' primary virtue. Still, he's glad he isn't going to be the one finding out firsthand what defenses the pod might raise when the accessory tether embeds its sharp claws. Chels thrusts forward to get safely in range, pressing ahead of Silv. Theo swallows past a dry throat as the accessory tether launches from Chels' right forearm, and a moment later, its metallic teeth bite deeply into the pod's dark skin.

No one speaks while Theo counts ten of his own rapid heartbeats. Then, he hears a collective exhale in the comms, and realizes he's part of that white noise, the puff of his breath briefly fogging the lower part of his helmet.

"*So far so good,*" Chels says evenly, but there's a grim note in her voice that belies her usual confidence. "*I'll reel in.*"

The tether on her forearm pulls her toward the pod, while the tether on the back of her suit feeds her more slack. Watching, Theo is reminded of a pendant on a necklace, strung over a delicate chain.

Silv thrusts after her. *"Theo, Mika, hold back,"* he tells them before they can follow. Chels doesn't hesitate to pull out her fire baton and depress the trigger. The device is a few handspans long, and the blue lance of flame that blooms from the end of nozzle is several times longer than that. Theo was never trained on the baton. In truth weapons make him nervous.

"Everyone fall in," Silv says tersely. Chels has cut a line through the pod's hull as long as she is tall, and the pod hasn't retaliated. Silv's been watching over Chels' shoulder, but now he turns his head. *"This door is closing fast."*

He sounds surprised, and so is Theo. He knows that pieces of the vine are self-repairing, but it usually takes weeks, not hours, let alone minutes.

Of course it's strong, Theo chides himself. *It's the spore.*

Theo looks over his shoulder at the *Destrier*, floating behind them, linked to them by their glittering tethers. He notes the similarities between the *Destrier* and the pod. The *Destrier's* skin is green too, if paler than the pod's, and its original body is also oblong, like an egg. Unlike the pod, it has been retrofitted with wings and thrusters and patches of clearide, the organic and mechanical stitched together.

But the first lance to touch the pod is Chels' baton. Except for the wound she's just opened, it remains just as it was grown by the vine. The pod can't be steered by a human crew like the *Destrier*. The pod isn't meant to be steered at all—it's meant to wait. It has waited here for a hundred years, and it would wait a thousand more. As long as it must, until some comet or other intergalactic coincidence cast it within reach of a fertile world, or until the right vessel came along and claimed it, carrying it on.

In his mother's stories, the last queen waited a thousand years. Theo wonders again why this one couldn't wait a little longer. Just a mere hundred years or so, until Theo was long dead, fealty to sleeping queens no longer his concern.

Theo is the blood of the vine. He should be overjoyed that the queen has been found, and honored to be the one to find her. But he also knows that before the vine was overthrown, its last long war in a series of wars had destroyed most of a star system. The new order may be just as corrupt as the rumors around the Aurora claim; Theo wouldn't know either way. All his information comes from the people on Aurora, and he doesn't place much trust in the veracity of pirates. But he knows most lies contain a grain of truth. *And* he knows for a fact the new order would happily kill Theo for the crime of his ancestry. He doesn't have to pick a side here; it was chosen for him before he was born.

But the ongoing conflicts are mere embers of the hot fire of even twenty years ago, to hear the old man's tales. If someone brings an imperial spore and its queen into the fray, how will that fan the flames? Can any cause, any lost empire, justify ravaging the settled worlds with another century or more of violence?

Theo can't dwell on his dilemma for long. It's time for the unit to thrust through the opening Chels carved, one by one. Even Theo has practiced this maneuver; one of the first lessons of piracy is how to breach a craft. Rarely do they engage with anyone who willingly opens their hull in welcome. Silv is first, steering himself with small, careful bursts from the thrusters on the backs of his calves and shoulder blades. Chels follows. She keeps the baton live so that its light pools inside the dark cavern of the pod's interior. Theo follows Chels, with Mika behind him.

He can't see more than a couple feet in each direction; the light is too bright and close. Mika has to duck her head as she eases through the rift in the pod's skin. As Silv warned, it's quickly knitting itself closed behind them.

"*Sweep complete*," says Silv softly in Theo's ear. "*Clear.*"

"*Clear*," Chels agrees.

They release and reel back their primary tethers, which barely slip through the opening before it seals over.

Theo knows the moment the pod has totally rejuvenated its skin because the internal environment quickly stabilizes. Instead of left afloat, his body is pulled firmly toward the floor until his boots make contact. A series of faint pops tell him the pod is creating oxygen.

Silv says, "*We have illumination, Chels. You can cut the fire.*"

Chels does, and for a moment Theo thinks Silv was imagining things. Then his vision adjusts and he finds Silv was right. A soft glow emanates from an inner wall of the small space they're standing inside. The pod seems to have generated a temporary chamber here to protect the rest of its interior from the effects of the hull breach. Theo presses his palm against the curved inner wall. It's soft. If he weren't wearing a suit, it would feel warm beneath his hand.

"Membranous," he confirms. Vine artifacts occasionally grow temporary parts which have varying degrees of usefulness. Theo is a janitor, not a real technician, but even he can't help feeling a degree of awe seeing an artifact's natural, perfect function rather than the random misfires of dying scraps.

The membrane is semi-transparent, filtering what appears to be a bright yellow light on its other side.

A candle in a dark chamber, left lit a hundred years. Theo shudders and pulls back his hand.

Chels steps past Theo with her baton powered up again and slices through the membrane. In a moment, Theo's vision is washed white by vivid light.

Once breached, the membrane withers away on its own. The pod appears to reabsorb it; after a few seconds it dissolves like it was never there, leaving the unit with an uninhibited view of the massive, vaulted chamber beyond.

Theo has no memory of any place except the old man's Aurora station, that sprawling, almost wholly mechanized, man-made island in ungoverned space. He has never seen a living organism with his own eyes that wasn't either human or a slowly withering artifact of the vine.

In short, nothing has prepared him for what he's seeing here: teeming, thriving, riotous growth. So much color, so much delicate organic shape. The entire space is plastered with vines, curving and interlacing, forming thickets in the corners of the tall, pentagonal chamber and a thick carpet over the floor and ceiling. And here and there, glowing muted red, soft and textured as a child's unmarred skin, are what can only be budding roses.

The ropes of intricate vine and the vibrant blooms all coalesce within a spinning net of light that emanates from nowhere and everywhere, casting everything in a warm golden haze.

27

Strangest and most riveting of all, in the center of the chamber, draped in vines and swathed in light, lies a woman. She appears deep in pleasant sleep, tucked into an oversized, black fur garment that strikes a sharp contrast to the pale hands linked over her stomach. Her serene face is framed by short, vivid waves of hair the same blood-red color as the flowers. Peeking through the vines Theo can glimpse her startlingly delicate, bare toes.

"*Holy wind and fire,*" mutters Chels, standing a step ahead of Theo, her eyes wide with shock. "*It's not just a pod. It's the imperial spore.*"

* * *

Grandmother abruptly stopped speaking, rose from the bench, and picked up her shears. Ruby got to her feet as well and stretched, unsurprised. Grandmother frequently paused mid-story; sometimes for a few minutes, sometimes for a few days.

From some not-so-great distance, a few lateral miles and far below where they stood in the tower, Ruby felt the unmistakable pulse of a K6 detonation like a needle in her heart.

Scarlet gripped the edge of the moonsalt pail. "Grandmother," she said tersely. "Should we not—"

"Come here, girls, and help me."

Ruby couldn't remember Grandmother ever asking for help with anything. She was born during one war and had fought a dozen others. She had the bearing of a warrior, and a perfect, ageless grace. The idea she could need something from Ruby and Scarlet was absurd. But she stared at them, her eyes steady and fixed, as though daring them to make her repeat herself.

If Grandmother had changed since Ruby was three years old, Ruby couldn't tell. Her unlined face neither frowned nor smiled. Her hair was still as red as it was silver. Ruby had always thought of Scarlet's hair as being like Grandmother's, but now she realized Grandmother's original color was muted by the silver strands. When she was young, it must have been just the shade of Ruby's.

Of course, Scarlet had immediately gone to Grandmother, and now they were both looking at Ruby expectantly, waiting for her to obey too. After another moment, Ruby joined them.

Grandmother handed the shears to Scarlet, then buried her strong hands in the dense carpet of dead vines on the floor alongside the bench. She grasped and pulled at two segments of vine bleached grey and lifeless, but still rigid and taut.

"Cut," she told Scarlet, who obediently placed the shears between Grandmother's fists, then paused, struggling with the handles. "Yes, there," said Grandmother. Scarlet slowly pressed the handles together and the blades bit into the vine. After a moment's struggle, the blades split the vine with a cracking sound and a puff of dust.

"Now, Ruby, pull them back."

Ruby hesitantly moved forward. She had to press close between her sister and Grandmother in order to reach, her arms and shoulders pressing against theirs. Ruby pulled where the vines were cut. Their surface was rough enough to abrade her palms, but she didn't so much as whimper. Then, Grandmother told Scarlet to cut again, and slowly they opened a furrow in the dead thicket. Ruby's hands and wrists were scratched raw, pebbled with small points of welling blood. Scarlet's palms were red and her fingers stiff from pressing the shears through ever more stubborn vines at ever more difficult angles.

Ruby did not ask Grandmother what they were doing. Grandmother never answered that kind of question. But when Ruby finally saw a flash of green deep in the path they had carved, she dared to hope they'd accomplished their painful task. A single young vine brushed Ruby's knuckles.

Grandmother reached her own hand inside the depression and tickled the new growth with her fingertips until it snaked loose and draped itself over the outermost layer of sheared, dead vine. While they watched, a single ruffled leaf burst from its green tip, and then it lay still.

Grandmother sat on the bench, and Ruby and Scarlet sank to the floor, exhausted by the last half-hour's work.

Then Grandmother picked up the thread of her story.

"The king's son knew his duty to the vine, but he was reluctant to fulfill it."

"Like I said," murmured Scarlet, brushing back her hair from her face. Despite the cold that had leached into the greenhouse, her temples were damp from her exertions with the shears. "No such thing as a worthy king's

29

son."

"Fortunately," Grandmother went on as though Scarlet had said nothing at all, "he was not the only king's son to find his way to her side."

* * *

After staring at the tableau before them for a frozen moment, Chels' whispered words a lingering echo in Theo's ear, Mika and Chels both point their batons at the queen. Theo just stares at the woman, who lies here as though asleep, seemingly oblivious to their arrival. She's really no more than a girl, her face as smooth as a child's, her mouth plush, her eyelashes dark red crescents on pink-tinged cheeks. The dense tangle of vines cradle her against a narrow, raised platform also drifted in leaves and blooms.

He'd already more than suspected what awaited them inside the artifact. And yet, seeing her is a blow.

The *Destrier* comm link transmits Pilar's voice to them, rough and distant. "*Report, any day now? Over.*"

"*We read you, Pilar. We're all inside and in one piece. Over,*" Silv answers.

"*The view in here just isn't exactly what we were expecting to see,*" Mika adds.

Chels snorts. "*That's a fucking understatement.*"

"*Um, what? Don't leave me in suspense. Not kind. Over.*"

"*We've found target A. Over.*" Silv speaks with the level of enthusiasm he might report a festering wound to a medic. Theo is confused. Shouldn't he be ecstatic?

While Theo knows better, the old man has long told the crews that when one of their number finds target A, he'll sell it to the highest bidder, making everyone on the Aurora fantastically rich.

"*The fuck? Repeat comm, there must be something wrong with the transmission. Over.*"

"*No, you're reading us. The pod is target A. We've found the spore. Over.*"

The comms are silent for a long moment. Theo might have thought Pilar was disconnected if he couldn't hear the fuzzy static of the connection staying live.

At last she says, "*Holy fuck.*"

"*My thoughts exactly,*" Chels murmurs. That's when Theo realizes she hasn't put away her baton. In fact, she's still pointing it at the woman—rather, the next Queen of the Red Vine—lying prone in the middle of the chamber. And it's half-lit, a curl of fire protruding from the nozzle like a tongue.

Theo isn't the only one to notice.

"*What are you doing, swab?*" Silv asks quietly. Theo glances his way. Silv is watching Chels carefully. "*There's no active threat.*"

"*The fuck there isn't,*" she snaps. "*Do you know what those monsters did to my family?*"

Theo doesn't know which monsters she means. The empire fell long before her parents were born. Maybe the old kings still scattered around the universe, each engaged in their own desperate quest for the spore. Any one of them could submit the richest bid to the old man in his hypothetical auction, so that even if Chels got rich, one of these "monsters" would too.

"*There's nothing more dangerous in the universe than* that," Chels continues, tone full of venom. She bobs the nozzle of her baton at the sleeping girl. "*We should burn it to ashes and pretend we were never here. We'd be doing all of humanity a favor.*"

A strange sensation seizes Theo. It's as though the entire chamber holds its breath; the sudden silencing of a small and constant sound, unnoticed until it's gone. The light radiating from nowhere and everywhere seems to dim.

And then the moment passes, almost as though it didn't happen at all, but leaving Theo shakier than he was before.

"*We need to get back and debrief with the old man,*" Silv says quietly. "*We're not going to set fire to the greatest prize in the universe,*" he adds in a harder voice. "*And that's an order, swab.*" The ice in his voice seems to finally touch Chels. She blinks and slowly lowers her baton, but stays rooted to the spot, staring at the queen. And she doesn't holster her weapon.

Theo may have misgivings about his role in what's unfolding around him, but the woman in the line of Chels' fire is still the sole source of hope in every children's story outside of the new order. An itch starts under Theo's skin, almost strong enough to make his feet move, but even if he could intercept Chels somehow, all he would succeed in doing is getting knocked on his ass. She outmatches him several times over.

He swallows; all he has is words, so he searches for some. *"Cap's right. We do need the old man,"* he agrees, pleased by how level and unaffected his voice sounds. *"We may not even be safe just standing in here. We need information before we take a closer look around, let alone light up a baton."*

Chels snorts. *"Like the old man will know where the traps are? All the lore we have about the Red Vine is just that—lore."*

That's not entirely true, and she knows it. Theo doesn't hide his irritation when he reminds her, *"Technicians have been studying the artifacts and utilizing them to keep us all alive for decades. They know more than nothing. And nothing is what we know, so again, I recommend we get off this pod before we break it and get ourselves killed in the process."*

"We did already cut a hole in it without any trouble," Chels points out, but she isn't really arguing. The fight seems to have gone out of her for now. *"Order received, cap. Let's fall back."*

While they retrace their path to the *Destrier* Theo recalls the moment before he realized what they were seeing from the bridge, that morning when his world had shifted from ordinary to anything-but in an instant. When his largest concern had gone from a squeaky wheel on the instrument cart to the beginning of a new epoch in history. One where he's center-stage.

Though, he thinks grimly, thinking back on some versions of the old stories he's overheard, it's very likely his appearance in the history about to be written will be brief. In stories of the vine, things rarely end well for kings' sons.

* * *

Theo and the rest of the crew wait in the corridor outside the bridge. Silv is alone on the other side of the hatch, making the call to the old man.

Pilar has been interrogating them about the pod ever since they came back aboard the *Destrier*.

"Fuck," she breathes after Mika repeats a careful description of the membrane. "It just created its own temporary airlock?"

The other two women shrug uneasily.

Theo doesn't pretend to understand the vine; no one does. Not even the technicians who've spent all their lives splicing half-dead pieces of vine to metal tech. It's like the difference between knowing how to tan and stitch leather, and knowing how to tend the animal that grew the hide. Two entirely fucking separate bodies of knowledge.

But the lore is full of examples of the vine having a mind of its own and anticipating human needs, and now Theo knows those stories have at least a grain of truth. Nothing else explains what he just witnessed with his own senses inside the spore.

Chels has been quiet, still clutching her baton. None of them have shed their suits, just pulled off their helmets. Theo finds his gaze drawn to the opaque hatch to the bridge, unconsciously hungry for the sight of the spore, so close and so far away, doubtless still framed by the bridge viewscreen. He wonders if Silv is staring, too, *his* view unfettered, even while he takes the comm.

Oddly unsettled by the thought, Theo bites the inside of his cheek and reminds himself that if Silv *is* looking, it's with riches, not destiny, on his mind. In this, as in all things, Theo is alone.

"So, we're all going to get filthy rich and retire, right?" Mika sags back against the wall with a dopey grin. "I'm going to buy my own satellite and never let anyone visit except to bring me chocolate and beautiful men."

"We'll get what the old man says we'll get," Pilar says judiciously, but then she wipes at her brow with a trembling hand. "Holy wind and fire, you lot," she says with an incredulous laugh. "I'm sweating."

Silv comes back out. He looks a little pale, Theo thinks. Not as excited as he should, almost grim. But then, Theo supposes they're still a long way from a payday. Though they're in a remote corner of an unsettled galaxy, if a rival crew finds them here, they can hardly defend their prize, and it will take weeks for the fleet to come to them.

Waiting for the fleet has to be the plan, Theo knows before Silv opens his mouth. They can't tow the spore in; it's several times the size of the *Destrier*, and they don't have an ounce of spare fuel. A simple return course to the Aurora is all they can manage. Every hour they idle here is dangerous.

"The old man says we batten the hatches and wait for the fleet to rendezvous with us here," Silv says, as Theo predicted. Then he goes on to say more that

Theo never saw coming. "They're eight weeks out. So, three of us will occupy the spore to conserve oxygen supply here."

Theo doesn't have to look at his crewmates to know they're all staring at Silv with identical expressions of shocked horror. A muscle jumps in Silv's cheek as he clenches his jaw, which Theo notices is dusted with a layer of dark gold stubble, an uncharacteristic lapse in Silv's careful personal maintenance regime. Understandable, given the circumstances. Theo only minds because it makes his jaw look even squarer than usual.

"Who?" Mika finally manages.

Silv doesn't hesitate. "Me, Theo, and Chels."

While the other swabs process this, Chels inscrutable and Mika and Pilar with visible guilty relief, Silv looks at Theo. "The old man wants you on the call. He's holding. Don't want to keep him waiting long, so you'd better hustle."

On the bridge, Theo doesn't let himself look out the viewscreen. He goes straight to the call console and picks up the earpiece, and just in case someone is listening at the hatch he keeps his voice low.

"This is Theo, sir."

The old man has never been one for pleasantries. "*Silv has already relayed my instructions to the crew, I presume?*" he asks without preamble.

"Yes, sir."

"*Then I won't repeat myself. Are you alone at this time?*"

"Yes, sir."

"*Good. When you are aboard the spore, find a way to attend the queen alone.*"

"What do I—" he began, but the old man cuts him off.

"*It is enough to be near her, breathing in the spore's atmo. Remember who she is. You shall not act without her permission. And you shall be perfectly obedient, no matter what she requests. You are of the blood. Fealty to the vine is your only purpose, whatever it should require.*"

"Yes, sir." Theo hates how small his voice sounds. And something in his tone clearly translates across the comm, because after a short pause, the old man lowers his voice, and instead of signing off, he issues a warning.

"*I remember how you looked when security plucked you out of the vents and pipes. Starved, small. I can only imagine how it felt, growing up that way. It was not a beginning befitting a king's son, but you are not the only one who was stripped of your birthright. The traitors' wars have taken their toll on all of us born of the blood. When I spared you, it was not out of mercy. It was out of my own fealty to the blood. The blood in your veins. Do you understand?"*

Ice creeps into Theo's spine, and he stands straighter. His gaze crawls inevitably back toward the view beyond the clearide, that fist of darkness, ringed by the pale moon, ringed by the fiery planet.

"Yes, sir."

* * *

That night, the tower glowed with effort, but it grew warm enough for Scarlet and Ruby to leave the greenhouse. By unspoken agreement, they went together to Scarlet's chamber, arm-in-arm.

"This is a good sign," Ruby murmured. She meant the warming—that the vine could spare energy from healing other portions of itself and elevate the temperature. There had been fewer warriors coming to speak to Grandmother. She allowed herself a small, cautious hope.

Scarlet pressed her lips together and shook her head. "I don't know." She gathered the blankets over them both, and they cuddled together. The tower was warmer than earlier, but still bitterly cold.

"What do you think of Grandmother's story?" Ruby asked, resting her cheek on Scarlet's shoulder. She gazed up at the high window and frowned. The vine had covered it over with a dense web of green, and it had shrunk to half its former size. If the warming was a good sign, disappearing windows was a bad one.

Scarlet didn't answer for a moment. Then she said, "I liked the way she told it when we were younger. When she didn't say much at all about the kings' sons. It was basically, 'then the princess awakened a queen, and she was strong and rained fiery death on her enemies, the end.'"

There had been a little more to it than that, Ruby thought wryly, but those *were* the high notes. The queen was the unequivocal hero of the story. In those early tellings, Ruby wasn't yet ten years old. She focused on the glory of the queen and not the misfortune of a few nameless men along the way.

35

"Why is she telling it this way?" Ruby asked, surprising herself with how fervently she wanted to know. "Why does she want us to care about them when we know they're going to die?"

"One of them lives," Scarlet said, matter-of-fact. She yawned. "Go to sleep, little sister. We should rest while we can."

Ruby didn't miss the ominous nature of that remark; Ruby saw the respite as a source of hope, but to Scarlet, it was only the calm before the worst of storms.

Exhaustion was a strange thing. Though fear and confusion and uncertainty were vibrant as fire in Ruby's chest, the tide of sleep was stronger still, convincing her there was nothing more important than closing her eyes and giving in. Or maybe that wasn't her body so much as it was the tower, sighing around her. Assuring her that it would protect her with its last breath. Not the comfort it once was, that promise; Ruby feared the vine's last breath was not so distant a prospect anymore.

* * *

The next morning, the sisters came to the greenhouse before Grandmother. Ruby could not recall that ever happening before. They stopped short just inside the door, for there, beside the bench where they had pried free the young vine the day before, the slender curling stem was weighed down by a single, red-tipped bud.

"Is that . . . ?" Ruby murmured, taking a halting step forward. Scarlet moved in sync with her, gaze just as riveted.

"A rose," Scarlet confirmed, a rough whisper.

From behind them, Grandmother spoke. Her tone was measured and low, the same as yesterday and all the days before that which Ruby could recall, as though nothing was out of the ordinary. "It has been ten years since I saw a flower on the vines."

Over one of her long, dark dresses, Grandmother wore a fur coat sewn from the sleek black pelts of fanged panthers. According to the lore, Grandmother had taken each pelt herself. It was disconcerting to think that even Grandmother was not impervious to the tower's bitter chill.

Ruby and Scarlet broke apart so that Grandmother could walk between

36

them. She studied the flower, then, lifting it with a forefinger, bent so her nose almost brushed the point of its yet-unfurled petals. She inhaled deeply.

Then she straightened and held out her shears. "Ruby, it is your turn to cut."

Like yesterday, Grandmother pried a portion of the vine apart beside the bench. Ruby's wrists and fingers cramped from handling the shears, but it was easy to be stoic when she wasn't the one thrusting her hands amongst the rough vines that occasionally bit through the skin. Scarlet gritted her teeth, uncomplaining even as she shed drops of blood. Eventually, she too reached a slender shoot of new vine, and Grandmother coaxed it out into the dim starlight. With a shudder, it unspooled a dark, ruffled leaf of its own, and rested.

Grandmother sat on the bench and gazed across the greenhouse, then at the girls.

"When the princess awakened a queen, she soon realized that she had more suitors than she required," Grandmother began.

Ruby went rigid, her ears ringing. Before she could stop herself, she interrupted.

"No."

Grandmother didn't seem surprised, but Scarlet sucked in a quick, startled breath.

Ruby didn't flinch. She watched Grandmother's calm face and the inky oblivion of her eyes, dark and ancient as the sky.

"No?" Grandmother echoed without emotion. "Why do you tell me 'no,' girl?"

Ruby's heart pounded, but somehow her voice emerged as evenly as Grandmother's. "I don't want to hear this story. Not this way. Not today."

Some emotion passed over Grandmother's face, quick as a shadow in firelight. "Today, this is exactly the way you must hear it."

Infuriated by the burn of tears in her eyes, Ruby gritted her teeth. "No! Not when we're in danger. Not when everything is about to—"

From the doorway, a quiet voice interrupted them. "Your majesty," gasped a warrior, leaning hard against the opening, bleeding from her temple.

37

"Forgive me, my queen, but I must make my report."

Grandmother appeared not to hear the warrior at first. She gazed thought-fully at Ruby. Ruby refused to look away, defiant even as tears sprang free from her eyes and streaked her cheeks.

After a few long moments of eye contact, Grandmother stood and crossed the greenhouse to speak to the warrior, and heard whatever news the woman had raced up the tower, hurt and bleeding, to deliver.

Scarlet stepped close to Ruby. They were holding hands; Ruby didn't know when that had happened. She felt numb everywhere except her head and her chest, like thought, breath, and a heartbeat were all her body could sustain, perception of touch an abandoned luxury. Like the vine, she thought, pouring the last of its reserves where they were needed and—

She shuddered as she realized why she was numb. Sensation flared back between her and Scarlet's clasped hands. She was shaking and had lost feeling in her limbs less from emotion, and more because the temperature had suddenly plummeted in the greenhouse.

* * *

The second time Theo casts himself out of the *Destrier*'s belly toward the pod, he's weighed down with a sealed parcel strapped to his back over the suit. It contains a blanket, a change of clothes, and three hand-copied paperback books. In other words, all his worldly possessions.

They don't need Chels' baton. The place in the pod's skin they opened with fire twice before opens of its own volition now, melting away to form a generous opening they can all thrust through with ease. They don't even need their harpoons and accessory tethers.

Inside, the membrane is in place until their point of entry closes over. Then, the artificial gravity engages and they hear the pops of restored oxygen a moment before the membrane dissolves slowly on its own. They're greeted with the familiar view of the large chamber where the queen sleeps, the vines crawling over her. Theo isn't sure but he thinks he notices more roses than there were before.

"*We aren't bedding down* here, *surely, Cap?*" Chels asks uneasily. Theo sympathized; it would be eerie, to spend weeks in sight of the otherworldly queen, sleeping and unchanging, cradled in her vines. Chels doesn't know yet that she will soon awaken.

Silv appears to think it over, then jerks his head toward a visible opening in the wall on the other side of the chamber. "*This way*," he murmurs over the comms, guiding them on a path that skirts the queen, clinging to the vine-matted wall.

Outside the opening, a corridor ramps upward, curving around the chamber they left, a staircase without steps. When they teach another opening, this one the corridor's outer wall, Silv steps through. Theo and Chels follow silently.

The space inside is only faintly illuminated at first, but the light becomes more intense as they all file inside. The chamber is bigger than any room on the *Destrier*, if only a fraction the size of the queen's chamber.

There are no tangled ropes of living vine, leaves, and blooms here. But it is as organic as the outer skin, more like what Theo is accustomed to seeing on the station from dormant or dead scraps. An oblong, seamless space with no corners or sharp edges, the floor slightly distended at the center, a pod within a pod.

"*Make yourself at home,*" Silv says with exaggerated cheer, reaching for the latch on his helmet.

"*This is creepy as shit, Cap,*" Chels mutters. "*We really gonna trust the atmo in here?*"

"*Yes,*" Silv says, no waver in his voice, "*we are.*" He unlatches his helmet and pulls it off.

For an instant Theo expects catastrophe—fears they were terribly wrong and the sleeping woman wasn't evidence the pod would support them after all. That they're actually in the same thing as open outer space inside this pod, and Silv will be freeze-dried in an instant.

But he's fine.

His nostrils flare with his sigh as though he too had some apprehensions he hadn't revealed about exposure, but then he recovers an instant later with a steady smile.

"Come on in, the oxygen's fine."

Theo almost laughs before he catches himself.

Feeling the need to get it over with—and, frankly, a little curious—Theo loosens the seal on his helmet and takes it off his head, Chels slowly echoing his actions.

The air tastes cool and clean. It reminds Theo of the time he drank some water in the old man's quarters, the precious kind, carefully filtered through the hydroponic system, not the raw version bathed in chemicals used by most of the fleet.

He hadn't known how good water could taste. Pure and faintly sweet. It seemed to cleanse his mouth and throat even as it sated his thirst.

He hadn't known how good air could taste either. The air aboard the *Destrier* is a little better than in the maintenance barracks on Aurora, but it still slides into his lungs with a faint burn. With each breath he takes here, he feels like his entire chest is expanding, easing a pressure he hadn't realized was there.

And then Chels gasps, clutches her throat, and collapses so hard and fast that she makes no effort to break her fall. She falls like a stone, striking the tangle of vines with a muted thud.

For a bewildered moment Theo only stares. Silv is already on his knees beside Chels, rolling her onto her back, speaking lowly and urgently into her face. She doesn't respond.

Theo looks down at her in horror. Her eyes are fixed wide, her lips parted, her last expression one of surprise.

Silv looks up at Theo desperately, his fingers searching for a pulse in her throat. He obviously isn't finding one; his expression is stricken. "Put your helmet back on," he says tersely. "We were—we were wrong."

"I think the danger was only to Chels," Theo says dully, the words coming out in lockstep with his thoughts. They're just forming, so he's speaking realizations aloud as he has them, startling himself and Silv in tandem. "She did threaten to light up the place, remember? It must have heard her."

Silv shakes his head with a hoarse, inarticulate sound. He leans over Chels and presses his mouth against hers, then pushes down hard on her sternum with the palms of his hands. Theo has never seen someone attempt manual resuscitation, but he knows that even if Silv is doing it right, it's too late.

Despite what he told Silv, Theo semi-expects each of his shallow breaths to be his last. For Chels' sake, he hopes whatever the vine fed into the air for her was quick.

Silv exclaims, and at first Theo is gripped with the panicked thought that Silv has been hurt too. But then he realizes that's not it; rather, Silv is cursing because Chels' body is being slowly encased by creeping vines.

One slides over Silv's boot, making him jump and scramble backward. Then, he lunges forward again to try pulling loose the vines that slowly grasp at Chels' waist, her arms and legs, her shoulders. He can grasp one and hold it only a few seconds before it snaps free and races back over the distance it lost in the struggle, and there are so many. With something like a sob, choked and furious, Silv falls back in defeat after just a few seconds, staggering to his feet. Theo moves to his side and together they watch in riveted horror as the moving vine pulls Chels' body, soft and silent as a doll's, straight down into the bed of green where she disappears with a low, wet pop.

"Holy..." Theo begins, but before he can finish, Silv distracts him by trying to force his helmet into place. "What the...?" Theo bats at his hands. "Stop."

Silv's eyes are wide, wild. He's so pale. Theo never noticed, but he has a few very light freckles on his cheekbones. They stand out now because his face has lost all other color.

"It isn't safe," Silv insists.

"There's only forty minutes of oxygen in that suit," Theo reminds him. "And there's not enough resupply on the ship for us to wait out our rendezvous," he adds. "We can't afford to play it safe."

"You could go back to the fleet," Silv murmurs, his eyes pleading.

Theo is still shaking his head. "*No.*" Then he pauses, really hearing what Silv said. "What do you mean, 'you'? Not 'we'?"

Silv seems to be getting his emotions back under control. He takes a half step back and frowns. "And what do *you* mean, 'no'? Did you see what just happened? You should be jumping at the chance to go. I know you don't really care about the payday."

They look at each other uneasily. And it dawns on Theo first.

Incredulity reduces his voice to nothing but a rough whisper. "You're..."

But Silv is sharper than Theo ever gave him credit for. His eyes widen a moment after Theo's epiphany and he is speaking before Theo can get far. "You're of the blood, too?"

They stare at each other, speechless. Two kings' sons. Plucked from the air vents and wherever the old man found Silv, placed on this crew at this time and sent to this ping. Theo feels sick.

He's heard a version of this story with more than one king's son. He remembers how the pod drank down Chels and wonders how much more voracious it would be for Theo and his king's blood.

He can't dwell long. Their comms light up.

"*Destrier to unit, status? Theo, Silv? We've lost our link to Chels. She okay? Over.*"

* * *

When Grandmother finished speaking to the warrior, she returned to them. Ruby searched her face for some sign of what she had been told, but like always, no ordinary emotion so much as flickered in Grandmother's face. Ruby wondered if the woman had ever felt joy or pain. Surely she did, but her mask was perfect, uncompromised even when a war had found its way to the doors of the supposedly untouchable tower.

Grandmother removed her fur cloak and put it over the two sisters. Scarlet put her arm around Ruby's waist so that they fit better under its warm cover. Grandmother did not react to the chill she must have felt, wearing only her gown, the air frosted with her breath. While Ruby and Scarlet looked at her, she looked at the ground near the bench. After a moment, the girls looked there too.

Beside the bit of vine Ruby had bled for, with its single, heavy budding flower, the bit of vine Scarlet had bled for had sprouted a glittering black thorn. Ruby had never seen one so sharp, fresh, or large—it was as long as her forefinger.

Ruby's bewilderment was interrupted by Grandmother's steady voice. "You say, girl, that you do not want to hear the story I am telling. What story would you have me tell?"

Ruby sucked her cold lower lip between her teeth, and when she released it, she felt the sting of frost split the delicate skin, but she didn't wince.

When Ruby didn't answer her, Grandmother went on. "There is a time for pleasant tales, just as there is a time for roses. And there is a time for dark tales, just as there is a time for thorns." Grandmother lifted her eyes to Ruby's for a moment, then she moved her attention to Scarlet. "In the story I have told you all these years, the princess wakes a queen, and makes her choice. Two kings' sons present themselves. She needs only one. And the vine is so young and hungry. Did the queen make a mistake, Scarlet?"

Scarlet glanced at Ruby, but didn't hesitate. "No, Grandmother." Ruby knew that Scarlet was not just appeasing Grandmother. The two were so alike. "The queen knew there were years of war ahead of her," Scarlet continued. "She did what made her strong."

Grandmother did not react to Scarlet's answer. Her gaze was as steady and unchanging as the tower. But when Scarlet was finished, she looked to Ruby.

"And what is your answer? Did the queen make a mistake?"

"Yes," Ruby said immediately. Once she might have chosen words with more care, always finding some balance between her true beliefs and what she knew Grandmother would rather hear. But she wasn't a child anymore. "The kings' sons were the blood of the vine, and only tried to do their duty—to help her. My sister says she did what made her strong, but I say she should have done what would make her *just*."

The most powerful blast yet rocked the vine. The tower lurched. Ruby and Scarlet stumbled to the floor, tangled together in Grandmother's cloak. When Ruby righted herself, the light in the greenhouse was so dim, she could see nothing through the cloud of her own breath but Grandmother's outline, a deep moving shadow bending to pick up the bucket of moonsalt.

"A new tale begins today," the queen told the princesses. The light was slipping further away; looking up with a squint, Ruby could see the pentagonal sky light slowly close over.

The new tale would be told, Ruby knew, of a queen named Scarlet, who bled for thorns. She squeezed her sister's hand tight and let a dark coil of fury unravel from her heart, fury at the faceless enemies who chose chaos over order, death over life. They poisoned the vine, the source of life for the many, to pursue the cause of the few.

But, Ruby thought with satisfaction, her sister would survive and one day restore the Red Vine, and with it the blood's order, once again. The anarchists would ultimately pay, even if it fell upon their descendants to settle the debt.

Ruby stood and pulled Scarlet up beside her. She looked at the figure of Grandmother as she upturned the heavy bucket and spilled the moonsalt over the deep fissures they'd carved in the vine, filling the crevices from which they'd pulled the rose and the thorn.

Grandmother held out her hand and spoke.

"Come here, Ruby."

Ruby thought she'd misheard.

It was Scarlet who moved first. Her fingers slipped through Ruby's so that she could put her hands briefly to Ruby's cheeks. Scarlet kissed her forehead, then pushed her toward Grandmother.

Ruby swayed and took only half a step. "What?"

"There is a time for thorns. And there is a time for roses," Grandmother said evenly, her hand still outstretched and waiting as though they had nothing but time, even as a wail reverberated through the walls of the greenhouse, plunging and soaring to notes no human voice could reach—the death knell of the vine. "This is such a time. Come here, my girl, and rest. You shall wake a queen."

* * *

Silv speaks into the comm, and for a moment Theo thinks he'll tell the crew what happened. But of course he doesn't. He simply says, "Chels was experiencing some feedback, so she turned off comms while Theo does some maintenance on her helmet. Over."

"*Copy that. Thanks for the heads up. Oh wait, you didn't give a heads up. Over.*"

Silv smiles faintly, but it fades fast. "Sincerest apologies. Over."

Theo is still processing the revelation that he and Silv have the same secret. Staring at the part of the floor where Chels disappeared, he's gripped by the same sensation he had when Chels threatened to set her baton on the queen.

There is something here with them. Waiting, watching, listening. Feeding them air and keeping the temperature ambient, helpfully bathing its chambers with light to illuminate their way. The vine is here, and alive, and a misstep now will be the end of them both.

Whereas the way forward will likely be the end of one of them, along with countless others who make themselves enemies of the vine.

Theo cocks his head, returning his attention to Silv, who is looking pensively at the opening they came through, probably thinking about the queen. Maybe thinking about the instructions he got from the old man, presumably the same ones given to Theo. Why didn't the old man tell them about one another? Did he think they'd see each other as rivals? And even if that was his reasoning, didn't he realize they would eventually get in one another's way regardless?

Or maybe he knew what Theo was realizing now: Silv is the true prince here. He is strong and beautiful and charming, the Captain of his vessel. There will be no contest between Silv and Theo. Theo must be nothing but a backup, a very last resort should something have befallen Silv.

He isn't even sure that the main feeling coursing through him is dread at what the next few minutes will surely bring. He's also relieved. He doesn't belong at the left hand of a queen and her monstrous vine. He wasn't built for the long war that has loomed since the moment the old man's ping registered the spore tucked alongside this faraway moon in this corner of the universe.

Silv glances at Theo. "We should... "

Theo nods. "Let's go."

Trying not to reflect on the likelihood he is walking to his own execution, Theo leads the way from the small chamber where Chels' corpse was swallowed, down the sloping floor that curves to the queen's chamber. He is conscious of Silv behind him, close enough that Theo feels the warmth that radiates from his big, capable body. Theo shudders, unconsciously shoving aside that old impulse, that unwelcome fantasy he has borne so long that repressing it has become second nature.

Then he pauses mid-thought. *Why not?* When all is lost, what's the value of pride and dignity? Why not indulge himself in his final moments?

Theo stops abruptly in the opening to the main chamber, and pivots so that when Silv collides with him, they are instantly chest to chest. Silv steadies himself by grasping Theo's arms, still surprised by Theo's about-face when Theo rises onto his toes, threads his fingers through the ridiculously long, pale hair at the back of Silv's head, and kisses him.

It doesn't last long, but in that short moment of closed-mouth pressure and startling warmth, a few impressions sear themselves into Theo's mind with an intensity he knows means he will carry them always. Even if "always" doesn't last much longer. The handful of hair is fine as silk. Silv's body is just as firm and perfect beneath the taut fabric of his suit as it has always looked. His breath is sweet as filtered water.

A second, maybe two, and then Theo lets go and steps backward, slipping free of Silv's hands. He turns and walks into the chamber, blinking fast.

The young woman who spells Theo's doom sleeps on, the vines draped now with countless blooms, clear and perfect red. They would be beautiful if Theo could look at them without imagining them as small, individual pools of Chels' blood.

"Theo," Silv says from behind him, voice gruff with shock. "Wait—"

But they are breathing. Panting, in Theo's case. And as the old man said, to be near and breathing is all it takes.

The vines covering the queen tremble, then lift, like a blanket shaken loose, and slide from her body. She is slender, almost ordinary, except for the perfect unblemished white of her skin, which seems to glow. Her breast rises beneath the heavy fur coat she wears, almost as though the lustrous hide is a part of her. Her eyes open; she gasps. Trembling hands travel down her hips and her thighs, then her face, her hair.

Finally she notices them and hastily sits up. The coat almost falls open, but she catches it at the last moment—though not before Theo sees she's at least mostly nude underneath.

Her eyes are black, the last bit of evidence as to who she is, if Theo had needed it. He stares at her, waiting for death. He hopes it's quick. For Chels, it seemed quick. And he still feels the sting of Silv's stubble on his lower lip.

There are worse ways and moments to die.

But Theo is still alive when then the first words of the freshly-enthroned Queen of the Red Vine are spoken. They lack the air of mystery that Theo unconsciously expected of a figure straight from lore and nightmare. Her voice might even have sounded ordinary—young—if the vines didn't tremble in a silent echo of her every word.

"*Two* kings' sons."

Theo's heart jumps into his throat, but he cannot make a sound. He's paralyzed.

Silv must sense his distress, because he takes Theo's hand in his—his palm is warm, his long fingers are smooth.

The queen's glittering black eyes fall to their joined hands. She does not smile. But she seems, somehow, softer. Her face is built of hard angles, her chin a point, her cheekbones and brow sculpted into broad planes. When the tension leaves her jaw, it changes her whole face. Her expression is almost kind, especially when she lowers her eyes, hiding their unnatural color.

"You need not fear me," she says quietly, tugging at the tufted fur lapels of the coat, her fingers disappearing into its dense pile. She glances up at them. For a moment, Theo's fears obediently subside. How can he fear her, seeing her like this: swallowed by her coat, her bare feet dangling over the edge of the platform, her lip snagged between her teeth and a lock of hair falling across her eye?

The vines suddenly lash tightly around his calves and *jerk*. The pressure and the angle pull him to his knees and bind him, ankle to knee, to the floor. Beside him, Silv is restrained in the same way.

Theo can barely hear the queen over the thunder of his pulse.

"Oh," she says, "that's right. You're supposed to kneel for this part."

Theo remembers now. The kings' sons kneel to await their queen's judgment. She comes toward them on silent feet. There is a rustling noise as she walks, soft as whispers, from the fur coat, so long it trails a foot behind her.

She holds her garment closed with a fist at her sternum, but her knees and slender calves flash with each stride. Her legs are painted with a constellation of faint freckles, like the ones on Silv's cheeks.

"Those of my grandmothers who were presented with more than one king's son chose one to live, and fed the rest to the vine. But this is my time, now."

You need not fear me, she had said. Theo clings to his fragile hope those words were true.

She reaches toward Theo. He resists the almost overpowering urge to flinch away. With her other hand, she reaches for Silv; her fingertips graze their heads in the same moment. Her touch is cool on Theo's brow, and feather-light. The delicate blue veins in her wrist show through her pale skin.

The queen is lore and nightmare, yes, but fragile youth and humanity too. She brushes one of Theo's curls back from his forehead. He cannot remember anyone ever touching him so gently.

"And now," says the queen, "I will decide how the tale is told."

3

The Fisherman's Catch by Chu Partridge

For many centuries, the Kingdom of Wan prospered: the nation's coffers were full, the trade was thriving, and the people were happy. The king met a beautiful enchantress whom he fell in love with and married. Together, they had many children, and the king loved her so much that he declined to accept any consorts and concubines. The queen was wise and caring, and dedicated her life to the governance of the kingdom. However, she passed away early, and the king fell into despair. Unable to live on without his love, he followed her into the afterlife shortly after. The kingdom was left without a monarch. Realizing that no one had been appointed as the successor, the royal princes and princesses fought to take the throne. The Kingdom of Wan was thrown into a chaos that lasted for many years. In the bloody battle for succession, the second prince slaughtered and maimed his siblings. He threw all but one into the great Yu River. The youngest princess was then nine years old and too young to be a threat, so he spared her.

Prince Ao ascended the throne and became the new king, but he was neither a just man like his father nor a wise woman like his mother. He removed all who opposed him and silenced those who questioned his rule. He turned a blind eye to his corrupt officials as long as they supported his reign. During the five years of his rule, the people of Wan grew fearful and the kingdom steadily declined.

Of those affected, the villagers and laborers suffered the most. In Mai, a village bordering part of the Yu River, several families fell into poverty because of the increased taxes. The patriarch of the Song family took on several new jobs to pay for the taxes. In an unfortunate incident while fixing roof tiles, he lost his arm. His wife, Madam Song, fell ill and was unable to afford medication. And thus, his son Song Xiaoyi took over as the breadwinner when he was 16. Song Xiaoyi was a gifted fisherman, and with his talent, he kept his family from starving. Despite his efforts, their family situation only got worse. His heart was bitter when he thought about the rising taxes each year. He grew to loathe the royal family and the corrupt officials. He thought of King Ao as a blight on the crops or a pus-filled pimple on the face.

King Ao and his courtiers were not just cruel and greedy, but also lecherous. The king took many concubines and when he visited the cities, he would bring back any beautiful man or woman who caught his eye. Xiaoyi often warned his sister to keep her face lowered so that her beauty would not be discovered.

"There is little to worry about. King Ao will not come to our village; he doesn't care about the people," Qiuyan tried to reassure her brother.

"It's better to be safe than sorry. Perhaps you should smear some dirt on your face," Xiaoyi replied worriedly.

"If I smear dirt on my face, I will lose my chance to marry into a good family," Qiuyan said, horrified. She was more beautiful than all the other girls in the village but struggled to find a good match because their family was impoverished.

"I'm saving up to pay for your dowry," Xiaoyi promised, "and I will keep my eye out for more jobs."

"And keep some for yourself," his mother reminded him, "so you can find a wife. You're already eighteen."

"There's a fishing competition in the next village, down the river," their father spoke up from where he was hunched over, fixing the leg of their table. "If you catch the largest or the most fish within a week, you can earn enough coin to feed our family for ten years."

"Oh, Brother, you must go!" Qiuyan said excitedly. "You're the best fisherman in our village."

Xiaoyi frowned. He knew he was good at fishing, but he was loath to leave his family alone for a whole week. However, his mother was still ill, and his father could not take on many jobs with a missing arm. Qiuyan could probably take on a few tasks, but it was not safe for his sister to go out and work. It still fell to Xiaoyi to bear the financial burdens for the family.

"When does the competition start?"

"In two days. If you take the raft, you can make it there in less than a day," his father told him.

The next morning, Xiaoyi checked his bags again. Aside from his trusty fishing rod, he had packed a few hooks and a flax-woven net. The bottom of his bag held some clothes and other necessities.

"Here," Qiuyan said, holding out a small box wrapped in a tattered cloth.

"What's this?"

"Some food for you. You won't be eating the fish you catch so I made you some buns and dried cakes that can last you for a few days."

"Thanks." Xiaoyi smiled and patted his sister's head fondly.

"Brother, I..." Qiuyan bit her lower lip and looked at her brother with obvious concern.

"Don't worry," Xiaoyi reassured her, "I'll be fine. You must listen to our parents, and do not be headstrong. While I'm gone, it'll be up to you to care for Mother. We have enough coins to last a full month if you are careful. If you continue making more baskets, Father can sell them at the marketplace next week."

Qiuyan laughed. "I know this already. You said it so many times last night. Careful you don't become a worrywart like Mum."

Xiaoyi flicked her forehead, then laughed when she protested.

"Alright, I'm heading off now," he said as he shouldered his bags, picked up his bucket, and waved goodbye to his family. It was a short trek to the riverbank where the family's raft was tied up. It was a dilapidated thing, made of wood, bamboo, and rope.

"Well, it's definitely seen better days," Xiaoyi muttered to himself. The raft had been used frequently before his father's accident but now lay forgotten. The wood had begun to rot, and it would not last many more trips. Xiaoyi decided to remake it entirely out of bamboo after the competition.

With a quick push off the bank, the raft floated down the river. Xiaoyi used a long pole and punted in the direction of the other village. As he made his way down the river, Xiaoyi allowed himself to relax. The stress had tightened the muscles in his shoulders. With the gentle sloshing of the water, he felt his worries slowly ebb away.

The River Yu was beautiful, the waters a shimmering cerulean that shone a deep purple under the setting sun. It was so wide that one could barely see the other side through the mist, and some distance beyond, it widened out into the ocean. Xiaoyi kept a leisurely pace, until a brilliant flash of gold in the water ahead caught his eye. Xiaoyi grounded the pole into the silt at the bottom of the river and slowed down the raft. He crouched down and squinted. It could be a fish, though one that shined so much must be worth a lot.

Sometimes though, small ships and pirates got into a scuffle and some gold would be lost overboard. Xiaoyi scarcely allowed himself to hope that it was a mound of real gold pieces. However, when he reached the area where he had seen the flash of gold, there was nothing in the waters.

Sighing, Xiaoyi straightened up and began punting again. Behind him, a pair of eyes in the depths of the water watched his raft drift down the river.

* * *

As the wind was blowing south, he made it to the village in good time. It was a much larger village, almost a small town, and was decorated with wooden signs marking the details of the competition. Xiaoyi smiled at the lively atmosphere and walked past a row of stalls selling 'fish rice,' 'fish bun,' and 'fish-shaped cups.' At the end of the stalls, Xiaoyi found a booth in front of a hut that held a sign saying 'Register Here.'

"Excuse me, I would like to register for the competition," he called out.

"Wait a moment!" came a gruff voice. Eventually, a large man walked out of the hut and grabbed a paper and a brush from behind the booth.

"Good evening, I've come to register for the fishing competition," Xiaoyi repeated politely.

"Cutting it close, aren't you?" he grunted. "I'm Kang Yugang, village chief. Give me your full name, age, and village name.

"My name is Song Xiaoyi. I'm eighteen years old, and I have arrived from

52

Mai village."

"Two coins to join. Pay up."

Xiaoyi pulled out two coins from his pocket and handed them to the village chief.

Kang grunted again, then pulled out a woven bracelet from a bag with a small token hanging from one end.

"Wear this, otherwise disqualified."

"Which fishing spots are available?"

"Up to three miles from this end and around to the west side from the other end. You will see the blue flags. You cannot fish beyond them," Kang said curtly.

"Is this large container for sale?"

"It's yours for five coins."

Xiaoyi considered the rather steep price for a moment before deciding to purchase it. He would have to make it back by selling the fish he caught, but hoped he could make a huge catch for which the container would come in handy.

"Thank you for your help," Xiaoyi said as the container was handed over to him. He bowed and walked away.

"Hey! You can buy more rods and fishing lures here," Kang reminded him, much friendlier now that Xiaoyi had parted with five additional coins. Xiaoyi smiled wryly and gave him a quick nod. He spent the next hour jogging around the edges of the river and deciding on which spots to claim for the competition. Even in the waning sun, he could see several dark shapes of fishes swimming in the water. While it was still part of the Yu River, this village seemed to have far more fishes than his own. It explained why the village could grow so much larger.

A flash of gold appeared at the corner of his eye. Xiaoyi turned quickly and walked closer to the water, peering about anxiously. But there was nothing. The river was even emptier here than at the other spots he had found. Was he imagining things? With a sigh, Xiaoyi marked the spot with a small stick and a smooth stone. He decided to check back tomorrow. Satisfied, he brushed his hands off on his trousers and headed back to the row of stalls. Next to the stalls, a group of people who were unable to pay for lodgings had set up makeshift beds and covers to sleep under. Xiaoyi drew closer to the group then thought better of it and walked a distance away.

Grabbing two sturdy branches from the ground, Xiaoyi took out his knife and with a deft hand, he began whittling down one end on each into a sharp point. He then plunged the branches into the soil and knocked them deeper with a stone. Pulling out a length of used cloth, Xiaoyi set it down between the branches, then lay down and folded the cloth back around to cover himself. He placed his bags below his head as a pillow and tied the straps to the two branches.

"Can I sleep nearby?" a voice came from behind him. Xiaoyi turned around to see a small boy whose height barely reached Xiaoyi's chest inching closer. He was dressed in rags and carried nothing more than his fishing rod and bucket. His hair was unkempt and his face so dirty that it was difficult to make out his features. However, his eyes shone with fierce determination.

The boy stared pointedly at the setup that Xiaoyi had made to secure his bags.

"Why not stay with the bigger group?" Xiaoyi asked.

"I'm an easy target," the boy said sullenly, "and you seem like a much nicer guy than those other people."

"Why thank you," Xiaoyi chuckled before waving the boy over and laying out his spare clothing for him. The boy looked gratefully at him and settled down on the clothes.

"What's your name?" Xiaoyi asked.

"Mingming."

"Have a good night's sleep, Mingming."

"Thank you," Mingming whispered.

* * *

At the first light of dawn, Xiaoyi woke. The skies were a pale pink and there were only a few clouds. Xiaoyi smiled. The weather would be good for fishing. He sat up and checked his bags, ensuring nothing had gone missing.

"Wake up," he called out softly to the little boy curled up near him. The child grumbled and Xiaoyi chuckled before gently shaking him.

54

"It's almost time for the competition. If you don't wake up you're going to lose out."

Hearing those words, Mingming shot up from where he lay and frantically grabbed his rod and bucket. Xiaoyi retrieved his spare clothes, now stained with soil and grass, and folded them together with the cloth he had laid on. A gong sounded from the other end of the stalls.

"Competition starts now! Ends at sundown!" Kang Yugang's booming voice carried over clearly.

"Well, good luck to both of us," Xiaoyi told Mingming cheerily. The areas he had marked out the night before were quickly occupied by other fishermen.

"Go away kid, or we'll break your neck," a group of rough-looking fishermen threatened him.

"Not a kid," Xiaoyi replied. Shrugging, he headed to the last spot where he had seen the flash of gold instead. It was an isolated area and the river ran clear and empty here. A small stream from the right stretched out and merged with the river. Xiaoyi sighed when he saw no sign of fishes but still, he settled on the grass at the riverbank. A fisherman needed to have patience. A swish of a practiced hand and the fishing line gently broke the surface of the river. Somehow, fishing out here, he felt transported into a different time and space. There was no one to bother him, and the peace and quiet was a welcome respite. Xiaoyi closed his eyes and enjoyed the cool breeze upon his face and the soft burbling of the stream.

Xiaoyi had begun for not more than ten minutes when he felt a tug. Surprised, he peered into the water as he reeled his line in. Clearly, there was a fish at the other end, and yet aside from the one, the river waters still looked empty. Puzzled, Xiaoyi pulled the fish off the hook and plopped it into his bucket filled with river water. It was fat and shiny and even if he couldn't win a prize, he knew this fish would make a good meal.

For many days, Xiaoyi fished and reported his biggest catch and sold the rest of the fish. He was glad he had bought a larger container, as his bucket was full and the container was also swimming with several large fishes. And yet none of the fishes appeared in the river until they had bit the hook. How mysterious! However, he did not find any particularly hefty fishes until the

NOT SO GRIMM: NEW TAKES ON OLD TALES

last day of the competition. It was a fish far bigger than he had ever seen, with great baleful eyes and a gaping mouth. It was so monstrously large that it barely fit into the container.

Pleased, Xiaoyi knew he had a good chance of winning and was ready to leave when again, a flash of gold passed by in the water. This time he was prepared and quickly threw out his flax-woven net which neatly landed around the rascal in the river that had been teasing him for almost a week now.

The thing struggled in the net, causing the water to splash out onto the riverbank.

"Got you," Xiaoyi crowed triumphantly. He pulled the net out and startled at the fish caught in it. It was unusual, with a brilliant gold back, a turquoise belly, purple fins, and spikes along its spine.

"What are you? I've never seen a fish like you before." Xiaoyi tilted his head curiously. Its bulbous eyes glared at him then rolled up. It proceeded to flop until it gave up and glared at him straight in the eye while making a little sound that sounded suspiciously like a snort.

"I don't know what I'm supposed to make of a fish's expression, but I suspect I'm supposed to feel insulted by that?"

"Yes, you are."

Xiaoyi yelped and fell backwards. He had been talking to the fish out of habit but he certainly hadn't expected it to talk back!

"Yes, yes. I'm an intelligent fish. Stop looking stupidly at me and release me back into the river."

"Ahhh! A talking fish!"

"Are you deaf as well? Put me back!"

Frowning, Xiaoyi picked up the net whereupon the fish began thrashing in it again. "I think you would fetch a very good price even if you aren't the largest in the competition. I'm sure someone in the market would pay well for an uncommon fish like you."

"Uncommon? Uncommon!? I'm a magical fish! Release me or else!"

"Magical fish. Now that's funny!"

"I'm not joking, you imbecile! They would skin me alive or roast me. I'm a highly intelligent fish and I have important things to do! I—I can grant you three wishes if you release me!"

"Now you're just pulling my leg. Three wishes. What sort of fairytale do you think you are in? This is the real world."

In truth, Xiaoyi thought that the fish was right. It did seem far too intelligent for a fish. While he was certain that talking fishes didn't exist in his village, perhaps they existed where rich people lived. Rich people seemed to have all the most unusual things. The fish must have escaped a noble's house. It was not worth getting into trouble for if the fish belonged to someone wealthy...

Sighing, Xiaoyi released the fish into the river. He rolled up his net and hooked it on the side of his bags before slowly lugging both bucket and container back to the gathering point.

"Hah! I knew it. Greedy human," the fish muttered when Xiaoyi was out of hearing range, not knowing that the three wishes had not swayed the young man.

Xiaoyi was a short distance from the hut and the booth when he saw Mingming sitting upon a flat rock and crying. His face was even dirtier now with a mix of mud and tears.

"What's wrong?" he asked gently.

Mingming looked up into Xiaoyi's kind face and cried even harder. The boy had met with trouble while fishing, and his catch had been taken by a group of rough men.

"I don't...I wouldn't care if it wasn't for my sister," Mingming cried, his little fists beating the grass in anger.

"What happened to your sister?"

"She's gone to work as a servant for an official to pay off our family's debts. He's a very cruel man, but we've lost our parents and Jingjing is doing her best for both of us. If I could win the first prize of five silver pieces, I could pay off the debts and bring her home." Mingming's body wracked with his sobs.

Xiaoyi sighed. It seemed King Ao had truly let his people down. During the reign of the previous king, children had been better protected. He handed his container to Mingming who grasped the handles and looked up with a confused expression.

"You can take mine. This fish is very large, and you'll stand a good chance of winning the first prize. And if you sell the rest, they should fetch you some coins."

Mingming stared down in the container that he could barely carry. A huge fish lay within, so fat that it reached the sides of the container and could not swim. There were several other fishes in it that looked meaty and had shiny scales.

"I—" Mingming began, but when he raised his head, Xiaoyi was already at the booth and reporting his catch to the village chief.

* * *

When Xiaoyi returned to his raft, he had more than earned back the seven coins he spent, but he failed to win any of the top prizes. He hoped his family would not be too disappointed. As he made his way back up the river, the raft suddenly broke down the middle. It was only with his quick reflexes that Xiaoyi managed to scramble up onto the riverbank instead of falling into the water.

"It should have lasted a few more trips," Xiaoyi mused. He dragged the raft up and rescued his bags but stopped to stare at the ropes in bewilderment. It looked as if it had been chewed through somehow. Xiaoyi groaned and looked around. He could walk back on foot, but it would cost him at least a couple more days. Rebuilding the raft would take him several more days and he would need to find bamboo as well. Xiaoyi gripped his hair in frustration.

"Looks like someone's in trouble," a gleeful voice called out from the river. Xiaoyi looked up to see the talking fish looking utterly smug.

"Are you laughing at me?"

"Of course. Your misery is my delight."

"Well then, go away. I have no time for you," Xiaoyi grounded out.

"Don't be too hasty. I could grant you your first wish right now," the fish said, grinning.

"You're actually serious about it?"

"What is your wish?" the fish asked.

Xiaoyi frowned then shook his head. "I don't need a wish. I just have to repair this raft or else start walking back home."

"Use a little creativity! You could wish for a ship made of gold and laden with treasures from all over the world."

Xiaoyi narrowed his eyes and replied to the fish with no small amount of suspicion, "I may not have been educated but I know a bit about boats and water. A gold ship would sink. Just what are you up to?"

"It was a joke." The fish laughed and looked about shiftily.

"Well I don't find any humor in this," Xiaoyi said and stood up huffily. He left the pieces of the raft where they lay and took off with his bags and empty bucket. If he walked quickly, he might make it home in two days.

"Hey wait! Where are you going? I didn't give you permission to leave!" the fish hollered after him. The young man did not turn back.

* * *

Xiaoyi returned to the sight of his parents in tears. Qiuyan was nowhere to be seen. He placed his bags and empty bucket on the floor before sitting by his mother where she rested on her bed.

"What's going on?" he asked in concern. "Where is Sister?"

His mother only cried harder.

"Mother? Don't cry. Let me know what's happened?"

"Qiuyan she—your sister, our dear Yanyan..." His mother choked and then shook her head, refusing to continue any further.

"Father?"

His father tried to wipe the tears at the corner of his eyes as discreetly as he could. He lifted his head and Xiaoyi reared back in shock from the large bruise on his father's left cheek.

"King Ao came to our village. We were caught unaware and Qiuyan was out helping me sell the baskets. He saw her and—" His father's face crumpled.

Xiaoyi did not need to listen any further to guess what had happened. He broke out in cold sweat and it felt like his heart had plunged to the depths of his stomach. His precious little sister, whom he had sworn to protect, was now in grave danger. He could not and would not accept that this was her fate. He would fight with the heavens if he must to bring her safely back home.

"I'll bring her back," he promised.

"No, it's too dangerous. And how could you convince King Ao to let her go?"

his mother objected, though she looked pained to say it.

"I won't be speaking to King Ao, of course. Besides, she's just one of many beautiful women he'd laid eyes on. He'd hardly remember if she disappeared," Xiaoyi argued. "I'll prepare to leave tomorrow. Which route did they take to the capital? The eastern one?"

"I do not know," his father admitted.

"I'll need to borrow a horse," Xiaoyi said, sighing, "which would use up a good half of the coins I earned from the fishing competition. But there's still enough left for you to feed yourselves for some months until I bring Qiuyan back."

His father looked at the ground in sorrow and guilt. "I'm sorry. I am such a useless father."

Xiaoyi shook his head. "You've done what you can for the family. And as you said, I'm eighteen now. I shall protect our family too." He stood up and began to prepare for the long journey ahead. He had no idea how much time he would need to retrieve his sister, but he would not give up. His parents exchanged worried glances before his father gave a defeated smile and got up to help him.

"You're always so stubborn. I don't want to lose you both," his mother sniffed.

"There's an unusual fish swimming in the bucket. Is this something you caught?" his father asked as he bent down to retrieve it. Xiaoyi froze where he stood. Unusual fish...

It couldn't be.

He hurried over and looked into the bucket. And there it was. The talking fish. Swimming in a bucket full of water. Looking smugly at him.

"Yeah that. That one's not edible." Xiaoyi laughed nervously and lugged the bucket out of the door. He dropped it carelessly near their old shed, and the water sloshed out.

"Hey! Watch it!" The fish gripped the side of the bucket with its fins until it was stable.

"Are you a ghost fish? Why are you haunting me?" Xiaoyi said angrily.

"Why! I'm just here to offer you your wishes! You still have three, you know?"

Xiaoyi folded his arms and glared at the fish. "Why should I be making any wishes with such a suspicious fish?"

"Desperate times call for desperate measures. You do want your sister back, don't you?"

"Yes, but—"

"You're not going to be able to snatch her from King Ao that easily. Likely you'll die, he'll still have her, and your parents will be devastated. But you could wish for an army to take her back."

Xiaoyi threw his arms up in frustration. "Why would I do that? Why do you not suggest I just wish for her to be back?"

"You could do that," the fish said with a nod, "since you lack the creativity for better wishes."

Xiaoyi fell silent and stared at the fish dubiously.

"Do you want to make your wish or not?" the fish asked impatiently.

"You would bring her back safe and sound? No tricks? Not missing anything, not dead in a sack, not an imposter. My actual sister, safe and sound, back home. Not with King Ao close behind."

"You drive a hard bargain." The fish sighed. "You have my word that your sister, your real sister in blood and bone, will be back here safe and sound. Completely unharmed except, I suppose, a little bit traumatized from seeing King Ao's ugly mug and being captured by him."

"Okay...alright. Please grant me this wish."

"It shall be done." The fish smirked in triumph and Xiaoyi had a terrible premonition before everything went black.

* * *

Xiaoyi woke to the sound of wood clacking on stone. It sounded like a carriage was passing by. Or he was on a carriage, because there was a rocking motion too and he was being bumped about...

Xiaoyi bolted upright.

He was on a bloody carriage!

He reached out to pull aside the curtains at the window and was shocked to discover that his hands were covered in a fluttering pink cloth. It looked like—

Horrified, Xiaoyi lowered his gaze and found that he was indeed dressed in Qiuyan's favorite dress. Prying open the curtains, he carefully peeked out and saw several guards both in front of and behind his carriage. There were a few ahead who were riding on horses, surrounding a second, more extravagant carriage with King Ao's banner.

"I'm going to kill that fish," Xiaoyi swore.

He smacked his face lightly to clear his mind before looking about the carriage. There had to be something useful he could utilize. He was rummaging about when he felt his carriage slow to a halt. Xiaoyi stiffened and then hurriedly removed the cloth used to cover the seat and threw it over his face. He heard the drapes shift apart and someone climb into the carriage.

"Hmm? What's this?" a man's deep voice muttered. Xiaoyi shrunk back against the side of the carriage. A moment later, the cloth covering his face was pulled off. Xiaoyi stared into the handsome but cruel face of King Ao.

"As I thought. You have the build of a man. Did you exchange places with her?"

Xiaoyi kept silent, his lips pressed together as he shook in both fear and anger.

"Who are you? The girl's brother?"

"Do you not even remember her name?" Xiaoyi shot back.

King Ao threw his head back and laughed. "Why should I remember the name of someone disposable? She's a beautiful woman, but your features are even finer than hers." The king reached out and gripped Xiaoyi's chin roughly, tilting his face this way and that as he studied it.

"Mm, I think I shall keep you."

Xiaoyi jerked back and the king relinquished his grip.

"What's your name, young man?" King Ao smirked.

"Why should you know the name of someone disposable?" Xiaoyi asked with narrowed eyes.

King Ao laughed again and patted Xiaoyi's cheek. "You're a cheeky thing. But be careful, there's a limit to how much disobedience I will allow." He then left the carriage in a swish of silk and walked over to his royal courtier.

"Find out everything you can about this man."

Xiaoyi peered anxiously at the king speaking to his subordinates but was not able to make out what they were saying. Soon after, the procession began moving again. A girl who appeared about the same age as his sister climbed into his carriage.

"Mister, my name is Jingjing. I was sent by my master, Lord Zhou, to care for you until you reach the capital. From there, you will travel to the palace with the King. Please let me know if you need anything."

"You look familiar. Are you...do you know someone called Mingming?" Xiaoyi asked.

The girl looked startled and nodded. "I am his sister. Is he in trouble?" she asked worriedly.

"No, he's okay. I met him at a fishing competition," Xiaoyi explained.

"I received a letter from him just a day ago, saying he won the competition because a kind man gave him his fish instead. Was that you?" Jingjing asked.

"Uh..." Xiaoyi scratched his head in embarrassment.

"I thank you, good sir, for your kindness towards my brother and I. This is my last task for Lord Zhou and I will be able to return home with the money that my brother won with your generosity."

"You're welcome, it was no trouble. Wait, we shouldn't be talking about this now." He leaned forward and whispered urgently. "Can you help me escape?"

"I..." Jingjing looked about worriedly.

"Please, my family needs me. My parents and my sister are waiting for me," Xiaoyi entreated.

Jingjing took a deep breath then said softly, "At the capital, they will settle the King's carriage first, then your carriage. Shortly after that, they will tend to the horses. That is the best time to leave. Run down the street until you see the first inn on your left and turn round the corner. There will be a backdoor and a koi pond there with some bamboo. You can hide behind the large rock."

"Thank you! I shall not forget your help," Xiaoyi said, grabbing her hands gratefully.

* * *

63

Jingjing's instructions were clear and helpful, and in less time than it took for an incense stick to burn, Xiaoyi found himself safely tucked behind the large rock at the koi pond. He hoped desperately that no one would realize he had escaped until much later, but his hopes were dashed when shouts rang through the streets.

"Where did he go? Find him!" King Ao commanded.

Xiaoyi winced and crouched even lower behind the large rock. The guards were coming closer to where he was hiding, their voices getting steadily louder.

"Where is he? You had better find him, or the king will have your head!" a guard yelled.

"He'll have all our heads! Mark my words. I will make sure you regret it if we're punished!"

"You little wretch, where did he go?"

"I don't know! I was helping at the stables! He must have slipped away then!" Jingjing cried.

Xiaoyi bit his bottom lip in worry. He wanted to escape but he hadn't thought about how he would have gotten Jingjing into trouble.

"Hey. Psst."

Xiaoyi startled, then looked about in fright. Did someone find him?

"Hey. Over here! Look down."

Xiaoyi lowered his head and through a hole in the large rock, he saw a familiar face.

"You again!" Xiaoyi exclaimed.

"Hush. You don't want the guards to find you, do you?" the fish chided.

"What do you want? This is really not the time!" Xiaoyi said. He peered past the rock to see the guard gripping Jingjing's hair. He was about to stand up when the fish spoke again.

"Are you going to run out and get both of you caught?" the fish asked.

"Then are you suggesting I watch her suffer because she tried to help me?"

"You do have two more wishes," the fish reminded him. "You could wish all the guards dead in this instant."

"I haven't even gotten back at you for pulling that nonsense with my first wish. You have the gall to ask me to wish again?" Xiaoyi said angrily.

Xiaoyi was about to retort further when the guard shouted, "Drag her away and beat the truth out of her!"

"You're running out of time," the fish pointed out the obvious.

"Okay! Please save Jingjing from the guards!" Xiaoyi said frantically.

"It shall be done," the fish said. A short moment later, the guards were in disarray for having lost Jingjing as well.

Xiaoyi collapsed from relief. He leaned against the rock and turned his head to look at the fish. "Where did you send her? Did you put her on a rooftop?"

"Better," the fish said gleefully. It swam backwards and used its fin to gesture to a koi swimming behind him. "Say hi to Jingjing!"

Xiaoyi stared at the koi in horror. Gritting his teeth, he made sure none of the guards were facing his direction before he swiftly scooped up both Jingjing and the meddling fish into the bamboo tub by the pond. He quickly ran out and down another street, taking several turns past other streets until he came by an inn that looked more rundown. He adjusted the carriage seat cloth which he had wrapped himself in. Reaching into his pockets, he found spare coins that he always made Qiuyan keep in her little embroidered pouch. Xiaoyi approached the innkeeper and paid for two nights. Once he received his key, he stomped angrily up to his room and slammed the doors shut.

"How dare you!" Xiaoyi shouted at the fish as he put the bamboo tub on the table. "Turn Jingjing back at once!"

"Is that your third wish?" the fish asked with a nonchalant air. Xiaoyi clenched his fist and went to the other side of the room to cool down. He took a few deep breaths and then shut the windows. He searched his pockets again, and found a small blade hidden in his sleeve. Qiuyan was indeed his sister. She knew better than to walk around without any protection.

He removed his sister's dress and began slicing the skirt off with the blade. Qiuyan would be miserable if she saw him tearing up her dress, but he had little choice. After a few modifications, he put it back on and pulled the cloth previously used as a seat cover over his shoulder like a shawl.

"You have a rather small waist and you looked good in a dress. King Ao must have been drooling."

Furious, Xiaoyi stalked over to the fish and pressed the blade at its throat. "Calm down!" the fish cried.

"You horrid creature! I've had enough of you. Tell me! What is your purpose? Why have you been messing around with me like this?"

"Remove the knife first! Okay, okay! I'm a prince! An enchanted prince. And a good guy like you surely would agree that it's not right to slit my throat!"

"An enchanted prince? Well right now you're looking like a fish to me and my job is to gut fishes! You better start telling me the truth!"

"I *am* telling the truth! I was a prince in the palace. Five years ago, King Ao, who was then the second prince, killed my siblings and very nearly killed me, and then threw us into the river. I survived miraculously. Now would you please remove that blade from my throat?"

Xiaoyi sighed and withdrew his hand but gave the fish a warning glare.

The fish slumped against the side of the bamboo tub and continued his story.

"That day the River Yu ran red with our blood. I was only fifteen, and the second youngest in the family. I was born with a weak body, but my mother, who was a powerful enchantress in her own right, cast several protection charms on me. Even though they had weakened since her passing, they saved me from death. But still, I had sunk into the river with little energy or life left to swim. When I woke, I found myself turned into a fish. There was little I could do but plot revenge every day. A few weeks ago, I came across a sage who informed me that I could turn back into a human if I granted three wishes to another. I would then return to the palace and take the throne away from my brother."

"I...I see. That is quite a story. And this is why you've been asking me to make wishes?"

"Yes. However, you haven't been cooperative."

Xiaoyi waved the blade in the fish's face and the latter backed away rather quickly. "Can you blame me? I've made two wishes, both of which were for good reasons, and you've found a way to mess both up."

The fish looked away guiltily.

"Perhaps you've developed a twisted personality spending five years as a fish. Perhaps you've forgotten what makes for acceptable humor and polite company. Perhaps you had a mean streak even before you turned into a fish. But let me tell you something. I will not make that third wish. King Ao is a horrid king, but you would not be a good ruler either."

Xiaoyi left him with those words and walked out of the room.

* * *

The next morning, Xiaoyi was in a foul mood. After their honest exchange the day before, he hadn't spoken to the fish at all, though he made sure to buy some fish food to feed Jingjing. However, he was running low on coins and he needed more if he were to arrange for transport back home. It was a long distance away without a horse.

While Xiaoyi had attempted to look for menial work around the capital yesterday, he was turned away by everyone he approached. He supposed even with his modified outfit, walking about dressed in blushing pink marked him as an oddity.

He rolled out of his bed and dejectedly walked over to the bamboo tub. He stared at it and it took him a full minute to realize what was wrong.

"Where's Jingjing? What have you done with her?" Xiaoyi exclaimed.

"She's fine," the fish said tiredly, "she'll be back soon." Right after the fish had spoken, there was a knock on the door, and it pushed slowly open.

Jingjing peered in, and upon seeing Xiaoyi up, she quickly entered.

"Mister!"

"Jingjing, you're...you're human again?" Xiaoyi asked in wonder.

"Yes, Lord Fish here turned me back. I have brought food and some supplies for you."

Xiaoyi carefully accepted the simple workmen's clothing and the packs of food on top of it. "Thank you, Jingjing. You must not tarry any further in case the guards find us. Go home to Mingming and I wish you both well."

"I'm sorry I could not do more, but I will remain grateful to you for the rest of my life." Jingjing bowed respectfully.

"You've done plenty. I am in your debt," Xiaoyi told her. When she left, he turned to look at the fish who was lazing at the bottom of the tub.

"Well I guess there is some good in you," Xiaoyi said.

The fish replied with a 'hmph' and turned away.

Xiaoyi smiled wryly then dressed in his new clothes before leaving the inn. He could now find work and earn some coins to return to his family.

This time, he was barely spared a glance before the chief workman shoved him in the direction of a pile of stones and wood logs. "Transport all of them to the other building there by the end of today," he was told curtly by the workman.

"I would get twelve coins after this, right?" Xiaoyi confirmed. He received a reluctant grunt and with a helpless shrug, Xiaoyi began a long day of manual labor. When he returned to the inn in the evening, he was exhausted and drenched thoroughly in sweat.

"One bath to room four, please," he requested. The innkeeper took a coin and left to prepare. Xiaoyi trudged up to the room in a miserable state and waited outside for the innkeeper. He would rather not risk them seeing the fish. Two assistants carried over a bathtub filled with hot water, another bucket of lukewarm water and a washcloth. Without another word, Xiaoyi brought the items in himself and then escaped into the room.

He moved the bathtub to a small area separated by a divider and stripped himself of his dirty clothes. With the lukewarm water and the washcloth, he washed himself as best as he could before stepping into the tub.

"Ahhh," Xiaoyi sighed happily as he sank into the hot water. It was heavenly for his sore muscles.

"Enjoying yourself? Could you not even give me a greeting when you came back?"

Xiaoyi screamed as the fish surfaced in the bathwater.

"Hey, stop screaming. My ears are fragile."

Xiaoyi grimaced and then flushed a deep red when he realized the fish was in his bathtub. His bathtub! He was naked! Xiaoyi frantically covered his nether regions.

"Y-you you..."

"I-I-what? Why are you so shy? There's nothing you have that I don't have too. I used to be a man, remember?"

"That's not the point! Get out!"

"No," the fish refused.

"Wouldn't you get cooked at this temperature?" Xiaoyi retorted.

"I would be fine if you made your last wish. I'd be a man again."

"I wouldn't trust you again." Xiaoyi narrowed his eyes. "Besides, have you thought about what you would do if you managed to defeat King Ao and take the throne? What would you do for the kingdom and the people? Or is it all just for revenge?"

"Revenge is a big part of it," the fish admitted, "but I also need to go back for my youngest sister."

"Your sister?"

"Princess Ling Yi," the fish said with a sigh, "my little baby sister. She was safe from the fight for succession, but since then she's been left at the mercy of Ling Ao. I fear that when she comes of age, he will barter her off to the northern barbarians."

"Does the king not care for his own sister?"

"Ling Ao murdered the rest of us in cold blood," the fish scoffed. "He would not care for the princess. Never mind, you wouldn't understand."

"I do understand. At least part of it. I have my own younger sister too, if you remember. I always worry she will marry a man who does not deserve her. My parents used to tell me that because of the Queen—your mother—people were becoming more accepting of women working and going into politics. But when King Ao ascended the throne, it was as if everything went backwards. And now my sister is suffering for it too."

The fish looked contemplative. "Perhaps you're right. Father and Mother created a wonderful legacy that has been left in the dust. Although my siblings fought for the throne and for power, the third prince and the eldest princess were well suited to lead. Now it has all gone awry."

Xiaoyi fell silent as he processed what the fish just told him. "What's your name?" he asked after a moment.

"Ling Dan."

Xiaoyi burst out into laughter. "Like the 'miraculous medicine pill' Ling Dan? Truly?"

"It just sounds like it. It's written differently." The fish sulked.

"So, what should I call you? Dandan?" Xiaoyi teased. Ling Dan laughed and then turned red. Xiaoyi watched in curiosity at seeing a fish blush for the first time, until he realized what he had just said. Then, he flushed even redder.

"I—er—I have to finish my bath..." Xiaoyi wringed his hands in the water.

"Y-yeah, of course. I will return to the tub—uh—have a good bath," Ling Dan replied awkwardly.

"Hey um, Ling Dan?"

"Yes?"

"Thanks for sharing that with me," Xiaoyi said. There was no reply. He was left alone in the bathtub as he awkwardly bathed in water that was only lukewarm now. Only as he went to bed for the night did he hear Ling Dan's response.

"Thank you for listening," the fish said.

Xiaoyi smiled.

* * *

"Now if you really want money without making a wish, which I'm telling you I would not mess up "

"Still not convinced," Xiaoyi interjected while rolling his eyes.

"—you should consider doing something you're more skilled at. Manual labor obviously isn't your thing. And I cannot believe I'm saying this, but catching and gutting fish is your specialty. So why not find a restaurant to work at? You can offer your cooking services to this inn. Trust me, you'll get the job. The cook here is terrible."

"Oh, that's actually a good idea!" Xiaoyi said excitedly, then his face fell.

"Why do you look so morose?"

"You'll leave after the third wish is made, right? You'll go back to the palace."

"Yes," Ling Dan replied, "at the least, I must retrieve Princess Ling Yi."

"Well if you...if you change your mind. You're welcome to travel back with me. Or after you've found your sister," Xiaoyi said nervously, his voice getting gradually softer as he spoke.

"I'll consider," Ling Dan said after a moment. "I'm surprised. I thought you disliked me?" The fish smirked.

"I-I'm just taking pity on you," Xiaoyi stuttered. The fish chortled and smacked its fins against the edge of the bamboo tub.

Xiaoyi shook his head. "You really are terrible, Ling Dan."

"Don't call me that," Ling Dan objected.

Xiaoyi stared at him blankly for a moment before he registered what the fish had said. "Oh. I'm sorry. P-prince? Prince Dan?" Xiaoyi tried awkwardly. What was he thinking? Calling a prince by his name without any honorifics was extremely disrespectful.

"No. Not that." The fish coughed embarrassedly. "The name you used yesterday. Call me that instead."

"Er. Fish?"

"No, the other one, the..." Ling Dan tried but couldn't seem to bring himself to say it. He began blushing again.

"Oh, you mean...Dandan?" Xiaoyi started turning red as well.

"Y-yeah. That. Yes," Ling Dan said, then flapped his fins about. "Well. You should get going."

"I. Yes. Right!" Xiaoyi stood up quickly and scampered out of the room. He shut the door and leaned against it, taking deep breaths. He lightly smacked his face with both hands. Somehow, he felt embarrassed, and a little flushed. But he also felt happy. His heart was beating faster, too... What was happening?

Xiaoyi shook his head to clear his mind and then headed downstairs. He found the innkeeper in the small area where guests were served meals. He was bowing and apologizing profusely to a customer.

"I'm very sorry, sir."

"And the meat is too tough! Are you trying to break my teeth?"

"Very sorry, sir."

"The tea was cold, and my wife nearly spat it out!"

"Our utmost apologies, ma'am." The innkeeper wiped the sweat off his brow nervously. "We will have the chef fry a new fish for you right away."

"Chef? More like a donkey at a stove! Shoo! Go away!" The angry customer waved the innkeeper off. The old man sighed and began heading to the back. Seeing an opportunity, Xiaoyi chased after him and followed the old innkeeper

71

to the backyard.

"Who are you? Guests are not allowed here," the innkeeper said, assessing him from head to toe.

"Hello, I am the guest staying in room four. I was hoping to offer you my services for some coins. I am very good at cooking fish," Xiaoyi said nervously. The innkeeper stared at him dubiously, his thick furrowed brows nearly meeting in the middle. He would have rejected this kid without a second thought, but the customer had just requested a freshly prepared fish and he knew the new dish would not be made any better. The cook he had hired was objectively bad.

"You have one chance. If you can cook a good fish dish for the customer there, I will hire you," the innkeeper said begrudgingly.

"Yes, sir!" Xiaoyi said delightedly. The old man led him into the kitchen where the cook was found asleep at a table.

"Get up, useless nephew!" the innkeeper yelled and then turned to Xiaoyi with a sour expression. "All the equipment you need is on this side. The new stock of fish brought over by the fishermen this morning was placed in that tub. Spices and all other things in this cabinet. Get started!"

Xiaoyi nodded and headed to the tub where he found a suitable fish. He picked out a knife and turned to the cook and politely asked, "May I use this knife?" The cook pointedly ignored him, yawned, and left the kitchen to continue his nap in the backyard. Xiaoyi sighed and began on his task, expertly slicing and gutting the fish.

"You really are good at this," Ling Dan observed from the bowl of water Xiaoyi had prepared. Xiaoyi jumped in fright and quickly placed the sharp knife down on the chopping board.

"Could you please warn me instead of appearing so suddenly? You're going to give me a heart attack! Also, I needed that bowl and water." Xiaoyi rolled his eyes and prepared another fresh bowl of water. He was getting used to the prince's antics and could not bring himself to be angry at him. He quickly hid the smile that had begun to form on his face. "What are you doing here anyway? Aren't you scared of watching me skin and cook fish?"

Ling Dan coughed. "What do you think I ate while swimming in the river?

THE FISHERMAN'S CATCH BY CHU PARTRIDGE

Other fishes of course. I used to love eating fish when I stayed in the palace. But I've been thinking, when I am a human again, I might turn vegetarian."

Xiaoyi laughed and continued bantering with Ling Dan while he steamed the fish with ginger slices. He also prepared a tofu and vegetable soup to serve it in. Soon, the kitchen was filled with the aromatic scent of freshly cooked fish and the innkeeper was drawn back in.

"Something smells amazing!" the innkeeper exclaimed. He hurried over to watch Xiaoyi pour the tofu soup over the steamed fish. The meat looked soft and glistening white, and the ginger slices removed any undesirable fishy smell.

"T-this..." The innkeeper was at a loss for words. The old man gulped and then carefully, reverently brought the dish out to serve the customer.

"Well done," Ling Dan said, "I would eat that. Make sure you get paid for it though. That innkeeper looks like a shrewd one." Xiaoyi agreed. Now was not the time to reject the money owed to him. When the innkeeper returned, he joyfully relayed the customer's positive reaction to the dish and proceeded to cajole Xiaoyi to work as his cook permanently.

"My family lives far away. I will only be here for a few more days. Perhaps in the future, I might consider this opportunity," Xiaoyi declined politely.

"Ah. What a pity. If only my useless nephew was half as skilled as you." The innkeeper stopped his attempts when he saw that the young man was firm. He persuaded Xiaoyi to cook for another week and offered him good pay and free lodging. Xiaoyi was hesitant, but it was hard to resist a bit more money which he could use for his sister's marriage dowry in the future.

After breakfast and lunch, Xiaoyi carried the bamboo tub and strolled down the streets with Ling Dan.

"What if someone sees me?" Ling Dan whispered from where he was hiding at the bottom of the tub.

"We'll be fine. I saw a shop down the street the other day. I might buy you a better bowl to swim in," Xiaoyi explained, "and here we are." He pushed apart the curtains at the entrance of the shop and headed in.

"Can I help you?" the shopkeeper asked with a smile.

"Yes, I'm looking for a bowl to put a fish in. It should be easy to carry and opaque around the sides. About this size would work. Perhaps a lid for longer journeys," Xiaoyi told him. The shopkeeper nodded and fetched a medium-sized fishbowl with a handle, a lid, and a strap.

"I should warn you that most fishes would not survive long journeys," the shopkeeper said.

"I understand," Xiaoyi replied, "but I would still like to purchase this." After he made the payment he headed out and down an empty street to pour the clean water and Ling Dan into the new bowl.

"I'm not like most fishes, so I'll survive. But I don't enjoy long journeys in any case," Ling Dan grumbled. Xiaoyi chuckled and gently rested the fish at the bottom of the bowl.

"I'll order a carriage when I go home, Dandan. I know you have business in the palace, but if you want to come with me, or visit me after, the offer still stands," Xiaoyi said. They returned to the main street and spent a few hours looking at trinkets. Xiaoyi quickly pushed away the thought that this felt like a date. He stopped in front of a stall selling accessories.

"I think Qiuyan would like this." Xiaoyi held up a blossom pink ribbon with embroidered peonies. He hoped it would make up for his destruction of her dress. Ling Dan swam to the top of the bowl and peered at the wide variety of necklaces, rings, bracelets, ribbons, and hair pins. He stared at one of the rings while Xiaoyi was choosing a ribbon.

"Psst," Ling Dan whispered.

"Yes?" Xiaoyi lowered his head towards the fishbowl and whispered back.

"Do you like the look of that ring? The light blue one?"

"Hmm." Xiaoyi picked up the ring to examine it more closely. "It's very nice. It reminds me of the River Yu. But it's too expensive."

"Buy it for me," Ling Dan requested, "I'll pay you back when I'm able to."

"You can't just magic up something similar?" Xiaoyi asked, bewildered.

"That's only possible with wish magic," Ling Dan informed him.

"Very well." Xiaoyi laughed softly while his heart beat faster. "I'll buy it for you."

* * *

The week passed smoothly, and Xiaoyi earned a considerable sum of money from the innkeeper for a task he felt was of little trouble to himself. He spent some of his coins buying small gifts for his family, and getting to know Dandan better. He wondered if Dandan had changed his mind about going home with him. Xiaoyi gave a wistful sigh. With how well things were coming along, he believed that his luck had finally turned. But it was too good to be true.

On the last day before he planned to return home, Xiaoyi was rudely awakened by a cacophony of shouts. He groggily sat up in his bed and pushed the window open slightly. Through the gap, he watched as several royal guards dragged the innkeeper out onto the street.

"I don't know what you're saying," the old man whimpered.

"Don't pretend to be ignorant! We've heard reports that he was seen working in your kitchens," one of the guards yelled.

"No, no. Only my nephew works as a cook here," the old man protested. He struggled against the tight grip that the guard had on his collar.

"Find the man and drag him out," the guard told another. Shortly after, the cook stumbled out as he was roughly pushed and prodded with the hilt of the guard's sword.

"Is he the right one?" one of them asked doubtfully. "This one isn't the slightest bit attractive." The guards unfurled a scroll and compared the black ink portrait painted on it with the cook's face.

"Not one bit similar. Surround the inn and we will search the rest of the building! If we can't find him then drag these two to the prison."

Xiaoyi withdrew from the window and turned to look at Ling Dan with barely concealed worry.

"No," Ling Dan said immediately, "I know that look. You can't save everyone. Your messianic complex is going to get you killed!"

"I'm not trying to save everyone, but this is a person I've directly harmed by staying here and working for him," Xiaoyi argued.

"Well, clearly he's chosen to keep quiet about your existence in order to save you. The least you could do is to escape and not waste his efforts," Ling Dan insisted. Xiaoyi turned to look out from the window again. He turned back around with a determined expression, picked up his belongings, wrapped them up quickly into a neat bundle, and grabbed the handle of Ling Dan's fishbowl.

"Oh, here we go again," Ling Dan sighed. Xiaoyi hurried downstairs and bumped straight into one of the guards who had begun to search the inn.

"Hey!" the guard yelled and angrily shoved Xiaoyi back.

"It's me. I'm the person you're looking for," Xiaoyi said quickly. The guard stopped and scanned him with a suspicious gaze from head to toe. Xiaoyi stood straight and tall, willing himself not to show any fear.

"Follow me," the guard said and Xiaoyi stepped out onto the streets. The head of the guards held the portrait against his face and nodded.

"This is the one," he confirmed. "Take him straight to the palace." The other guards roughly shoved the innkeeper and his nephew aside. They stumbled onto the ground and cried out in pain. The old innkeeper looked up at Xiaoyi with a complicated expression as he was roughly pushed into a carriage. Soon, the carriage was in motion and Xiaoyi was once again en route to the palace. He winced as he rubbed his wrist where the guard had gripped too tightly. A bruise was quickly forming.

"Are you alright?" Ling Dan asked quietly.

"Nothing too bad," Xiaoyi murmured.

"I wish you were a more selfish person," Ling Dan said. Xiaoyi did not reply.

It took a day for them to reach the palace gates. Xiaoyi was provided no food or water throughout the journey and his throat was parched by the time he arrived the next morning.

He was unceremoniously thrown into a room that had nothing more than a bed and a lamp. A leering guard told him to wait for King Ao to visit before he was shut inside.

"It's an iron lock," Xiaoyi said as he struggled with the door. It was not made of simple, thin wood and paper strips, but of thick and sturdy wood. He could not break it apart and tear through a paper screen as he would most doors.

"Iron?" Ling Dan asked worriedly. "My powers do not work well on iron."

"If I could find a metal bar or something to wrench it open..." Xiaoyi paced about the room, trying to look for something useful.

"You need to listen to me," Ling Dan said hurriedly. "Now's the time to make a last wish. Wish magic is very powerful, and with it I can easily get you out of the palace."

"No," Xiaoyi stubbornly refused.

"Why?" Ling Dan asked in frustration. "I promise you I will not mess your last wish up in any way, if you would just trust me this time—" Ling Dan stopped talking midway when the door shook.

"Someone's outside," Xiaoyi warned. "You need to hide!" The next moment, there was a click of the lock and the sound of metal sliding on metal. Xiaoyi raised his arms, prepared to fight as much as he could. The door creaked open slowly and an eye appeared in the gap. Then, a hand firmly gripped the side of the door, pushing it open, before a large woman entered the room.

"Who—who are you?" Xiaoyi asked in confusion with his arms still raised.

"Yiyi!" Ling Dan cried as he surfaced the water again. He leaned out of the fishbowl and stared in wonder at his sister.

"Yiyi?" Xiaoyi asked, walking closer to Ling Dan, but not shifting his line of sight away from the stranger.

"This is my sister, the royal princess Ling Yi," the fish said, sounding choked up with emotion. The woman quickly stepped forward and stared at the fish in shock.

"You...that voice. You couldn't be my brother, Ling Dan?"

"Yes, yes I am! You still recognize me!" Ling Dan cried happily.

"I recognized your voice but...it's been many years. You're a fish now?" she asked uncertainly.

"And you have grown very large," Ling Dan observed.

"Never comment on a woman's size," the princess chided. Ling Dan laughed, and his fisheyes looked wetter than ever. Xiaoyi lowered his arms and backed away to give the two siblings space.

"Where have you been?" the princess asked tearfully. "Why did you not come back?"

"I almost died," Ling Dan admitted. "I've been stuck as a fish these five years and only made it this far because of this young man here."

The princess turned to look at Xiaoyi with curiosity burning in her eyes.

"This one is named Xiaoyi, family name Song. This one pays his humble respects to Your Highness," Xiaoyi knelt down and gave a full kowtow reserved for royalty.

"You may rise," the princess said.

"Actually, all things aside," Ling Dan said, "we're in a bit of a hurry. That scumbag Ao could come at any time—wait. Why are you here, Yiyi?"

"I have spies in the capital," Princess Ling Yi revealed. "One of them is an innkeeper. He sent a message saying King Ao had his eye on a young man for longer than he usually would. I had come to see for myself if there was something special about you."

Xiaoyi blinked in surprise. He hadn't expected the old innkeeper to be a spy.

"It must be fate that I got to meet my brother again. For that you have my thanks," the princess said.

"What should we do now?" Ling Dan asked.

"I will get you both out of here. I will send your friend back to his home and then I will find a way to return you to your human form, Brother. It is time to take the throne from that tyrant."

"Indeed," Ling Dan agreed, "but more than anything I am glad you are alright, Sister."

The corner of his lips had just begun to curve into a smile when Xiaoyi froze. He could feel the presence of someone standing behind him.

"My, my. What a touching reunion," King Ao said as he walked past Xiaoyi to look at his two siblings. His face was twisted into a cruel expression and his eyes mocked them.

"I was just thinking that it was time to send my lovely sister off to the North, where she would be of far more use to the barbarians. And now my brother has come back in the form of a fish," King Ao sneered. There was a beat of silence and the next moment the King viciously backhanded the princess.

She screamed and collapsed on the floor from the force of the slap. Her face bled and her cheek swelled quickly, an ugly red bruise forming.

"Yiyi!" Ling Dan shouted. King Ao reached into the fishbowl, pulled Ling Dan out, and threw the fish against the wall. He strode over to Ling Dan again when Xiaoyi threw himself in front of the prince.

"Move away, you worm," the king snarled.

"No!" Xiaoyi cried and held his arms out to shield Ling Dan who lay helplessly on his side, gasping in pain. King Ao bared his teeth and grabbed Xiaoyi's throat, lifting him up. Xiaoyi thrashed and kicked about, choking from the brutal grip and the lack of air.

"Leave him alone! Xiaoyi, *Xiaoyi*!"

He could hear Ling Dan shouting. The corners of his vision had begun to dim. As he started losing consciousness, Xiaoyi could finally admit to himself—he had kept from making the last wish because he was selfish. He did not want his time with Ling Dan to end so soon...

Before he lost consciousness, Xiaoyi made his last wish.

And everything went dark.

* * *

A fish splashed in the water. The sun's rays scattered across the surface of the River Yu. Its light blue and cerulean waters sparkled and the wavering depths that distorted the world that lay beneath the surface of the water made the river look surreal. The mist across the river seemed as paradisiacal as the mythical Penglai. Xiaoyi cast his rod into the water and smiled as the fish swam closer.

"Hey, are you done fishing?" came a cheerful voice from behind him.

"Shh...you will scare the fishes away," Xiaoyi murmured.

"Good. We're not poor anymore. You should stop working so hard. You'll get sick if you're not careful." Qiuyan came into view and began tugging on her brother's sleeve. "Come on, help me choose a ribbon for my wedding."

Xiaoyi sighed. He was always helpless against his sister's requests. He pulled his fishing rod back and stood up to follow his sister back to their hut.

"Ah, Son. You need to stop skipping out on lunch," his mother said as he entered their home. Her health had improved greatly over the years and Xiaoyi was delighted to see her walking about so energetically.

"I already ate when I went to the market earlier today." Xiaoyi gave her a quick hug.

"Oh, right! I forgot to move the rest of the eggs to the back," Qiuyan said, and she bounced off to the kitchen. Xiaoyi looked at her retreating back fondly.

"Can't let go?" his father asked from where he sat at the table.

"She's my little sister. I'll always worry. That Yuan kid better treat her well or I will skin him alive."

His mother laughed and patted his shoulder. "Before you think to threaten your soon-to-be brother-in-law, how about you think seriously about finding yourself a wife?"

Xiaoyi shook his head. "I have no plans to and I will not change my mind any time soon."

"Is there no one who caught your eye? Not even at the Zhao's party last weekend?" his mother asked.

"It's improper for the younger sibling to marry before the elder," his father said, "but more than that, we are worried about you."

"I already have someone in my heart," Xiaoyi confessed, "but the person has many things to do and lives in a different world from ours. Do not worry about me! I'm satisfied with life the way it is now," Xiaoyi replied. He smiled reassuringly and left to help his sister in the kitchen.

"He looks alright on the outside, but I'm not convinced," his father said. "It's been three years since he returned from the capital and he still hasn't told us what happened."

"Didn't he exchange letters with some fellow from the palace when he came back? For a whole year, there was always a messenger running back and forth," Madam Song mused.

"And it only lasted a year. Well, we can't expect anything from the people there. They have more important things and more important people to bother with," her husband sighed.

"I heard rumors," Madam Song added, "they say the new King Dan may abdicate the throne."

"So fast?" Mister Song asked in surprise. "It's barely been three years. Although he's done a world of wonder for the people..."

In the kitchen, Xiaoyi frowned as he heard his parents' conversation. He felt concern for Dandan and bitterness for having been forgotten but he chose not to dwell on it. Xiaoyi busied himself instead by helping his sister with her incessant requests on choosing the right ribbon and the right accessories. It was nearly evening when Xiaoyi was alerted to the sound of hooves outside their house. They rarely had people come through the village on horses.

He walked out and looked around warily. There was a horse tied to the pole outside their hut, but no rider. The horse's saddle was made of simple leather and looked rather common. Xiaoyi felt the painful hope that had begun to bloom fall away again. How could he think so highly of himself?

Xiaoyi walked on further and there, on the gentle grassy slope towards the river, a lone figure with a noble bearing stood, his hair blowing gently in the breeze. When Xiaoyi walked closer, the figure turned around and upon seeing the man's face, he felt his heart stop in his chest.

"Dandan?" Xiaoyi choked out.

"What are you doing, standing over there? Come over here." Ling Dan smiled. Xiaoyi sobbed and ran over, throwing himself into Ling Dan's open arms. In the man's tight embrace, Xiaoyi felt that the world which had been thrown off its axis had now righted itself again.

"Hush, don't cry," Ling Dan soothed him.

"Why did you stop sending letters?" Xiaoyi looked up at him accusingly.

"Things were still unstable then, and we suspected a spy in our midst. I didn't want to risk your safety if an enemy intercepted your letter," Ling Dan explained.

"And now?"

"I've stabilized the Kingdom and the palace affairs. Once I was done with the inspections at the trade route the next town over, I rode out at first light to find you."

"Well, I'm happy you came but..." Xiaoyi pushed Ling Dan away and stepped back from his embrace. He kept his head lowered to hide the pain and resentment on his face. "You will leave again anyway. It's not right for a king to be gallivanting out here instead of tending to the country's matters."

"About that." Ling Dan reached out to hold Xiaoyi's hands, pulling him closer again, "I'm no longer king now."

"What?" Xiaoyi stared at him, stunned. "Then..."

"Ling Yi has taken over as the Queen and the announcement will be made throughout the Kingdom soon."

"But why?" Xiaoyi asked, bewildered.

"Do you remember your last wish? You said, 'Dandan, I wish for you to be well and happy.'"

Xiaoyi looked away, his cheeks flushed red. "Must you repeat that?"

"Well." Ling Dan grinned. "The wish wasn't completed. I am well now, but I am not happy."

Xiaoyi turned his head back to look at Ling Dan in confusion. The man then reached into his sleeve and pulled out a ring, which he slid onto Xiaoyi's finger. It was the same ring that they had bought in the capital's market three years ago. The light blue hue was still a perfect match for the River Yu's waters, though there were a few gems now added to the ring. Xiaoyi tilted his hand, mesmerized. When the gems caught and reflected the sunrays, it looked just like the scattering of light across the surface of the river water.

"Will you make me happy by marrying me?" Ling Dan asked gently, his hands still cradling Xiaoyi's. His eyes were filled with both hesitation and hope.

Xiaoyi stared at him, and then broke into a beaming smile and pressed his lips to Ling Dan's in a soft kiss.

"Yes, and for the rest of our lives, Dandan."

4

Meadowsweet, Woodbine, and Lavender
by Arlo Blackwood

The few lacy clouds were tinged pink and gold by the rising midsummer sun, smearing color into the grey predawn world. Mist rose like ghosts from fields of winter wheat just starting to turn golden. It was already quite warm—the day promised to be another hot one.

By the time the Miller family reached Eastfold village square, a crowd was already gathered, nervously awaiting the time of Choosing. The Millers lived at the edge of the Nameless Wood, just outside the village proper. The father was—in conflict with his name—a woodcutter. His wife was a midwife, and their thirteen children ranged in age from twenty-two to seven.

Eighteen was the age at which the people of Eastfold village became eligible for the Midsummer Tithe: an offering of flesh and blood to the Witch of the Wood. In exchange, the Witch granted protection from the demons of the forest and ensured a bountiful harvest. The elders of the village still told stories of the year the sky went black at midday and a plague of frogs descended upon their crops, destroying everything in their path. Everyone knew it had been the Witch. And so, every year, a man and woman were chosen, bathed, and crowned with wreaths of meadowsweet, woodbine, and lavender—the sweet scents of which were said to entice the Witch—and sent into the forest as a sacrifice.

This was the first year the Miller twins, Nikolai and Lorelei, were old enough for the Tithe. Their older siblings had insisted that there was nothing to worry about—the Tithe always seemed to avoid their family—though their mother and father were far more grim.

Lorelei huddled next to her twin. She wasn't cold, but she'd awoken that morning with a premonition that still clung to her mind like the mist in the fields. One look at Nikolai over the breakfast table had confirmed he'd had the same feeling.

The mayor stepped out into the square just as sunlight spilled over the square. He was a short, round man with wispy grey hair and a suit that stretched across his large belly. He wore several gold rings and an expensive blue silk sash of office. The mayor's assistant, a youth of twelve or thirteen, hauled two wooden chests onto the dais. Inside each chest were slips of parchment with names written upon them. One chest contained the names of men, and the other, those of women. The mayor flourished his hands, wriggling his fingers in mystical-seeming passes over the chests, and then plunged his arms into them simultaneously, sending bits of parchment sailing.

Nikolai rolled his eyes at the Mayor's showmanship, but still squeezed Lorelei's hand tightly. The Mayor raised his arms triumphantly, a bit of parchment sticking out from each side of his plump fists.

"The Chosen of this year's Midsummer Tithe are..." he said, his voice carrying clearly across the crowded square. He opened his palms with a theatrical flourish.

The thrill of premonition that had plagued the Miller twins rose to a crescendo. Lorelei and Nikolai exchanged resigned glances. The rest of the gathered crowd broke into excited murmurs.

"Lorelei and Nikolai Miller."

* * *

Their mother raged and their father wept. Their three older siblings silently clasped the twins' hands in turn, their faces pale with sorrow. Their eight younger siblings cried and clung to them as if that could prevent them leaving. They spent the rest of the day saying their goodbyes. The butcher's son and the baker's apprentice mournfully said they'd miss the sweet sound of Lorelei's singing at the fair. The candlemaker's son shyly asked Nikolai for one of his drawings by which to remember him.

That evening, as the sun blazed bloody-gold in the west, and the heat of the day still lingered, the Miller family made their way once more to the village square. The twins had bathed and dressed in their finest clothes but had left their shoes behind. Shoes were expensive, and they had eight younger siblings who could grow into them.

The common had been transformed. Many large wooden tables had been set up, each one laden with food. A large, crackling bonfire burned in the center of the square, and the parchment slips bearing the names of the rest of the adults of Eastfold village were cast into the fire, symbolically rendering them safe for another year. Lorelei and Nikolai, as the guests of honor, had seats at the head of the mayor's table. The mayor's family and friends toasted them with goblets of wine and mugs of ale. Roast pig, fresh bread, and fine cheese were sliced and served, along with berry pies and pastries. The Miller twins sat sullenly while the rest of the village rejoiced. Neither of them touched the food.

Children wore flower crowns and laughed and danced; they didn't truly understand the horror of what was to come. They'd learn eventually when they were older, or lost a loved one to the Tithe. The younger Miller children were red-eyed and somber this year.

"It's a great honor!" the mayor said, clapping them both on the shoulders. "You're doing your part to protect the rest of your family!" Then, he wobbled off, face flushed with wine.

"Strange how the mayor and *his* family seem to be exempt from the Tithe," Nikolai muttered. He'd gotten a bit of charcoal and was mindlessly drawing designs on the table.

The waxing moon cleared the treetops of the forest, a pale crescent that hung in the night sky, unremarkable except that it heralded the time of Tithing.

The mayor made a show of crowning the Miller twins with the wreaths. They were allowed to embrace their parents and siblings one last time. And then were sent off. A procession of villagers followed them with the mayor in the lead, carrying a rowan-wood torch that had been lit by the bonfire. The edge of the Nameless Wood loomed above them, a great wall of blackness that swallowed the starlight.

Lorelei and Nikolai gazed up at the dark woods, their hearts pounding in their chests. They held hands gone clammy with fright, and without even a backwards glance, strode forward into the Wood.

* * *

The Wood was even darker once they entered. They were somewhat familiar with the shallowest edge of the forest, as they'd helped their father and older siblings cut wood during the day. But the trees took on sinister forms at night, twisting into demons that reached with grasping wooden claws to rip their clothes and bloody their exposed skin. Roots seemed to writhe around their ankles to trip them, and sharp sticks and stones rose up from the loam to bite the soles of their feet. The twins held tight to each other's hands as they traversed terrain rendered unfamiliar by the dark.

Silence pressed on from all directions. Even the animals and insects were quiet, and the air still, as if the world were holding its breath. The only sounds were the twins' footfalls on last year's leaves and their faint breathing. Somewhere in the distance, a lone frog croaked, and they both startled at the noise.

After a while, when the silence became too oppressive, Nikolai asked in a low whisper, "Do you think the Witch of the Wood actually *eats* people? Are we to just keep wandering until the Witch finds us? Are we allowed to go home if morning comes and the Witch hasn't got us yet?" He was babbling but couldn't seem to stop himself.

"None of the Tithed have ever returned," Lorelei said. "Maybe they made it through the woods to the other side and found a new life there?" She tried not to sound too hopeful.

"Or maybe they were eaten by wolves," Nikolai said. "I wonder what's worse—being eaten by a pack of wolves or by the Witch?"

"It's not much of a choice," Lorelei replied, resigned.

* * *

86

From high in the branches, a purple lizard watched as two young people traveled deeper into the forest. The lizard leapt from one tree to the next, silently following them. The one who watched from behind the lizard's sharp eyes was intrigued.

* * *

They must've been walking for hours, though with the trees blocking out the moon and stars, there was no way of telling how much time had passed. Their eyes had adjusted to the darkness, yet they still stumbled occasionally over hidden deadfall or exposed roots. If there had ever been a path, it had been lost long ago. As they went deeper into the forest, the nature of the Wood itself changed. The trees grew taller, wilder, and more twisted. The air was redolent with the scents of loam and rot. The forest floor became spongier, and soon, they were struggling to pick their feet up out of sucking mud. Here and there, clumps of odd, greenish, glowing mushrooms sprung forth from the ground and decaying logs. Walking near them left sickly yellow-green smears on their clothes and skin.

* * *

As the night wore on, the existential horror of the Tithe gave way to something more mundane: they were both ravenous.

"Do you think those are safe to eat?" Nikolai asked, pointing at a gently-phosphorescing cluster of mushrooms.

"Do they look safe to you? I'm not about to eat something that glows in the dark," Lorelei retorted.

"What about that?"

"That's a stump."

"It looks a bit like a cake if you squint,"

"It doesn't even slightly look like a cake, Nik."

"Roast goose," Nikolai said. "Fresh bread, soft cheese. Apples, the slightly sweet kind."

"Stop that," Lorelei's stomach growled at the thought of food.

Nikolai sighed. "We should've eaten more at the feast."

"We should've eaten anything at the feast." Lorelei sighed. "Knowing you're going to be sacrificed rather ruins one's appetite."

Nikolai stumbled over another hidden root and swore. "I do wish the Witch would just get on with it. I'm getting bored."

"We'll die of starvation at this rate." Lorelei paused to brush a glob of phosphorescent mushroom off the hem of her skirt. "Or perhaps thirst? I think people die of thirst first, don't they?"

"We might die of boredom first," Nikolai said. "I never thought I'd want to meet the Witch, but anything would be better than this." He kicked a bit of mushroom. They seemed to be multiplying.

"I don't remember seeing these before," Lorelei said, gesturing to the mushrooms. By now, there were so many that the twins could see quite well in the gloom.

"Well we've never been in the Wood at night before, have we?" Nikolai said.

They kept walking. The mushrooms kept multiplying. The trees became more twisted and rotten. Lorelei hummed a little tune—a nervous habit that had the effect of calming herself. The sound of it seemed to form a little bubble around them, as if song alone could hold back the dangers of the forest.

"Blackberry tart. Currant jam. Honey cakes," Nikolai listed, as if the words were a magic spell that would make food appear. "I think I would actually fight a pack of wolves for a blackberry tart right now."

"Me too," Lorelei admitted.

Just then, Nikolai stopped in his tracks. Lorelei walked a step further and almost lost her grip on her twin's hand. Lorelei turned to see what caused him to stop. Nikolai looked at her with wide eyes.

"Do you smell that?" he asked.

"Smell what?"

Then, she did. At the same time, they turned to each other. "Gingerbread!" they shouted. They tore off through the woods, all care forgotten, only the hunger in their bellies driving them on. Glowing mushrooms streaked by in yellow-green blurs as they ran, heedless of fallen branches and exposed roots and knotted brambles.

At last, the smell of gingerbread peaked, and they stumbled into a small clearing—so small, the trees still blocked out most of the night sky above. Before them stood a little cottage surrounded by all manner of plants, mossy stones, and a pond. Dozens of frogs croaked from the pond, followed by the occasional splash. The cottage was built right against the bole of a large tree, as if it were some strange growth from the tree itself.

Candy-colored smoke rolled from the chimney in glittering pink and blue clouds. The white eaves glistened as if they were made of sugar. The siding of the house scalloped in a gingerbread pattern.

Lorelei and Nikolai exchanged glances, and then, as one, they stepped into the clearing. The moss was soft and seemed to waft a sweet, minty scent when trod upon.

They reached the cottage. None of the windows—which seemed to be made of many-colored, mismatched panes of real glass—were open, as they were expecting. The smell of gingerbread seemed to be coming from the walls of the cottage itself.

"It's a gingerbread house!" Nikolai whispered in awe.

"That can't be right," Lorelei said. But it was true. The walls themselves smelled of gingerbread. Even the glass windows smelled like sugar.

"I'm so hungry, I could eat it even if it were made of wood and plaster," Nikolai stated. And then he leaned forward and licked the wall.

"You look stupid doing that," Lorelei told him, even as her stomach growled loudly. What if the house really were made of gingerbread? She leaned forward and tentatively touched her tongue to the mullioned glass.

"I wouldn't do that if I were you," a voice said from behind them. "The green glass is made with arsenic."

The twins jumped as one and spun around. The speaker had a deep, pleasant baritone, though all they could see was a tall shadow standing at the edge of the pond.

"What do we have here? Could it be the village Tithe? Strange siblings who show no fear?" the voice said. "Siblings who are trying to"—the shadow person paused, as if he was trying to hold back a laugh—"eat my house?"

The shadow stepped closer, resolving into a tall, strikingly handsome man with long, jet-black hair, pale skin, and eyes which flashed emerald green in the dim light. He wore a long black robe and several thin silver chains around his neck. The robe hung in such a way that it exposed a good swath of skin at his chest.

Lorelei and Nikolai put their backs to the house—the Witch's house, for this person had to be the Witch—and watched with wide eyes as he stepped closer. He stopped, standing barely a handbreadth from Nikolai. Nikolai averted his gaze, his cheeks darkening with embarrassment. The Witch studied Nikolai for several long moments, before nodding to himself, as if satisfied with something. Then, the Witch moved on to Lorelei. She did not avert her gaze. She clenched her jaw and stared straight into the Witch's very green eyes in challenge.

The Witch held her gaze for several long moments, as if staring into her very soul and weighing it. Then, he smirked and gave her a wink. That flustered her, and she looked away, feeling her own cheeks heat up.

The sounds of the night came rushing in once more. The frogs in the pond croaked and splashed and the crickets chirped. Leaves rustled in the night breeze. The twins felt as if they'd passed some kind of test.

"Now, I suppose I don't need to tell you that my house is not actually food," the Witch said. "Though with as much of the Green Lady mushroom on your bodies as you have, I'm surprised you're not convinced you can fly." The Witch looked pointedly at the twins' feet. Smears of yellow-green phosphorescence still stained their bare feet and legs. Bits of it clung to the hem of Lorelei's skirt and the legs of Nikolai's trousers. Two pairs of yellow-green footprints softly glowed in a line back to the forest.

"Come in, then," the Witch said. "You need to get cleaned up before you climb a tree and try to eat the moon."

The Witch ushered them through the front door of his house. The inside was crammed with dried herbs, potted plants, and an assortment of oddities bursting from every cupboard. Clusters of garlic, onion, and several varieties of dried flowers hung from the rafters. More of those yellow-green mushrooms were growing in a glass terrarium guarded by a small violet lizard. They nervously eyed the large black cauldron which hung by the strangely purple fire, some kind of potion merrily bubbling away in it. There were more frogs inside the house, croaking at them from countertops and hopping along the large wooden table.

"I have many names, but you may call me 'Mattias,'" the Witch said, after he'd shut the door. He strode past them into the kitchen.

The twins stood close together in the entry, uncertain of what was going to happen next, and a little bit frightened. The cauldron *did* look large enough to cook a person.

The Witch—Mattias—crossed his arms and leaned back against the large wooden table. He raised an expectant eyebrow. "And your names are?"

"Nikolai," Nikolai blurted.

"I'm Lorelei," Lorelei said reluctantly.

"Nikolai and Lorelei," Mattias said, as if trying their names on his tongue. "Welcome to my home."

The twins did not leave the foyer.

Mattias sighed. "There's a bath through that doorway, down the hall and to the right," Mattias said, gesturing. "But please wipe your feet on the moss mat, first."

They looked down; beneath their feet was a welcome mat that did appear to be made entirely of moss. They dutifully wiped their feet and went through the door Mattias had indicated. There were four steps formed from stones set into tree roots, and beyond that, a hallway paved with flagstones. The walls seemed like they were made of living wood, as if this part of the house were actually inside the trunk of the giant tree.

Shelves carved into the walls housed all manner of oddments: crystals, feathers, books, carved bits of wood. Frogs hopped and croaked from various corners. The small bathroom was dominated by a fair-sized stone basin half-set in the earthen floor and filled with steaming water. Another moss mat lay in front of the basin, presumably to catch water.

Nikolai and Lorelei exchanged glances.

"He wants us clean before he cooks us," Nikolai said.

"Definitely," Lorelei said.

But the prospect of a hot bath was too good to resist, so they took turns washing the worst of the muck and mushroom off.

By the time they were fully clean again, their old clothes had been spirited away and plain black robes left in their place.

They exchanged another glance and dressed quickly. Lorelei stomped up the hall back into the kitchen, with Nikolai following much more cautiously behind. Mattias was lounging in a wicker chair with his head tipped back and feet propped on the table bench.

"What happened to our old clothes?" Lorelei demanded.

"I've burned them," Mattias stated. He gestured languidly to the fireplace without looking up. "They were covered in toxic spores."

Nikolai exchanged a glance with his twin. "Toxic spores?" he asked, the words unfamiliar on his tongue.

Mattias lifted his head and favored him with a look. "The greenish glowy bits of the Green Lady mushrooms, which were all over your feet and clothes."

"Oh."

"They are highly poisonous and powerfully psychoactive, causing hallucinations, paranoia, and delusions of grandeur even when absorbed through the skin." When Nikolai and Lorelei gave him blank looks at the unfamiliar words, he clarified, "They make you see things that aren't there. Or perhaps smell, in your case, since you were both going on about gingerbread when I found you trying to eat my house."

Nikolai flushed, Lorelei glared, and Mattias smirked.

"These robes have protections woven in. They'll keep the worst of the spores off you when we go through the forest."

Lorelei looked up sharply. "We?"

Mattias directed that inscrutable look towards her this time. "Of course. You managed to find my house despite the wards and misdirections I've placed around it. I've taken it as a sign." He unfolded himself from the chair and smiled wolfishly at them, his green eyes flashing. "You're both my apprentices, now."

* * *

Mattias led them up a staircase tucked behind the fireplace which opened into a loft. The upstairs was mercifully frog-free. There was a door on either side of the loft; they were shown to the rightmost one. Beyond it was a small room with a narrow bed. Mattias considered the bed for a moment and then grabbed the edge and *pulled*.

The bed stretched.

Lorelei and Nikolai gawked. This was the first time they'd seen actual magic done. The bed stretched into double-size and then split apart down the center with a fabricky pop and a puff of straw. In the end, there were two identical narrow beds, each pushed against a wall.

"I trust you two can share the rest of the space," Mattias said. He ran his fingers through his long hair. He didn't even appear to have broken a sweat. "Get some rest. Your apprenticeships start at dawn."

The twins nodded mutely, staring after him with wide eyes as he swept from the room and gently shut the door behind him.

Only after they'd extinguished the candles and climbed into their beds did they speak.

"This isn't how I expected the day to go," Nikolai said, breaking the silence at last.

"Neither did I," Lorelei said.

Nikolai turned over to face his sister. "So, instead of being a witch's dinner, we're his apprentices?"

"Apparently." Lorelei frowned. "I wonder what happened to the other Tithes. Did he eat them?"

"Maybe he turned them into frogs," Nikolai said, yawning. "I don't know what makes us so special though."

A long silence followed.

"I'm still hungry..." Nikolai said.

Lorelei shifted in her bed, trying to get comfortable. "Me too," she admitted.

* * *

Morning came far too early. Mattias burst into their room without even knocking.

"Up you get! We've a long day ahead of us."

He seemed inordinately cheerful. For a moment, the twins didn't know where they were. Lorelei pulled the blanket over her head until all that could be seen of her was a lump with curly brown hair. Nikolai pulled the pillow over his head and groaned.

93

"No apprentices of mine are going to be lazy layabouts," Mattias warned.

When neither twin moved, Mattias stepped between the beds and placed a hand on each frame. A mild jolt of electricity surged from his fingers and along each bed frame. The twins leapt straight into the air with identical yelps and gave him identical glares. He gave *them* both his brightest smile.

"Dawn comes early at Midsummer." Then, he swept from the room. "If you don't hurry, I shall feed your breakfast to the frogs!"

They nearly got stuck in the doorway trying to get through it at the same time.

Downstairs, the frogs were ever-present, always underfoot and croaking. They swarmed the countertops, clambered across the large wooden table, and even lurked in the cupboards in tea cups and bowls. The only thing they left alone was the terrarium with the mushrooms.

"Your house seems to be...um...overrun with frogs," Lorelei said to Mattias.

Mattias, who was over by the cook stove, with his long hair incongruously pulled into a sort of bun, gave her a look out of the corner of his eye and hooked a stray lock behind his ear. "It's not overrun. They live here."

When neither twin said anything, he continued, "They're useful. They eat bugs." Then he gestured to the sleeping purple lizard. "Augustus eats bugs too, but he's too lazy to catch them, usually."

"Rude," the lizard said, cracking open one startlingly orange eye.

"The frogs came here because something terrible has befallen their king, and they've asked me to help," Mattias went on.

"Frogs can talk?" Nikolai asked.

"Frogs have kings?" Lorelei asked.

The frogs responded by breaking into a chorus of angry croaking.

"Everything can talk if you know how to listen," Mattias said, sending a glare at the purple lizard, Augustus, "and sometimes they never shut up."

"Only because I'm always right and yet you never listen to me," Augustus said.

"Don't listen to Augustus. He's only my familiar."

Augustus responded by flicking his orange tongue out.

"As for frogs having kings," Mattias continued. "I'm not sure about all frogs, but these do."

The frogs croaked in agreement.

"Here." Mattias ladled some thick, sweet-smelling porridge into wooden bowls and slid them to the twins. "The porridge has lavender in it. It should help stave off any lingering Green Lady poisoning."

The twins devoured their porridge helpings ravenously, even going so far as scraping their bowls with their fingers. Mattias, nonplussed, spooned more porridge into their bowls and they devoured that too.

"Don't they feed you in that village of yours?" he asked.

Nikolai blushed, embarrassed, and couldn't meet the witch's eyes. Lorelei met his gaze squarely.

"We had enough," Lorelei said. "Our family wasn't rich, but our parents loved us and gave us the best life they could."

Mattias sat down at the table across from the twins. "Yes, they loved you so much they let that mayor send you into the woods to die."

"That's not—" Nikolai started. When Mattias turned his gaze upon him, he blushed to the roots of his hair, but didn't look away. "They didn't have any choice! I...we...*you're* the one who demands a sacrifice!" At that, Nikolai stood from the table, his hands clenched into fists at his side. "How do we know you're not just...just being nice to us to lull us into a false sense of security? How do we know you're not just...fattening us up to...to eat us!"

Mattias shot a quick glance at Lorelei—who was also rather shocked at her normally soft-spoken brother's outburst—and then stood up with an almost inhuman fluid grace. Lorelei sat frozen at the table, uselessly clutching her empty bowl of porridge as Mattias stalked around to where Nikolai stood.

Nikolai's hands trembled but he didn't back down or look away even as Mattias closed the space between them. Mattias was a good foot taller than Nikolai, and yet Nikolai stood straight and tall as he could.

Mattias' hair had come loose from its binding and writhed down over his shoulders and back in a fall of pure shadow. His eyes seemed to catch the light of the room and blaze as green as the arsenic-stained glass in his windows. Almost faster than the eye could see, Mattias gripped Nikolai's chin in his hand and tilted his face up.

Nikolai blushed even redder, but didn't—or couldn't—look away.

"I bring you both into my home, and this is the thanks I get?" Mattias said, soft and dangerous. "I merely study the tides and currents of the natural world. I did not ask for any Tithe, and I am not in the business of cursing villagers or destroying crops. I am in this forest because something is making it sick and I must discover the cause and eliminate it."

There was a long, strained moment that seemed to stretch on for eternity.

"If I wanted to kill you," Mattias continued, gazing deep into Nikolai's eyes, "rest assured, I would have done so already."

Then, he released Nikolai, and stood back. Nikolai remained where he was, red as a tomato and trembling.

"And as for eating you, well..." Now Mattias smirked, and his tone grew distinctly flirtatious. He reached out and tucked a lock of curly brown hair behind Nikolai's ear. "Maybe later."

Then, he turned his gaze to Lorelei and winked at her. "I'd have quite the feast—breakfast and supper!"

Now it was Lorelei's turn to blush as tomato-red as her brother.

* * *

After breakfast, Mattias set them to work grinding fragrant dried herbs with a pestle and mortar, scrubbing out the big cast-iron cauldron, heating water, and applying pungent oil to soft leather boots and gloves.

"I don't suppose either of you know how to read and write?" Mattias asked that afternoon, when he came in from outside covered in pollen and hauling an armful of strange plants.

Lorelei and Nikolai shook their heads and Mattias sighed. "Well, I suppose I'll have to teach you that, too, or you won't be able to write our findings in my field journal." He dropped the plants down into a washbasin and fished a small, leather-bound book from the inside of his robe, which he then tossed carelessly onto the table. "There are pictures in it, too, but I'm no artist," Mattias said, mournfully.

"Drawing?" Nikolai asked. "I draw a bit."

"He's spectacularly good at drawing; don't let his humbleness fool you," Lorelei said, swatting Nikolai on the back of his head. "His drawings look like the real thing."

Nikolai reached over and let his hand hover over the beaten up and stained cover. He looked to Mattias with a question in his eyes. Mattias nodded once and Nikolai picked up the book and flipped through it. It was full of wriggly, messy script and rather crude drawings. Bits of dried plant fell out from between the pages. Nikolai pulled over a stem of lavender that had avoided the mortar and pestle and looked around for something to draw with. Mattias produced a charcoal stick from his voluminous sleeve and handed it to Nikolai.

Nikolai sketched the lavender stem quickly and with a fine attention to detail. When he was finished, he slid the journal across the table. Mattias inspected it with interest.

"You have a deft hand, Nikolai," he said. "It looks so lifelike."

Nikolai flushed with the praise.

Mattias looked over to Lorelei.

She gazed back. "I can't draw, if that's what you're wondering."

"Then what hidden talent *do* you have? For surely you must."

"She can sing," Nikolai supplied.

Lorelei glared at her brother.

"Really?" Mattias folded himself gracefully onto the bench and propped his elbows on the table.

"I won't sing for you," Lorelei said, flatly.

"Oh? And why not?"

"Because her voice beguiles men." Nikolai snickered.

Lorelei threw a bit of lavender at him. "It does not!"

"It does too! Remember the butcher's son? The baker's apprentice?"

Mattias laughed. The sound was like water over river rocks, and wind through summer leaves. "You don't need to sing for me if you're afraid you might beguile me, Lorelei," he said.

"I'm not afraid!" Lorelei replied, indignant. "I just...don't feel like singing right now, that's all."

Mattias held Lorelei's gaze until she flushed and looked away.

"Nikolai," Mattias said, "Would you be so kind as to sketch those Green Ladies in Augustus' terrarium?"

Nikolai looked puzzled. "Sure," he said, gathering the journal and the stick of charcoal.

He gave a wary glance at Augustus, who was still curled in the terrarium, and opened the journal to a fresh page.

"Don't get too close," Mattias warned. "The spores are contained, but you don't want to take any chances. We can't all be as lucky in our biology as Augustus."

"I'm not affected by them," Augustus said, smugly gesturing with his tail to the mushrooms. "I'm not actually a lizard, you know. I just take this form while I'm bound to Mattias."

Nikolai nodded, and tried not to think of what Augustus actually might be if not a lizard. He began sketching the mushrooms and the bit of rotting wood they grew on. They were oddly formed, narrow at the top and then flaring out into a bell shape. They rather did resemble the shape of fancy ladies wearing fine dresses.

He scowled at his drawing and scribbled it out. He tried again. All of his renderings of the Green Lady mushrooms looked as childish as Mattias' drawings. He finally threw down the journal in frustration.

"I can't draw them! I can't capture their forms at all!"

Mattias only sighed. "As I thought." But he didn't elaborate further.

* * *

The next few days were spent doing much the same. Mattias would wake the twins up at the crack of dawn, feed them lavender porridge, and then have them clean, organize, and grind herbs while he went out into the woods. The frogs had learned to stay clear of the kitchen after being almost stepped or sat upon by the twins.

Mattias spent a good deal of the day outside, but told the twins to stay indoors as much as possible. When he came back to the house, covered in pollen and smelling of trees and rot, he'd taken to messing with a small, wooden box that was crusted with melted wax.

"Do you think he keeps a demon in there?" Nikolai whispered to Lorelei one day after Mattias had left.

"I don't know. He keeps Augustus trapped in a box too," she replied.

"I'm not trapped," Augustus said with a yawn. "I'm merely keeping these specimens under observation. I can leave whenever I wish."

Nikolai exchanged a glance with Lorelei. They seemed to be having a wordless argument. Finally Nikolai turned to Augustus. "So..." he began, trying to keep the nervousness from his voice. "What happened to the other Tithes?"

Augustus regarded him with a fiery orange eye, and then made a show of stretching. "He ate them, of course."

Nikolai blanched and Lorelei dropped her pestle.

Then, Augustus flicked his tongue over his eye and said, "That was a joke. I was joking."

When neither twin said anything, he sighed.

"What happens outside this forest is no concern of ours. We don't meddle in the affairs of normal folk," Augustus said, examining one of his shiny black claws. "But once the Tithes are inside the forest, Mattias must feel some kind of responsibility—the sentimental fool. He sends me to find them so we can get them to Westfold village on the other side of the Wood." Then, he paused. "That is, if the thing in the forest doesn't get them first."

Lorelei stood and walked over to the terrarium. "The thing in the forest?"

Augustus flicked his tail at the Green Lady mushrooms in annoyance. "Whatever it is that's going around making these. He thinks it's some kind of demon."

"Like you?" Nikolai blurted.

Augustus' expression was one of reptilian offense. "I," he said, with as much dignity as a lizard could muster, "am *not* a demon. I am a spirit of fire and air."

"Are the frogs spirits too?" Lorelei asked, curious.

"No, they're just frogs."

"So they're definitely *not* the Tithes of previous years?" Nikolai asked, feeling the need to clarify.

Augustus made a strange sound and it took the twins a moment to realize he was snickering. "Is that what you thought? That the infamous Witch of the Nameless Wood turned the Tithes into frogs?"

"Um..." Nikolai began. "Something like that."

Augustus favored him with an indecipherable reptilian look. "No, you thought he ate them."

Lorelei and Nikolai exchanged a guilty glance.

"That is, of course, what the previous Tithes thought, too," Augustus went on. "Sometimes they'd be so overcome with fear we had to adjust their memories before escorting them out." He sighed again. "Annoying."

"So you sent them to Westfold?" Lorelei asked. "Why?"

"Mattias has no use for gibbering idiot villagers," Augustus said, contemptuously. "And sending them back to Eastfold would only panic that superstitious lot."

"So if the Tithe isn't to Mattias," Nikolai asked, "then who or what is it for?"

Augustus gazed at them for a long while. "That's what we're trying to figure out. It has something to do with what's poisoning the forest," he said at last.

That gave the twins something to think on for a long while.

* * *

The wreaths of meadowsweet, woodbine, and lavender that they had worn during the Tithe now hung over the mantel of the fireplace. When Lorelei asked Mattias why he kept them, he only cryptically answered, "Even a stopped clock is right twice a day."

He had Nikolai draw the wreaths next, on a clean two-page spread in his field journal. Nikolai drew them in such great detail that they almost looked as though they could be plucked from the page.

Nikolai had taken to trying to draw the Green Ladies every chance he got, and yet it was always the same. The mushrooms could not be captured by an artist—not even one as skilled as Nikolai. After his fifth or sixth attempt, he flopped down at the table and put his face in his charcoal-stained hands.

"Why can I not draw these damned mushrooms?" His voice was muffled by his hands but his frustration was obvious.

"Have you tried sneaking up on them and taking them unawares?" Lorelei said, holding back a smirk.

"Yes!" Nikolai's forehead thumped onto the table. "I don't understand it."

"It's because they're the product of a curse," Mattias said from right behind Lorelei.

As usual, his entrance had been utterly silent. Nikolai sat up quickly, his face red. Mattias leaned down to set more herbs on the table and his arm brushed Lorelei's shoulder. He was so close behind Lorelei she could feel the heat of his body. She sat very still and willed herself not to blush.

Mattias moved around the table with liquid grace and folded himself onto the bench beside Nikolai. "Let's see, then," Mattias murmured, reaching across Nikolai to pull the journal over. His green eyes roved over the pages of failed mushroom drawings. Everything else had been rendered beautifully: the rotting log, the pebbles and twigs, and even Augustus, peering out from one of the drawings with one eye cracked open. The only thing that looked out of place were the shapeless mushroom-blobs.

"The Green Ladies are resistant to magic," Mattias said.

Nikolai looked puzzled. "But I'm only drawing them. I'm not trying to do magic to them?"

Mattias smiled and reached one elegant hand up to wipe a bit of charcoal off of Nikolai's cheek. His hand lingered. "Your magic manifests in your drawings."

Lorelei looked away, vaguely embarrassed to be witnessing this moment between them.

"Now," Mattias said, "I have something else I'd like for you to draw, if you would?"

Nikolai nodded. Mattias crooked a finger and the mysterious wooden box lifted off the shelf and floated over to the table.

"What is it?" Nikolai asked.

Mattias smiled. "Something that I have a feeling will come in handy later."

Nikolai flipped open the journal and began sketching. The box took shape after a few rapid strokes. "This is much easier to draw than the Green Ladies," Nikolai commented. "And it feels...friendlier too, if you catch my meaning?"

"Yes, it would be," Mattias said. "This box is made of rowan wood and lined with lead and silver. Its purpose is to trap curses within."

Nikolai nodded as if he understood.

"Keep drawing it from different angles." Mattias stood and stretched languidly. "Until you can draw it in your sleep."

Then, he turned to Lorelei. "I'll leave the room, if you wish, Lorelei, but I'd like for you to sing at the box while Nikolai sketches it."

Lorelei gave him a dubious look. "You want me to sing to a box."

"If you would."

"Is this a magic thing?" Lorelei demanded.

"Yes, it is a magic thing," Mattias said.

"What will it do?"

"I'm not sure yet, but I've got a feeling about it." Mattias winked at her. "And I've learned to trust my feelings."

Lorelei chewed her lip for a moment. "What should I sing?"

"Hmm. A lullaby, perhaps?"

Lorelei thought for a long moment, considering the box in front of her. True to his word, Mattias left the kitchen and disappeared into the back room that served as his study and shut the door.

Feeling faintly ridiculous, Lorelei took a deep breath and began to sing a lullaby their mother used to sing.

Oak and Willow, twining deep
River rocks beneath the stream
My darling dear, you now must sleep
Stars watch over as you dream

* * *

It had been a fortnight since Lorelei and Nikolai came to live with Mattias. In that time, they'd learned basic skills with herbs that could be applied to witchcraft, and had even begun learning how to read and write. Mattias left more of the black fabric that made up their robes on the table one morning and instructed them to sew face coverings from it.

The Green Lady mushrooms remained stubbornly immune to being captured in drawing, to Nikolai's endless frustration. Lorelei had taken to singing as she worked. It was only after she caught Mattias gazing at her with a strange intensity that she stopped. She'd sent a guilty glance at Nikolai and resolved to stay quiet after that.

They both missed their home and family. It was strange to live in a house shared with a multitude of frogs, a snide lizard, and a handsome witch instead of their parents and a horde of siblings. But neither twin could deny that they were almost happy living with Mattias. Mattias seemed to be glad of their company, at least. Augustus tended to sleep often and be rude when he was awake, and the frogs were not great conversationalists.

* * *

"I think you're ready to go into the woods with me today," Mattias announced that morning over breakfast.

"What?" Nikolai and Lorelei exclaimed at the same time.

"What about the poison mushrooms?" Lorelei asked.

Nikolai went a bit pale. "Aren't there wolves?"

Mattias made a gesture with his hand and the oiled gloves and cloth masks sailed over from the shelf to land on the table. "That's what these are for," he said. "They're now saturated enough with oil that they'll protect you from the Green Lady spores."

"And the wolves?" Nikolai prompted.

Mattias gave him a small, wry smile. "There aren't any wolves in this forest anymore. They left when the sickness first began."

"Good," Nikolai said.

"No, not good," Mattias told him. "Wolves are necessary for maintaining the natural balance. Although, most other things have left, too."

He looked troubled at that.

"Well, once we deal with the forest sickness, we can set to work getting the forest to rebalance itself," Mattias continued. "I've been tracking where the Green Ladies spring up, and I've discovered a pattern." He leaned closer across the table, his green eyes pinning first Nikolai and then Lorelei in place with their intensity. "I have a theory...but I can't do this alone. I'll need the two of you with me." He reached across the table with both hands, taking Lorelei's hand in his left and Nikolai's in his right.

A surge of tingling warmth sparked from where their hands touched, like that time the first morning Mattias woke them at dawn, except warmer and more intimate, somehow. Mattias looked just as shocked as the twins were.

His green eyes widened, and, for the first time since they'd met him, a slight blush suffused his face. He released their hands immediately and stood up.

"Yes," Mattias said, visibly flustered. "Well! Gloves, boots, masks, and cloaks on!"

* * *

In the daylight hours, it was obvious that something was very wrong with the forest beyond Mattias' clearing. Once they'd stepped beyond the ring of healthy trees, the rest of the forest looked almost decayed. Moss had gone black and slimy. Bark sloughed off the trees, revealing squirming, pale things that shied from the light. A brittle, browned fern crumbled to dust when Lorelei brushed by it. The Green Lady mushrooms covered every available surface. Even with their oiled cloaks and boots and gloves, and cloth face masks stuffed with dried lavender, the twins found the stench of decay nearly overpowering.

"It's worse than it was the night we left," Nikolai said.

"Whatever is causing the sickness didn't get its Tithe for the third year in a row," Mattias explained. "It's making its anger known."

Lorelei stopped cold. "The village..."

"Our family..." Nikolai whispered.

Mattias turned to them. "The best thing we can do for Eastfold is to get to the root of the problem."

The color drained from Nikolai's face. "The root of the problem is Lorelei and I were Tithed. We should've died. This wouldn't have happened if we'd died like we were supposed to!"

"Enough." Mattias grasped Nikolai's shoulders. "You'll not be playing sacrificial lambs now." He straightened and looked around. "In fact, if we do this right, the Tithe won't need to happen ever again."

Lorelei swallowed. "What do we need to do?"

Mattias gestured. The Green Ladies were thickest in a line curving off to the west. "We follow the trail."

* * *

They followed the trail left by the mushrooms. As they went, the forest became less dense and yet somehow darker. Leaves rotted off the trees, falling around them with wet-sounding splats. The gnarled branches clawed at the pale midday sky like skeletal hands. The ground itself had a thick layer of green-black slime coating it—decayed plant matter, Mattias told them. Even their lavender masks couldn't hide the fetid stench of rot.

It was hot. The air was rank and dense. The sun was a burning white disc in the hazy grey sky. After an hour of following the mushroom trail, they were all sticky with sweat. Biting flies buzzed around their faces and no amount of swatting would dissuade them. The ground became spongier and spongier until they were ankle-deep in rancid grey water, and reeking mud sucked at their feet. Still, Mattias urged them on.

"We're getting close now," Mattias said.

"Is this another one of your 'feelings'?" Lorelei asked tartly.

Mattias said nothing.

* * *

At last, they reached a long ledge of stone that stood a few feet above the forest floor and stretched several yards in either direction. By now, it was less a forest than a swamp. Mud and greyish water stretched as far as the eye could see, dotted by clumps of decaying plants and columns of blackened, dead trees.

"What...happened here?" Nikolai asked. "I didn't know there was a swamp here."

"There isn't," Mattias said, grimly. "At least, there isn't supposed to be. Swamps exist in the lowlands and by rivers. There shouldn't be one here."

As he spoke, something out in the waste made a large splash. The muddy water rippled as something large moved beneath it. A line of bubbles followed in its wake. They watched the bubbling trail get nearer.

"Get back!" Mattias shouted.

He shoved Lorelei and Nikolai away from the outcropping, and darted to the side just as a huge, mud-covered creature broke out of the water. It landed with a wet, muddy plop on the bit of stone they'd just vacated.

The monster resembled a gigantic frog, but wrong somehow, as if it were as twisted and unnatural as the swamp it inhabited. Open sores wept putrid green ooze from its body. It stood almost as tall as Mattias' cottage, though its massive bulk didn't seem to slow it down at all. Its eyes burned that same sickly green as the Green Lady mushrooms as it rounded on Mattias. Mattias had found a large stick, and brandished it like a sword, as if it could protect him from the beast.

The twins landed in the mud among the roots of a rotting oak tree. The soft ground threatened to pull them under. Phosphorescent globs of light bubbled up from the mire and burst into spores around them. Nikolai pulled Lorelei's arm and they scrambled away from the spores onto the higher ground of the tree's exposed roots. They stood dripping with muck and helpless, clinging to the crumbling tree, and watched as Mattias fought the frog demon.

"Witch!" the demon bellowed.

"That's me, yes," Mattias said, as he dodged the frog demon's massive black tongue.

"What have you done with my subjects?" the demon demanded. "My children should be with me!"

"They sent me to help you break this curse you're under, Your Majesty." Mattias danced away from the frog demon's lashing tongue. "You were not easy to find until recently!"

"Where I go, the rot follows," the frog king croaked. "I've been hard at work, gnawing the roots and bringing the putrefaction to the surface!" The frog king laughed. It was an ugly roaring sound. "Now it is too late to stop it!"

"We'll see," Mattias said.

He swept the stick upwards and a wind followed. The wind smelled sweet, as if it had come from a distant meadow. It blew away the reek of decay. Mattias leapt and climbed the air currents as if they were stairs.

The frog king swiped at Mattias again and bellowed in rage as its tongue fell far short. "You insolent fly! I shall crunch your bones myself!" Then, it heaved its bulk around. "Or perhaps," it said, turning its malevolent green gaze upon the Miller twins as they clung to the slimy oak, "I shall crunch the bones of your apprentices, if I can't have you."

"Lorelei!" Mattias shouted. "Sing!"

"What?" Lorelei shouted.

"Just do it!"

The frog king leapt from the rocky shelf and landed with a splash that sent reeking water over Lorelei and Nikolai. But instead of going after them, he burrowed down into the mud, leaving trails of glowing green in his wake.

"Get onto the rock!" Mattias shouted, his voice now edged with urgency.

"How do we—" Nikolai began.

"Jump!" Mattias said. "I'll send the wind to catch you!"

The twins exchanged a quick look and then clasped hands and leapt. The wind caught them and bore them up to the ledge. No sooner had their feet left the roots of the tree, than the entire oak crumpled in on itself and sank beneath the muck with an awful sucking sound. The frog king burst up from the mud where the tree had been standing only a moment before and bellowed his rage at being thwarted. The twins sailed through the air to where Mattias stood.

"Lorelei," Mattias said when they landed. "Sing. Now!"

Lorelei coughed and cleared her throat. She tore the mask from her face, and began to sing the lullaby she'd sung to the box back at the cottage.

> *Oak and Willow, twining deep*
> *River rocks beneath the stream*
> *My darling dear, you now must sleep*
> *Stars watch over as you dream*

The frog king made as if to leap, but swayed on his feet.

"Keep going!" Mattias shouted.

> *Rose and lavender for your bed*
> *Moon and cloud, earth and sky*
> *My darling dear, rest your head*
> *Stars watch over where you lie*

The green fire of the frog king's eyes dimmed, and his translucent eyelids drooped.

"Nikolai," Mattias murmured, landing lightly next to them on the rock. "You have our field journal, with you, yes?"

Nikolai, not trusting himself to speak, nodded.

"Good boy. Open to the page where you drew those Tithe garlands, quickly now!"

Nikolai flipped to the page, and looked to Mattias.

"Take your gloves off."

When Nikolai sent him a puzzled look, Mattias said, "Just trust me."

Nikolai took his gloves off.

"Put your hand on the page. Concentrate on the drawings. Remember how they looked and felt. The smell of the flowers. The way they were woven," Mattias said.

Nikolai closed his eyes. The feeling of the fresh wind Mattias had summoned ruffled his hair, and Lorelei's voice wound through the breeze, weaving a melody of sleep. He could hear the frog king still moving through the swamp, but his movements were sluggish.

Nikolai concentrated, and soon, the smooth page of the journal seemed to take on a leafy texture. The sweet smells of meadowsweet, woodbine, and lavender rose up from under his fingers.

"Good, good. You're doing very good. Now, *pull*, Nikolai," Mattias said, whispering very close to Nikolai's ear. "Not just with your hand, but with your mind as well."

Nikolai's fingers curled, and he *pulled*. There was a strange, disorienting sensation of his hand reaching through space but when he opened his eyes, he held the wreath.

Nikolai stared at the wreath. "I...did it?"

"Good," Mattias said, sounding very pleased. "Now, the other one. Quickly!"

This time, Nikolai got the feel of it quicker. He pulled the second wreath in half the time and handed it to Mattias.

The frog king had gotten closer to the ledge, but it looked as if every movement cost him. Lorelei sang until her voice went hoarse. Mattias strode towards her.

"Lorelei," he murmured into her ear. He put his hand on her shoulder. "You can stop now."

Lorelei started at the contact, and cut off abruptly mid-song. As soon as her voice stopped, the frog king came fully awake again.

"How dare you work witchcraft against me!" the frog king roared. "I will crunch your bones for my supper!"

As the frog king raged, Mattias flicked his wrist and sent one of the wreaths flying high into the air. The frog king stopped mid-tirade and followed it with his eyes. Animal instinct took over and his tongue darted out to catch the wreath as it made its downward arc to the ground. He pulled the wreath into his mouth and swallowed in one motion. The frog king's body rippled and he let out a croaking howl.

"What have you done to me, witch?" he roared. "I will destroy you! I will destroy this whole forest and devour the world! I will—" But what he was going to say next was cut off as Mattias sent the second wreath sailing into the frog king's gaping maw.

Nikolai came up to Lorelei and Mattias, watching the scene with wide eyes, the field journal still clutched in his hands. The frog king's body rippled violently, as if something inside were trying to escape. He spun his bulk around and heaved. Putrid, glowing green slime issued forth from his mouth.

Mattias gathered Nikolai and Lorelei close, with an arm around each of their waists, ready to call a wind to carry them away if needed. With every convulsion, the frog king shrank, until at last he was about the size of a rat terrier. He gave one last, mighty heave, and a small, glowing green stone flew from his mouth to land upon the rock at their feet.

Mattias drew the twins back away from it. It glowed malevolently, marked all over with curse runes. The frog king gave a final croak and collapsed into the muck. The cursed stone rocked weakly from side to side, as if it were a beetle that had been knocked onto its back.

"Nikolai," Mattias said, "I need the curse trap box."

"Did you bring it?" Nikolai asked.

"No, but I brought you." Mattias smiled at him. "Pull it from the journal for me. Please."

Nikolai smiled hesitantly back, and flipped open the journal to the page where he'd drawn the box. He pulled the box through the page of the journal and handed it to Mattias. Lorelei's eyes went wide when she saw it.

"Nikolai...you're a witch!"

"You're the one who sang the frog king to sleep. If I'm a witch, then so are you."

But they were both grinning.

"Yes, yes. You can accuse each other of witchcraft once I've dealt with this curse," Mattias snapped.

"We're not—" Lorelei began.

The stone rolled over once and hopped like a flea, trying to avoid Mattias.

"Oh no you don't," Mattias muttered. He slammed the open box down over the stone just before it could leap off the rock. He slid the cover beneath and lifted the box in triumph. A faint melody emanated from the box—it sounded like Lorelei's lullaby, but muffled. The box wobbled in Mattias' grip for a moment and then went still. He stowed the box in the sleeve of his robe and turned back to the twins—and nearly fell backwards as they both rushed over to embrace him.

Then, Mattias tipped Lorelei's chin up and kissed her mouth. Her eyes widened in shock, but she melted into the embrace all the same. By the time Mattias pulled away, Lorelei was red-faced but smiling.

Then, before Nikolai could react, Mattias put his hand around the back of Nikolai's neck and kissed him, too. Nikolai slid his hands up Mattias' shoulders and deepened the kiss himself. When Nikolai pulled back, he was also very red.

Lorelei and Nikolai exchanged a long, wordless look. Then they both nodded, as if reaching an understanding. Mattias waited patiently.

"We've shared everything our entire lives," Lorelei started.

"We might as well share you, too," Nikolai finished, grinning sheepishly.

Mattias smiled, and pulled them both close once more. That spark surged again, enveloping the three of them in warmth.

There was a weak croak from the mud below, followed by the sound of a very muddy amphibian body sliding over stone. Nikolai and Lorelei backed up a pace as the frog king—now much smaller, though still larger than a normal frog—climbed onto the rock they stood on.

Mattias crouched down next to him. "Will you be alright?"

"Yes, I believe I will, now. Thank you, Mattias," the frog king said.

"Excellent." Mattias beamed. "Would you like a lift?"

"Please," the frog king croaked.

Mattias stood. The wind had worked his long hair free of its binding, and it rippled with the breeze. He took off his cloak and made a kind of sling with it, and the frog king climbed in.

"I'm going to raise a wind to take us back. I don't fancy trudging through all this mud to get home, do you?"

Nikolai and Lorelei nodded.

"Here," Mattias held the sling to Lorelei.

"I'm truly sorry I tried to eat you," the frog king said to her. "You have a lovely voice."

"She has the loveliest voice," Mattias agreed. He snaked his arm around Lorelei's waist, and his other around Nikolai's. "Keep your lips closed unless you want a mouthful of bugs," Mattias advised. "And don't let go of me!"

The wind came and tore away the last of his words. They all leapt off the rock and the wind caught them.

* * *

Back at the cottage, the frog king was greeted with a great deal of joyful leaping and croaking from his subjects. Mattias herded Nikolai and Lorelei into the cottage and, once the last frog had left, shut the door firmly.

"It went well, I take it," Augustus said from his terrarium.

The Green Lady mushrooms had withered away to small black globs, and were dissolving into oily smoke as they watched.

"Well enough," Mattias replied. He still held tight to Lorelei and Nikolai's waists.

Augustus gave them a knowing look. "I suppose it did."

Mattias let go of the twins and strode over to set the curse trap box on the mantel. The wreaths of meadowsweet, woodbine, and lavender no longer hung there.

"The frog king did a lot of damage to the forest while he was under that curse," Mattias began. "I could use your help setting the forest to rights again..." he trailed off, and for the first time ever, he looked unsure.

The Miller twins exchanged looks.

"I...we..." Lorelei began.

"Our family," Nikolai said. "We need to see if our family is okay."

Mattias gave them a smile tinged with sadness. "Of course. I'll take you to Eastfold, if you like?"

* * *

The trek back to the village was a complete reversal of the one they'd taken from it two weeks before. Mattias walked ahead of them through trees that were budding with new growth. An honor guard of frogs leapt from tree branch to tree branch on either side of them. Not a single Green Lady mushroom could be seen.

The frogs accompanied them to the very edge of the Nameless Wood and bid them good luck in their own croaking way.

Nothing could've prepared Lorelei and Nikolai for the shock of how much the land around the village had changed in the time they were gone. Whole swaths of pasture were slimy with mud, and more than one unfortunate cow had gotten stuck. Wheat withered in the fields, and vegetable gardens had gone black and wilted, as if they'd been taken by a frost.

To their horror, the Miller family home was deserted. A symbol of warding had been painted on the front door.

Lorelei and Nikolai exchanged alarmed glances. Mattias only looked grim. Without speaking, they turned and headed towards the mayor's house. The villagers' pale, gaunt faces peered from behind windows just before they were shuttered. Many people made signs of warding against evil as the three of them walked through the desolate village.

The formerly green common was brown and dusty. Dead grass crackled under their feet as they made their way to the mayor's residence.

Mattias strode to the door and knocked.

No one answered.

He knocked again.

Again, no one answered.

After the third knock he said to the twins, loud enough for his voice to carry, "This door seems stuck. Perhaps we should break it down?"

The door suddenly opened a crack.

"Begone, you vile creature!" a voice hissed.

"I will not!" Mattias said. "I'm just here for a friendly chat."

Mattias reached for the door handle and sent a shock through it. The voice yelped in pain and wrenched the door open.

The mayor stood there. He was much changed from the last time Lorelei and Nikolai saw him. He was thinner; his clothes hung off him and his skin had taken on a sallow, waxy look. "What do you want?" he demanded. "Is it not enough that you destroy our village?" His eyes locked onto the twins. "Was our Tithe not good enough for you? Were they not to your liking?"

"Lorelei and Nikolai are both very much to my liking. That's not the point," Mattias said. He advanced a step, but the mayor stood his ground. "I came to tell you the demon that had been plaguing the forest has been defeated."

"Oh, so you defeated yourself then!" the mayor sputtered. "Perhaps those witch brats we sent you did it, eh?"

"I never demanded any sacrifice. You lot are the ones who decided that. I saved who I could when you started this. I sent them on to Westfold if I found them before the demon did." Mattias' eyes glittered with anger, though his voice remained deadly calm.

"Where is our family?" Lorelei demanded.

The mayor sneered at her. "They were run out of the village once it became clear that Tithing the two of you brought only misfortune upon us, girl."

"Maybe the Tithe is the problem, then," Nikolai said.

"No family of witches is welcome in my village!" the mayor spat.

Lorelei stepped close to the mayor and raised her hand in what she hoped was a witchy-looking gesture. "Where. Is. Our. Family?"

The mayor cowered. "North! We sent them on the north road!"

Mattias glared at the mayor, who visibly flinched.

"Augustus," Mattias said.

Augustus climbed down the wall from beneath the thatched roof of the mayor's house. Neither twin had seen him there a moment before. "Yes?"

The mayor blanched and made another sign of warding, which Augustus ignored.

"Would you be so kind as to locate the Miller family?"

Augustus flicked his orange tongue. "Perhaps. But I'll demand payment."

"I'll give you as many crickets as you can eat," Mattias assured him.

"Make sure they're fat ones," Augustus said. Then, the lizard scuttled to the edge of an exposed wooden beam and leapt into the air. Two thin membranes of skin stretched between his fore and hind legs. They caught the updraft and he was borne away on the wind.

"So," Mattias said to the mayor, "I was going to offer to help set your land to rights again, but I see my services are not needed or wanted."

Before the mayor could say anything, Mattias held up a finger to silence him. "The land will right itself before next spring. You'll have a lean winter, but I'm sure you can manage without the help of a witch."

Then, he turned on his heel and strode off. Nikolai and Lorelei cast one last glance back at the mayor before following Mattias.

"One last thing, mayor," Mattias said, his voice ringing clearly across the square as if it had been amplified. "If you ever Tithe innocent people again, or anyone at all, I *will* rain destruction upon this entire wretched village."

They left the mayor trembling on his doorstep, and the Miller twins never looked upon the village of Eastfold again.

* * *

On the outskirts of Westfold village lived a woodcutter, a midwife, and their family. The three eldest of their thirteen children had already married and left home. The eight youngest still lived at home, and helped their parents. The remaining two, twins, had left home as well, but their fates had taken them elsewhere. They still visited from time to time, bringing herbs for their mother to help in her midwife practice and magical trinkets for the younger children.

Deep in the Nameless Wood, life abounded. Deer leapt and wolves hunted. Owls flew and mice and foxes and rabbits ran and chased beneath verdant ferns and over thick mosses. Trees grew strong and tall, and flowers bloomed in profusion. If one were to walk through the Nameless Wood and were lucky enough, they might just glimpse a small clearing, where the unlikely combination of meadowsweet, woodbine, and lavender grew thick in the garden. One also might hear the joyous sound of frogs croaking and splashing in the pond in front of a small cottage. And, if one were very lucky indeed, they might just spot one of the three witches who lived in the cottage and worked tirelessly to keep the balance of the forest.

5

The Tower Girls by Kate Vitty

Princess Magdalene held her chin up high as she strode into the stone tower that awaited her. Once upon a time, it had been used as a watchtower on the outskirts of the kingdom. Now, it was to be her prison. She turned around, skirts fluttering behind her, and sat down on the hard wooden chair, full of the grace she had been taught all her life.

"I will not change my mind. I will marry Prince Bertram or I will not marry at all," Magdalene proclaimed.

Her father, the king, gave her a nasty glare. "Stone up the entrance," he commanded the stone mason, then signaled to one of his knights to nudge the man with his spear. The mason was too enraptured by Magdalene's beauty to pay the slightest attention to his king. "Stone up the entrance!"

The stone mason hesitated and looked between the princess and the king. He considered it a crime against nature to hide away such a treasure.

"Now! Or you will lose your head!"

It was not the threat, but rather the barest of nods from Magdalene, that stirred the stone mason into action.

The man crouched and laid the stones in a line, slathered them with lime mortar, and repeated the process for the next row. It took the craftsman hours to build the wall. Whenever he tried to rest, one of the knights would jab him with their spear, and he would have to resume his work.

The whole time Magdalene sat perfectly still in her hard wooden chair, looking more a queen than a princess. Her eyes stayed unwaveringly on her father. She ignored the guilt from the craftsman and the pity from the nobles, who had been forced to witness the consequences of disobeying the king. Their beloved princess was to be locked away in a tower for seven years, as if her status and royal blood meant nothing.

Those who had a choice departed when the stone blocked their view of the princess. Magdalene's mother and brothers were among those who left. The king stayed as did his closest retinues. He feared that without his supervision, Magdalene would convince the stone mason to tear down his work and set her free. He was well aware of his daughter's charm and knew most of his subjects would prefer her to be on the throne.

"Give Prince Bertram my love!" Magdalene cried out when there was only one more stone to put into place, breaking the silence that had lasted a sunset and a sunrise. The king's face turned red. He pushed the stone mason out of the way and, with a hissed word, placed the final stone himself.

* * *

Magdalene slumped back in her chair and sighed. She was disappointed her ploy had failed. The king had placed the final stone; there was no possibility of escape. This lightless void would be her home for the next seven years. When her father had threatened retaliation for refusing his choice of bridegroom, she had not thought that he would imprison her like this. She had not thought that the court would allow it.

A soft feminine voice rang out from the pitch black, "Are you well, your royal highness?"

Magdalene barely refrained from jumping in surprise. She had forgotten that a chambermaid had been made to serve her during her imprisonment until the girl spoke. Even in these hostile conditions, it was unthinkable to force a princess to do servants' work.

"I am well," Magdalene responded. She was quite glad the girl had chosen to speak to her. Most of the servants lived by the motto "neither seen nor heard," a policy which annoyed Magdalene when she was starved for company. Solitude would have been the worst part of this imprisonment. Her father knew her character and would have sent some of her ladies-in-waiting if he had not intended to torture her. Magdalene was sure that he never thought a servant could bring her comfort. She decided that this person would be her friend. "And you? Are you well? What are you named?"

"I am called Amila, my lady." The chambermaid curtsied. Magdalene could hear the ruffle of fabric although she could not see the act itself. "I am as well as one can expect, given our situation."

"Try not to fret too much," Magdalene consoled. "I doubt it will be more than a fortnight or two before some young hero decides to free us, even if it means betraying my father."

"You truly think so, my lady?" Amila asked skeptically. "I would be surprised if any dared defy our king."

"What is your thinking on the matter?"

Amila stayed silent.

"You may speak freely," Magdalene assured. "I will not punish you. I rather prefer honest conversation."

"After our king was so ruthless to his own daughter, the most beloved in all the land, I think few would risk raising his ire."

Magdalene made a noncommittal motion, forgetting Amila would not be able to see in the dark of their new home.

"Your theory has merit," Magdalene admitted and stood up carefully, "but I believe it is more important to have hope when caught in a situation such as this than to let dread take over our hearts and minds." Magdalene stretched her arms out in front of her and turned around, remembering the bed was somewhere behind her. She was exhausted from staying up those long hours to stare down the king.

"That is very optimistic."

Magdalene failed to hear the bitter sarcasm in Amila's voice and hummed in agreement. She fell onto the bed, having tripped over it despite her best efforts.

* * *

Time passed oddly in the tower. Without the ability to see if it was night or day, they had no perspective of how much time actually passed. When a day felt like a week or a week felt like an hour, they did not have the sun or a clock

118

to tell them that they were objectively wrong.

Still, it is only human nature to desire things to progress logically and linearly, so they devised their own standard to measure the passing of time. Magdalene and Amila decided that their sleep schedules were regular enough to count by. Outside the tower, sixteen days had passed. Inside the tower, twenty sleep cycles had passed. By either measure, it was long enough for the occupants to settle into a routine and their eyes to adjust to the lack of light.

Amila woke first. After the first couple of sleep cycles, Magdalene had offered to share the singular bed in the tower with her. Amila agreed. In other households, even those of minor nobles, it was common for all the occupants to share one bed, no matter their age or status. As a princess, Magdalene never had to share before. She thought she was being remarkably gracious.

After she woke, Amila would go down to the cellar to bring up water from their well. She would then wake Magdalene and help her dress. The princess was still awaiting rescue and wanted to look proper for whatever hero saved them.

When it was time to breakfast, Amila would once more go down to the cellar to prepare their meal. In the tower, there was some food meant for a princess and some fit for a servant. They did not eat according to their station. When Magdalene saw Amila eat food of inferior quality to hers, she insisted they share. At each meal, there would be a combination of basic and rich food.

After they had eaten their first meal, Magdalene would lounge back on the bed or walk around the perimeter of the tower to get some exercise. Amila tried to keep herself busy by making their prison more hospitable. She was not successful.

* * *

"What do you see?" Magdalene asked suddenly, pointing up towards the ceiling. Magdalene was obviously restless and an outburst like this was not uncommon. She would frequently engage Amila in conversation to put an end to her boredom.

"Stones, my lady," Amila deadpanned. She reluctantly humored Magdalene by staring up at the top of the tower. "I fear for you if you see anything else."

Magdalene laughed. It sounded far more joyous than the setting deserved.

"I am shadow gazing!" she pronounced happily. "That one"—she lifted her hand to point to a shadow on the opposite side of the square tower—"looks a bit like my mare and that one"—this time, she pointed down and to the side—"looks like a rabbit."

Both shadows were indistinct blobs. Amila indulged her lady's good mood anyway. "That one"—Amila pointed to a round blotch of darkness halfway up the tower wall—"looks like a shield."

Magdalene laughed happily. "And that one looks like a sword!" she exclaimed, pointing to a long shadow not too far from Amila's shield. "Do you suppose they are fellows or enemies?"

"I do believe they are rivals, my lady." Amila squinted and struggled to continue the story. "See how the shield stands against the sword?"

"They must be fighting over your hand." The two shadows seemed to move and clash against each other. Amila startled and looked over to the princess, who had already moved on to another shadow. "I believe that one looks like a book."

"I believe you may be right, my lady." She agreed, thinking the shadows' movement just a trick of the light.

* * *

The familiarity with which Magdalene treated Amila broke down barriers that should have been insurmountable between the two girls. Amila did not suppose they were friends—there were no friendships between a princess and a servant—but it was hard to think of the princess as untouchable now. After Magdalene's prediction of rescue proved to be untrue, Amila could hold her tongue. She had to ask the question that had been on her mind since she first heard of the princess' defiance. "Why did you choose this fate, my lady?"

"Pardon?" Magdalene turned to face Amila.

"Why did you choose to be locked in here?" Amila clarified.

"I did not *choose* to be locked away like some kind of criminal." Magdalene was offended by the very idea that she would willingly have her freedom ripped away.

"You could have married your betrothed."

"You are speaking of the foreign king my father selected for me to marry?"

Magdalene's voice was harsh, and her posture changed to that of a bristling cat.

Still, Amila pushed on. "Yes, my lady."

"I would not marry that poor excuse for a man even if death were my only alternative!" Magdalene snapped venomously. "It would only bring me shame if I lowered myself to marrying that beast! There was no choice for me. I will never marry that man." The end of her tirade sounded flat and rehearsed. Magdalene had defended her choice several times before, and she was resigned to do it again and again although she knew nobody would understand. "If this is to be my prison, I shall bear it. If this should prove to be my tomb, I will die satisfied with my decisions."

Amila bit back the resentful replies that jumped to her lips. "You entreated me to speak honestly, my lady," Amila said slowly. "Do you still hold that desire?"

Magdalene looked at Amila shrewdly. "I do." Magdalene's words were also spoken with caution. "I may voice opposition to whatever opinion you are so hesitant to express, but I still rather you speak it than not."

"My lady, you had two miserable choices, but there was still a decision for you to make, and you chose the poorer of the two options."

"You believe that I would have been better off acquiescing to my father's wishes?" Magdalene asked incredulously.

"Yes," Amila admitted, "for no matter how distasteful you find your suitor, he would have made you a queen, which is a better fate than a prisoner's."

"In some situations, there is no difference in fortune between them," Magdalene said, voice low and serious. "You must not forget, Amila, a queen's main duty is to provide the king with an heir."

Amila blinked, startled by what seemed to her to be a change in topic. "I am aware it is a queen's duty to provide the king an heir, just as it is a wife's duty to give her husband sons. My lady, that will not change even if your rebellion succeeds, and you are permitted to marry another. It is the way of the world. If you were to marry Prince Bertram, do you believe you would be exempt from this responsibility? I understand lying with your betrothed would be more arduous than lying with Prince Bertram, but I do not see how the act itself can be a factor in your decision."

"Bertram knows I find the business of reproduction to be repugnant," Magdalene explained. "Bertram also wishes for a wife that will not begrudge him his relationship with his groom. He has siblings and is perfectly happy to raise one of their children as his heir. I believe he finds the idea of lying with a woman as repugnant as I find the idea of lying with anyone. My suitor, as you call him, would never respect my wishes. I know what people say of my beauty, and I have heard his boastful talk." Magdalene's face twisted with revulsion. "I dare not repeat the words he used to speak of me. It makes me sick to even think of such things."

"You reject nature, my lady," Amila replied softly.

"I reject having someone else's will forced upon me," Magdalene snapped back. "I tire of this conversation." She laid down on the bed and turned so her back was to her chambermaid, signaling that the time for talk was unquestionably over.

"I tire of living in this dank tower," Amila muttered, once she was sure her lady would not hear her comment.

* * *

Magdalene was startled awake by the sound of mortar being scraped away. She sat up in surprise and saw a thin trickle of light enter their dark abode.

Magdalene shook Amila awake. "I told you it would not be long before someone came for us," she said, voice hushed. The two girls watched as a stone was slid out of place, exposing their tower just the slightest bit to the outside world.

The sunlight did not feel soothing or refreshing as they had dreamed. Rather, it was an assault on the pair's eyes. Both shielded their faces. The sounds of birds chirping were less offensive to their senses and both relished in the evidence of life outside the tower.

Magdalene was ecstatic. She should have never doubted her friends, she thought. Of course it would take time to get a rescue mission together. She gestured impatiently to Amila. She needed to dress. Were her braids undone? How embarrassing it would be for Magdalene to be caught in such a state.

The king's voice boomed into the room. "It has been a year. Will you accept the marriage I have chosen for you now?"

All of Magdalene's joy vanished. Her eyes grew wide and grief-stricken. "No." Magdalene mouthed the word inaudibly. "No!" Magdalene turned and yelled at the half of a face that was visible, "No!" Her cries became more and more hysterical.

The king said he would be back the next year to ask again, but neither of the two could hear him over Magdalene's rabid denials.

"No!" Magdalene howled as the stone slid back into place, plunging them into a darkness that was worse than before. The glimpse of sunlight had stolen their ability to see in the dark. "No." Magdalene collapsed into a fit of tears on the dirt floor of the tower. Nobody had come for her. "No," she whispered, defeated.

Amila did not know what to do as she watched the princess break down. She wanted to rage. She wanted to cry. She wanted to scream and shout and despair. But she could not waste time on her own emotional distress when she could take advantage of Magdalene's. She now only had six years to convince the princess to give in to the King's wishes. Otherwise, her life was forfeit.

* * *

Amila was six years old the first time she accompanied her mother to the castle. Her mother worked as a laundress, and Amila was expected to follow in her footsteps. She would have taken on the role gladly, but when she was twelve, one of the princess' chambermaids was injured. An unfamiliar servant ran in, all in a tizzy, desperate to find a substitute. Seeing her idle, the servant grabbed her and dragged her up to the princess' rooms. Amila excelled at her assignment and what began as a temporary duty became a permanent job.

However, Amila was still the most inexperienced and disposable of the maids. The other servants of the princess never quite fully accepted Amila, despite the six years they had worked together. So, when Princess Magdalene disobeyed the king, Amila was chosen to be shunted away with her.

A week before Amila was to make the journey to the tower, the king summoned her. He promised her a marriage to his youngest son if she were able to secure Princess Magdalene's agreement within the first year of their stay. He offered her family land and a noble title if Amila were able to secure

Princess Magdalene's agreement to wed within the first three years of their stay. He offered her a position as the princess' lady's maid if she were able to get the princess to agree within five years. If Princess Magdalene agreed before the end of seven years, Amila would keep her head. If the princess still remained defiant at the end of seven years, Amila would face her death. Although Amila dreamed of securing the princess' agreement and the rewards she was promised, she did not actually believe the king would promote her among the servants, let alone elevate her to nobility or marry her to his son! However, she knew he would not hesitate to carry out his threats of violence.

Amila had become distracted with the princess' inane talk that first year and fell for her charm like so many others before her. The visit from the king, however, reminded her of what was at stake. She could not afford the sympathy she had begun to develop for Princess Magdalene.

* * *

"My lady"—Amila knelt down next to the crunched over figure—"let me attend to you." Her vision in the dark was slowly returning, and she could make out some shapes. It was fairly easy to locate Magdalene. "I will wet a cloth to clean your face." Amila gently wiped away the tears and snot from Magdalene's face. "Do you see now, my lady? We are not going to be let out of this tower unless you give in to the king's demands. Is it not more sensible to obey your royal father than live in this state for any longer? The next time his majesty comes to call, it would be more prudent to submit to his wisdom than continue this rebellion."

Magdalene took the rag out of Amila's hands. "Is this truly how peasants think?" she asked, mystified. "I was always told we rule because the rest have too weak a mind, but I had never truly believed there to be such a contrast in the hearts of people."

"Pardon, my lady?"

"My tutor taught me about the differences God made between the nobility and general populace. God made the nobility to govern in matters of state and as such the nobles have stronger minds than the peasants. It is in the peasants' nature to follow where the court leads and take their superiors' opinions as their own. I had never believed someone could truly be without

124

their own notion of the world, but I see now that she was accurate in her teachings. I was just sheltered from the world at large."

Amila stood up and took a step back in offense. "My lady, just because we peasants have to bow to the opinions of those with more power than us does not mean we do not have thoughts of our own!" Amila defended passionately. "We may expect our lords to govern for us, but we do not need them to think for us! Peasant or not, God gifted everyone with a mind of their own which they might use to have their own private thoughts and desires!"

Magdalene raised an eyebrow, doubt evident on her face. "Your inner thoughts just happen to perfectly align with my father's?"

"I believe in the Church's teachings and thus our duty to respect our parents and elders," Amila hedged. "While I might be more hesitant to endorse an opinion contrary to my own, even if it were from the elders, when one's life depends on their notions, they can quite easily bend to accept that which they would typically find repugnant."

Magdalene stilled and looked at Amila entreatingly. "'When one's life depends on their notions'?" she repeated. "It is hardly in my nature to be violent, but even if it were, your notions oppose mine. They would not grant you my favor. Might I be so bold as to venture that it is my father you fear so desperately?"

"I am not a royal, my lady," Amila said dryly, "nor am I a noble, nor is my family of any significance. It is quite easy to behead a servant without fuss. As you said, we expect a monarch to rule and judge us fairly. If a king says a chambermaid betrayed her country and deserves to be executed, not even the chambermaid's mother would dare stand in her daughter's defense."

"I would not let my father do such a thing to you," Magdalene said fervently, leaning towards Amila. "You have kept me fine company in my seclusion, and I quite enjoy you."

Amila remained unmoved. "Nobles have no need to keep a promise of loyalty to one below them. Forgive my saying so, my lady, but you do not have the king's favor at the moment. If he is willing to lock you away in a tower, I doubt he will grant a stay of execution on your behalf."

* * *

Magdalene went silent.

Amila, unwisely, believed Magdalene accepted her rebuke and would choose differently the next time the king came.

And so the second year continued as a mirror image of the first. Magdalene hid her pain by clinging onto Amila. Amila dutifully pretended she was Magdalene's friend instead of her maid. While Amila's spirits were higher than they were the first year, Magdalene's were lower.

This peaceful unreality came crashing down as soon as the king asked Magdalene his question for a second time a year later: "Will you marry him now?"

"No."

This time she said it with greater poise. She did not break down and sob, although her eyes did start to water. She did not yell her refusal (of the situation, of the man, of everything). Instead, she stood straight-backed, reminiscent of when she was first locked in the tower. She stared into her father's eyes that were just visible through the window created by the removed stone. Magdalene ignored how the light pained her eyes, and let him see it all. She let him see her hurt, her grief, her feelings of betrayal. She let him see her resolution, her determination, her pride, her stubbornness.

The king took the stone and slid it back into place, ignoring his daughter, who was still standing there staring at him.

The silence was deafening.

Amila continued to do her chores and did not say a word. She should not have felt betrayed. Magdalene had never said she would concede to her father. She had never shown any sign of softening her stance towards marriage. Amila was the one who took Magdalene's silence as agreement. Nevertheless, it was confirmation for Amila; a peasant should never trust a noble's word.

* * *

"When my father comes calling, I do not deny his demands to spite you." Magdalene had taken notice of Amila's distant and cold demeanor after the previous year, and she worried Amila thought she did not care about her. Amila was the only company she had; inevitably, a bond had been forged. "I deny him because, unlike you, I cannot force myself to accept something so ghastly to me even if it may ensure my survival. Being the wife of that man—of *any* man with crude expectations of me—would be a fate worse than death. I do not want you to think I do not care about your life and livelihood. I care about you a great deal more than I have cared for any friend before, but there are some things that are too horrid to contemplate. What my father asks me to do is one of them."

Magdalene turned and smiled at Amila. "I no longer believe I will escape with my life. I am sorry your death will come with mine but if I have to die, I am glad it will be you by my side."

Amila stepped back. "I do not believe accepting death's embrace is preferable to any other fate. I appreciate the sentiment, my lady, but it does not change the fact that you also are killing me."

* * *

Despite Magdalene's hopes, her confession did not prompt a closer relationship with Amila. Instead, their friendship chilled once more. Amila did her chores and was ostensibly polite to Magdalene, but she kept an appropriate distance between them. For months (eons to Magdalene), Amila refused all overtures of friendship. When Magdalene pointed out an interesting shadow, Amila made a polite but curt comment. If Magdalene tried to start a conversation, Amila made vague noises of comprehension but did not engage further. When Magdalene was desperate and tried to do chores with Amila so she could not be ignored, Amila would firmly put an end to it by reminding Magdalene of their positions in society.

Magdalene was persistent, however, and they had endless hours alone together. Amila did not last a year before she gave into Magdalene's efforts. It did not take long to build their relationship even stronger than before.

Their relationship would cool for a dozen or so sleep cycles surrounding the king's visit, but it was not torn to pieces as it had been previously. By the fifth year, Amila and Magdalene were close confidants.

* * *

It was a surprise when after so many years of repetition (deny the king's request, lose their minds in the darkness for a year, then deny the king again) the pattern broke. The fifth year, the king did not come to ask for Magdalene's surrender. It was her younger brother who came instead. Unknown to Magdalene, her refusal to marry the foreign king had started a war. The young prince pleaded for Magdalene to accept the marriage. Magdalene pleaded for her "favorite" brother to let her out of the tower. They were both disappointed by the other's response.

Shortly afterward, life became worse for the girls. For all the discomfort inherent to life in the tower, it was survivable. There was always enough food, and it never went bad.

Until it did.

On the surface, their meal looked fine and nothing tasted off. They only discovered the food had gone bad when Magdalene took a bite of the meat, then doubled over and regurgitated her undigested meal.

Amila scrunched her nose up in disgust, but a moment later she did the same thing.

Magdalene gagged, then waved her hand, and the sick vanished.

Amila blinked in surprise. She had heard the unkind rumors accusing nobles of using strange and unusual powers, but she had never seen evidence of such a thing in all her years working at the castle.

"You are a witch."

"I prefer the term 'blessed,'" Magdalene replied, wiping her face and mouth clean. "I am not a witch."

"I know witchcraft when I see it performed in front of my very eyes. That, my lady, was certainly witchcraft." Amila stepped back and crossed herself. Just speaking with a witch could get one executed. Amila had no money to buy repentance for a sin such as this.

"To perform witchcraft, one has to make a deal with the devil. Members of my family are born with our powers, so quite obviously we are blessed by God. I understand how you could mistake it for witchcraft. It is a very easy error to make, which is why we keep quiet about our gifts. I was always told that the general population would not believe we are so beloved by our Creator—instead, they would believe we had turned our backs on Him. It always seemed odd to me. I know even the slightest hint of witchcraft causes hysteria, but I still do not understand why they would not believe He gave us our gifts. He chose us to rule. Why would he not give us blessings to help with our task?"

Amila looked at Magdalene doubtfully. "That is truly what you believe?"

"No," Magdalene scoffed, "I believe we are all the descendants of changelings, if not changelings ourselves, no matter if the person displaying gifts is peasant or noble. We are all abominations in the eyes of our Creator, but if the priest says differently, who am I to contradict such a learned man?"

Amila drew back a bit. "Fae ancestry would explain your beauty," she mused.

"It could also be evidence of how favored I am by God," Magdalene said with a careless gesture, clearly showing her derision.

"I do not believe your beauty could be from God when you possess it even now, after poking fun at God's ambassadors and rebelling against your father. It must be from the fae." Amila told her. "I have no doubt that you are not in God's favor. He lets you languish here to punish you for your sins!"

"That is similar to something my father would say." Magdalene looked at Amila suspiciously. "Did he also feed you that line?"

"No, my lady." It had been four years since Amila told Magdalene of the king's threats, but the princess never forgot the confession. Whenever Amila voiced a dissenting opinion that might vaguely resemble what the king might think, Magdalene would accuse her of repeating an idea that the king had demanded she voice. Amila doubted her numerous denials did anything to change Magdalene's mind. "It is quite an easy conclusion to come to on my own. If God did not approve of your punishment, you would be able to use your powers to escape from this imprisonment. Since I have not seen you even attempt to rescue yourself, I will even go so far as to speculate that deep down, you know this punishment is just!"

Magdalene's face went blank.

Amila took it as a sign of affirmation and continued, "You revel in going against nature. Frankly, my lady, I am surprised God's wrath has not come down upon you sooner! Our spoiled food is an obvious sign of His displeasure—"

"What is your sin then?" Magdalene interrupted. "My meal is not the only one deceptive in its appearance and taste. What did you do to displease your Lord so much He felt the need to punish you like this?" Magdalene's eyes were cold and she drew herself up to her full height. "What did you do to deserve the same punishment as such a sinner as I? And what entitles you to judge me? You are not a priest or nun, although your attitude would suggest otherwise. Tell me what gives you the right to judge me and find me lacking?"

"My sin is my failure to guide you back to the path of the righteous!" Amila exclaimed. She wanted to shake Magdalene but was too scared to get any closer. "My sin is enjoying the company of one of the faithless!"

Magdalene inhaled sharply. "That is an awfully bold accusation." She stared at Amila. "One that could have you hung for heresy." Magdalene stepped closer to Amila. "I am not someone who can be accused with impunity. In case you have forgotten, I am the daughter of a very powerful king. He is displeased with me but he would be even more displeased if one of his subjects implied he raised me so poorly that I do not have faith in our Lord. I would not let anyone else hear you say that.

"Now, let me put your foolish ideas of being punished by God to rest. I am not the only one in my family with powers." Magdalene stressed, "I may resent my father, but I can acknowledge that he is a powerful and strategic man when he wants to be. He knows of my gifts and indeed, possesses them himself. He would not lock me in here by only mundane means. As long as the tower is intact, the curse will not allow me to escape. Our food lasted this long only because of an enchantment. As for why I never even tried to rescue myself? I tried once while you were asleep, but I am not strong enough. I was not permitted to become as trained or powerful as the men in my family. There is no chance I can overpower a curse such as this!" She raised a hand, and bright silver-toned light was cast from the tower walls. It was a rash choice and a poor one; the light caused them both agony. Magdalene exhaled in frustration. "There is nothing I can do against that."

She released the enchantment that made the magic visible to both of them, and the tower was plunged into darkness once more. They were newly blind, and Magdalene didn't even attempt to stumble her way towards the bed. She laid down where she was and prepared to sleep there. "This is not a punishment from God but a cruel torture devised by someone who will use most every means to get his way," she said quietly. "I do believe it will all be over soon, however. Sleep well, Amila."

* * *

For the first time, Amila abandoned her duties. She did not wake Magdalene. She did not bring her water. She did not prepare any meals. She did not speak to Magdalene. Amila completely ignored Magdalene for the next two dozen sleep cycles. The revelation of Magdalene's magic and their quarrel was too much to deal with. She spent her waking periods praying for guidance from the Lord above.

To Amila's scorn, Magdalene made no move to take care of herself. She was growing frailer and frailer. Even the most hard-headed of individuals (which, make no mistake, Magdalene was amongst) would have given into their base need to eat by now. But Magdalene did not order Amila to bring her food and she did not move towards the cellar. Magdalene just sat and stared blankly at the stone walls.

After five days of observation, Amila could not bear to see Magdalene in such a state any longer.

"None of the food I have eaten since was spoiled," Amila said softly. "Would you like to try an apple?"

Magdalene gave her a dirty look. "I refuse to poison myself," she said weakly. "Naturally the food *you* eat would be good." Magdalene attempted to sneer. Her facial muscles twitched but could not fully form the expression. "You are the saint. I am the damned."

Amila recoiled. They were really nothing more than Amila's own words spat back at her, but hearing them while not in a moment of anger felt different. She had meant them, she was sure she had, but suddenly she did not *want* to believe them anymore. Magdalene had her flaws (and after five years locked up with her, Amila could give you a long list of them), but she was rarely purposefully malicious.

"*...not a divine punishment but from God but a cruel torture devised by someone who will use most every means to get his way.*" At that moment, Amila decided it must be the truth. If it was, then there was still hope.

131

She slung an arm around Magdalene's waist and positioned one of Magdalene's arms over her shoulder. Taking most of Magdalene's weight, she started to drag the princess down to the cellar. Their difference in height made it awkward, and going down the stairs was perilous. Nevertheless, she succeeded in getting them both to the cellar, minor miracle that it was. Amila set Magdalene down against one of the cellar walls and hurried to the well. She drew up the water and brought it to Magdalene. The princess was so weak that Amila had to hold the bucket up to her lips for her to drink.

"Why did you bring me down here?" Magdalene asked once she had finished

"You said you could sense magic, my lady." Amila was proud that her voice did not even stutter over the m-word. "Since I have eaten without becoming sick, some of our food must have escaped the curse." Magdalene opened her mouth, to object or throw Amila's words back at her again, but Amila did not let her speak. "I have indulged you frequently these past five years. Please, humor me. What is cursed and what is safe to eat?"

Magdalene's eyes fluttered shut. Amila wasn't sure if she was falling asleep or truly dying. Before Amila could panic, Magdalene answered, "Only the best food is spoiled. The curse was meant for me. It seems we will have to survive off of black bread." Her nose wrinkled in disgust. "We will not have any more meat."

"We will just have to split my ration," Amila said firmly. It was not a hardship for Amila to share her food. She had grown up with a simple and small diet, shared with many siblings. Amila went to carry Magdalene back to the main floor of the tower but Magdalene brushed her off.

"It is easiest to stay here until my strength returns to me."

Amila frowned. "It will be unpleasant."

"It does not matter where I stay," Magdalene said, shrugging carelessly. "It is darker down here than it is up there, but the environment is not any more hostile. If you wish, you can bring me the blanket off the bed, and I shall be as comfortable down here as I would be anywhere else in this tower."

Amila did not relax her frown, but she also did not protest. She brought the blanket down as Magdalene requested and stayed in the cellar with the princess until her strength returned.

* * *

"Why did you not use your magic earlier in our captivity?" Amila asked once they were residing on the main floor of the tower again, "You could have given us light all this time."

"And have you accuse me of being the devil's spawn even earlier into our imprisonment?" Magdalene asked incredulously. "No, thank you. If we had not gotten sick, I would have allowed you to remain blissfully ignorant of the royal family's true origins."

"I do not care about your origins!"

Magdalene gave Amilia a look of exceptional doubt. "You really showed how much you did not care when you crossed yourself after seeing me perform magic."

"Perhaps I cared a bit," Amila admitted. Truth be told, in most other circumstances, she would still care. But her fear of being alone outweighed her fear of magic. Magdalene had been good to her. She could forgive this flaw if it kept the princess close.

"And you would have cared more if you were not familiar with me," Magdalene pressed. "Even after all the time we spent together, you were still quick to label me a sinner. If I displayed my gifts near the start of our imprisonment, how much worse would you have reacted?"

"I can accept your point," Amila said with a frown, "but I still think it would have been worth the risk to have an actual source of light in this place. Now, I am so used to darkness, I am not sure if I will ever be able to bear sunlight again."

"It takes energy." Magdalene held up her hand and summoned a small ball of dull light. It was still a shock to the system, but it did not hurt them as it had when Magdalene previously lit up the room. "I cannot keep it going constantly and would rather not give myself this small gift to just have it taken away moments later."

Amila nodded. "Perhaps that is a good notion, but even having this weak shine would have made our games with the shadows more interesting." She positioned her hands in front of the light then started to twist her fingers in strange ways. "When I was little, my ma would use this to amuse my brothers and me." Amila stopped to point at the wall. "Watch the shadows, not my hands." Once she was sure the princess was avidly watching the wall like she instructed, Amila began to move her fingers and hands into different shapes.

The shadows created all sorts of animals and figures. Amila glanced to the side and saw the princess' eyes lit up in joy and a wide smile on her face. Despite the dull skin and under-eye bags Magdalene had developed during the past five and a half years, the delighted expression she wore made her look truly exquisite. Even now, anyone would be able to see why Magdalene was a legendary beauty. Amila thought it was truly her charm that drew people in. Even if she were the ugliest troll on Earth, her bright smile would still turn heads.

Amila amused the princess with shadow puppets until Magdalene could no longer support the globe of light.

"You simply must teach me how to do that next time!" Magdalene said with excitement. Her tone was cheery, but her words were slurred from exhaustion. She had used up all her spare energy by wielding her magic. It would have been wise for Magdalene to refrain from using magic again, but both girls were too delighted by their experience to consider that course of action.

"Of course." Amila hesitated. She knew it was unlikely that Magdalene would object to her blatant disrespect but it was still unnatural to her. "M-Magdalene."

The princess stopped short. Amila feared that she had gone too far. Even though Magdalene frequently insisted that they were friends, there was still a class difference between them that should be unconquerable. "No one but my *family*"—she spat out the word like it was a curse—"has called me that before."

Amila inhaled sharply.

Magdalene turned around and smiled at Amila. "I think I like it. Yes, I think I like it a great deal coming from you. From now on you should only refer to me as Magdalene, not 'my lady.'" Some things were too deeply ingrained in a person to be erased. Magdalene's dictatorial attitude was one of those things.

The last of Magdalene's energy faded away. "Thank you, Amilia." Her voice was even more tired and slurred. "Good sleep."

"Good sleep to you also, Magdalene."

* * *

The sixth year, Magdalene and Amila did not get a visit. The war had grown so severe that no one could be spared. Magdalene was rendered worthless. Marrying her to the foreign king would no longer stop the fighting.

It took the two prisoners a while to notice that something was wrong.

"We are running out of food," Magdalene said half-way through their sixth year in the tower.

"We have been running out of food for a long while," Amila responded dryly.

"We should have been visited a while ago."

"You cannot know that."

"Maybe not, but I know there is *something* wrong, Amila!" Magdalene burst out, startling the other girl. Magdalene was restless. That, in of itself, was not strange. Magdalene was not meant to be confined. She would occasionally go through periods where their imprisonment felt particularly suffocating to her, but she had not been this upset in years.

"We need to escape!" she declared. Amila raised her eyebrows. That was quite the reversal from the girl who had accepted the tower as her crypt.

"How do you suppose we do that?" she asked. "I thought you were unable to overpower the magic keeping us here."

"Yes," Magdalene nodded, "but there is always a loophole when it comes to magic. In this case, I believe if you dislodge one of the stones, the curse will break—more or less. It uses the stones to define the boundaries that keep us contained, but if part of that boundary is broken, the curse should be rendered ineffective."

Amila was outraged. "Why did you not think of this previously? Perhaps when we were not so weak and would have a better chance of escape? Or when the king removed the stone each year?"

"I did not think of it." Magdalene admitted shamefully. "But now I can't take it any longer. I can not stand for black bread to be my last meal." Magdalene sighed. It was obvious Amila was not about to accept that as an answer. "I have a chance at real freedom. My family has forgotten me.

Not even my brother came to offer me a chance to be released this year. If we escape, nobody will notice or care." She looked up at Amila with a half-smile. "No one will come after us; we will truly be free."

Amila was not going to point out the flaws in Magdalene's logic. "How do you suggest we do this?"

Magdalene took some of her portion of food and pushed it towards Amila. "It will be mainly you who will have to work at it. My father's magic would sense me through my own magic, even if I do not use it, and know my intent. Then, his spell will defend itself. You need to remove one of the stones."

"How do you expect me to displace a stone? The walls seem to be built strong."

"I would suggest using your nails to wear down the mortar."

Amila looked at Magdalene in horror, then down at her nails. Her nails were long, but that did not mean they were strong or healthy. Chances were good that they would break the moment they came in contact with the mortar. "You honestly think this will work?"

"I do not know," Magdalene admitted. "But I think we are both desperate enough to try." Amila was unable to disagree with that, so she allowed Magdalene to give her the bigger portion of food and resolved to break them out of their prison soon.

* * *

Amila placed her nails against the mortar and began to tap them idly as she considered the best course of action. She started to scrape her nails side-to-side but cringed at the sound it made. Unfortunately, every other method of scratching she tried yielded the same results, so she went back to her original plan. Her nails were less likely to break moving horizontally than vertically. Just attempting to scratch vertically caused one of her nails to bend back. This was their only escape plan. Amila did not want it to fail so soon.

After about two dozen sleep cycles—during which Magdalene got progressively weaker and Amila got progressively more frustrated—a faint indent formed in the mortar. It was only a tiny bit larger than the width of a strand of hair and so shallow it could be mistaken as a trick of the eye, but it was something. In the effort to get them this far, Amila's nails were filed down to half their previous length. The plan was untenable. But it was still the only idea either of the girls had, so Amila continued to scratch at the mortar until her fingernails were worn away. She then grasped at the mortar with her fingers, still trying to dig her way out, until the tips of her fingers bled and Magdalene forced her to stop.

Both Magdalene and Amila searched the tower for any rock or metal that could be used to wear the mortar down. The straight pins from Magdalene's clothing helped deepen the small scratch, but did nothing for its width, and broke before they could do much. Without anything else left, Amila desperately pushed at the rock, hoping that she had weakened the mortar enough to dislodge the stone with sheer strength. The pushing did nothing, not that Amila expected it to, but Amila kept trying every day until she exhausted herself.

Magdalene was sleeping more and more often. Her portion of food was enough to keep her alive, but with no spare energy. Amila was losing hope. At this point, she was unsure if Magdalene would survive, even if they did escape.

* * *

Miles away, a war had ended and a king had fallen.

Magdalene woke with a gasp.

Amila turned from where she was taking advantage of Magdalene's sleep to try to use her fingers to dig their way out again.

"It's gone," Magdalene whispered in wonder. "The curse is gone!" She looked up at Amila joyously. "Both of the curses broke! We can escape! And eat!"

Amila's jaw dropped in disbelief. "You are sure?"

"Absolutely." Magdalene gave her a weak smile. "Once I have my strength back, I will be able to bring this tower down." Her eyes fluttered shut, but she was able to win the battle against her exhaustion to say one final thing. "The enchantment that kept the food fresh ended too, so we only have a little while before it spoils."

Amila's stomach hurt at the idea of eating the rich food of the nobles after the poor meals they had been eating, but she still nodded her head enthusiastically. She hurried down to the cellar, using the wall to support herself and prevent her dizziness from making her fall.

It took Magdalene several sleep cycles to work up the energy to bring the tower down.

Despite her poor health, Magdalene could not resist making their escape into a spectacle. Magdalene gathered her magic in her hands. She compressed it into a tight ball, letting the pressure build up. Then, in one fluid motion, she let it go, flinging her arms out to the sides to direct it. There was a dull thud.

Then the tower exploded.

The stones hit directly by her magic turned to dust. Others shattered into pieces as they flew away outwards. The only sign there had ever been a tower were a few stones close enough to the ground to escape the blast.

Magdalene laughed, delighted with the destruction she caused.

Then she fainted.

Amila rushed to Magdalene's side to check her breathing, sighed in relief when she saw Magdalene's chest moving, and collapsed next to the other girl. She closed her eyes against the sunlight that assaulted her then put a hand over her closed eyes. With these precautions, Amila tilted her head towards the sky and enjoyed the warmth of the sun on her skin.

It took three days for Magdalene to awaken, which Amila knew for certain because she could actually see the sun and moon again. She found that the light of the moon was much easier on her eyes, but the novelty of the sun made daytime her favorite. It took a week before Magdalene could move in the slightest, during which time Amila would bring her water and hand-feed her freshly picked berries. As soon as she was able, Magdalene had Amila help her stumble out of the ruins of the tower. Even with the sunshine, neither wanted to be inside the corpse of what once held them prisoner. Magdalene had this irrational fear that the tower would suddenly spring up around them and never let them go.

"We can not go back to our land," Amila said softly.

"That was never a question." Magdalene was finally able to sit up independently. She ran her fingers through the grass. It seemed to be a great source of comfort to her as she rarely stopped the motion when she was awake. Amila could understand needing the reassurance that they were truly free. When the night came, she would have to keep her eyes set on the moon to avoid panic.

"Where else could we go?"

Magdalene smiled in response to Amila's question. She was only just starting to regain her health, but already her legendary beauty was returning to her. The more fresh air she breathed in, the more life returned to her. Magdalene looked more content than Amila had ever seen her, even happier than before the tower. Her joyful eyes and beaming smile stole Amila's breath away.

"Why, on an adventure, of course!" Magdalene exclaimed. "I think we deserve to bask in our freedom!"

Amila's thoughts raced. They were still women, and it was still their duty to follow their relatives' orders. They should reassure their families that they were well, or at least Amila should. If they were not to return to their former homes, then it would be best to find a nunnery to take them in. It was improper for a woman of the peasant class, much less a princess, to go on an adventure!

Then, she looked at Magdalene. The princess was only dressed in her chemise, her hair loose and blowing in the wind. Amila saw her sparkling eyes and gorgeous smile, and she was certain Magdalene must be some sort of fae. If Amila were to keep herself a good, proper woman, she would leave Magdalene in the wild and seek a sisterhood where she could work towards repentance. Amila would leave all this magic and sin behind.

But she would never see Magdalene again. This brilliant girl would be forever lost to her. Amila wanted to stick to the principles she was raised with, but, even more than that, she wanted to stay by Magdalene's side. After seven years together, Amila could not imagine living without her.

"Where do we start?"

6

Of Silver and Dragons by Elysia Song

"Ash, Ash, Ash, wake up!" A heavy weight pounced on the bed, shaking Ash out of a deep sleep. He opened his eyes to see Calla al Sena, his little sister, sitting on his blanket-covered legs. Her curly black hair was half-pulled into the beginnings of an elegant bun, pastel beads and ribbons already woven in, and her cheeks were flushed.

"Did you get into the candies again?" Ash asked with a yawn, wiggling his legs until Calla shifted her weight to the side.

"No, silly. How can you still be asleep? Today is going to be the best day ever. Get up! You have to prepare!"

"I told you I'm not going," Ash said. He might be a masochist, but only in specific circumstances, which absolutely did not include humiliating himself in front of Rosenia's elite. Ash had accepted that he would only ever make collars, never wear one.

"I know, I know, but I had an idea! For your shop, I mean. You want more customers, don't you?"

Ash stared at her warily. "Calla, what did you do?"

She pulled out an envelope and presented it to him proudly.

The front was addressed to Ash el Cin in elegant calligraphy. Ash flipped it around and saw the au Nari wax seal stamped on the back.

"Open it!" Calla said when Ash froze.

He obeyed with clumsy fingers, breaking the seal and pulling out a thick invitation.

Ash el Cin

You are cordially invited to

House au Nari's Masquerade

On the eighth night of

The Long Summer

In the year 871

Seller Status Granted: Metalweaver

"How did you get this?" Ash asked.

"I know, right? It's amazing. I didn't tell you because I didn't want you to be disappointed if it didn't work out, but it did! I know you've been worried about your shop, so I talked to Flora, who's currently the Zenith of Oliver au Nari, and showed them one of your collars, the one with the emerald butterflies? They loved it so much that Oliver added you to the guest list at the last minute. You'll come, right?"

His refusal was on the tip of his tongue, but the thought of making enough sales to help him pay next month's rent stopped him. At the hopeful look on Calla's face, the last of his resistance died a silent death. "Of course, after all the work you put in," Ash said weakly. "But I don't have anything to wear." Because he had never planned to go to the au Nari masquerade. Though technically both in the same city in Rosenia, the outer court district where Ash made his home and the inner court district of the wealthy vastly differed. They had different cultures, different upbringings, and different lifestyles. He didn't know how to even *talk* to someone from the inner court. Calla didn't count; they had been siblings for the last five years, and Ash knew she didn't care if he made a mistake that would be considered an irredeemable social faux pas by the elite.

Calla's face fell. "I know. I got you a mask, but it was too late to buy something nice for you to wear. I was thinking you could wear that outfit from 869?"

Ash cringed at the thought of dusting off the ill-fitting shirt and pants, but that was the only formal wear in his wardrobe. "Fine," he agreed because he was helpless against Calla. "Can I see the mask?"

Calla beamed again and darted off. She came back with a beautiful mask that would cover the top half of his face. The artist had painted whorls of red, blue, and purple on black, creating the illusion of a dancing blue flame. "Isn't it amazing? I found it when I went shopping in the market last week, and I instantly thought of you! And don't you have a matching collar to go with it? Imagine if you meet someone at the masquerade, and they find the perfect collar for you because you made it!" She sighed dreamily, eyes distant. Calla, sweet and seventeen, still believed in the stories of love—and by default, a perfect Zenith/nadir relationship—at first sight.

"I don't live in a romance novel."

"Hush, you. Don't be so negative. Now, get up, and we'll get you ready for the party!"

* * *

Ash tugged at his pale-blue sleeves, trying to pull them over his wrists, and smoothed out nonexistent wrinkles on his pants. Thank the gods for stringweaver stepmothers and last-minute repairs that made him marginally more fashionable. Tracing the holes of the white buttons nervously, Ash surveyed the crowd in the ballroom of the au Nari manor.

There were so many people here. He saw flashes of bright colors, which marked the wearer as a nadir, mixed with the dark Zenith outfits. There were Meridians, who switched between nadir and Zenith roles, wearing a blend of bright and dark tones. At tables in the back sat several Horizons, who never engaged in a Zenith/nadir relationship, in white and black clothes. All were elite, probably from an al, ar, or au family.

He didn't fit in with them, not when he was just an el Cin. More than once, Ash had thought about leaving through the secret halls through which he had glimpsed servers slipping in and out, but Calla would casually brush by his stand once every half-hour or so to make sure he was okay.

Ash could catch glimpses of her through the crowd, her pastel-green dress spinning around her as she met Zeniths. Calla belonged here, in a way he never would, not even if he lived a hundred lifetimes.

"Hello."

The sudden voice made Ash jump. He tore his attention away from Calla to see a Zenith standing by his table. Not just any Zenith either. Even under the stormy mask of crashing waves, Linford au Nari, the Zenith Ash's generation of nadirs had grown up pining over, was easily recognized. He was handsome in his dark blue coat and grey pants, his presence imposing the way only a Zenith's could be.

And he was focused solely on Ash.

"Sir," he croaked out when he remembered how to speak.

"Are you the creator of these beautiful designs?" Linford asked.

"Yes, sir." Ash had learned metalweaving from his mother before the wasting sickness took her and she passed on to the stars. She had poured herself into her art to create fragile, intricate collars, each unique and easily broken by a too-hard tug. They made collars for ownership, not collars for play. Tradition dictated that a nadir must have the ability to end a relationship at any time with a symbolic break of the collar.

"They're amazing. I'd ask how you made these, but I'm afraid I'd under-stand none of it, and I'm trying to impress you right now." Linford winked and grinned.

"Would you like one, sir? Free-of-charge." Ash hoped Linford would say yes. The thought of this Zenith liking his designs enough to keep a collar was making Ash irrational. Gods, each collar here cost him thirty crowns to make and sold for forty, the profits a tenth of a month's worth of rent and supplies.

"Ah, I'm afraid I like to buy my collars *after* I meet a nadir. Would you like to dance?"

Ash choked. He couldn't mean what Ash thought he meant. His mouth opened and closed a few times, no sound coming out.

"Yes, he would!" Calla appeared from nowhere and pushed Ash forward. "I'll watch your table for you, dear brother. Remember, share limits and don't do anything I wouldn't do!"

Ash's cheeks burned, but he let Linford lead him away. "Sorry," he mumbled.

"Nadirs or not, little sisters are a force of nature," Linford said, a warm smile on his face. "But I can't say I'm upset at her for giving me a chance to spend time with you. I'm Linford au Nari. What's your name?"

Ash froze again. Gods, that should be his name—Frozen el Cin. "Cinders," he said after a too-long pause, deciding to go with his play name rather than his official name. If this went badly, he definitely didn't want Linford to spread news of the nadir who couldn't hold a conversation. Ash didn't think Linford would do that, but he was a stranger despite all the tabloid stories about him.

"It's a pleasure to meet you. Remember, tell me to stop at any time and I will."

"I know how to respect my limits and use a safeword, sir. It's silver, by the way," Ash said dryly.

Linford laughed and placed a hand at the nape of his neck, a shocking, dominant touch that made Ash want to sink to his knees right there and then. Of course, then he'd humiliate himself when someone tripped over him. "I like to check. Cinders, you never answered me. Do you want to dance?"

"Yes." Ash's cheeks burned a little. "But I'm not very good."

"Let me lead, and you'll be fine."

Always. Ash bit down on the word before it could escape. They walked to the large ballroom floor together, and Ash could feel eyes on him as he heard loud whispers about "that nadir with Linford." It was almost enough to make him safeword then and there.

"Ignore them," Linford whispered against his ear as he led Ash in a slow dance that circled the room. "It's been a while since I've shown interest in a nadir, and my friends feed off gossip."

"Why haven't you?" Ash asked.

"Found a nadir? I struggle to hold on to contracts. My job gets in the way of relationships, and by the time the preliminary six months are up, my nadir is ready to find someone who works less. What about you? Why doesn't someone as talented as you have a Zenith?"

"My last potential Zenith expected me to give up metalweaving and my shop once I entered a contract," Ash said as neutrally as possible, biting back his irritation at the memories. He had been hurt at first, but the pain had died as the months passed. Now, the idea that a nadir should be wholly dependent on their Zenith just made him roll his eyes.

"That's horrible! Did they try to violate the contract?"

Ash shook his head. "It came up during negotiations, but I list giving up my business as a hard limit." And a Zenith who refused to respect limits was a horrible Zenith.

"I'm sorry you had to go through that. Did you report them?"

"I didn't want to be a bother."

Linford shook his head. "If they tried to pressure you, they definitely tried to pressure others too."

Ash shrugged, uncomfortable with the conversation. Maybe it would have mattered if an au Nari had made the report, but he was an el Cin. He was starkly aware of the social divide between him and Linford, and he'd have tugged on his too-short sleeves again if not for the fact that Linford was holding on to his hands.

"Tell me about yourself," Linford said with a smile. "Who are you beyond the best metalweaver I've ever met?"

His cheeks burned from the praise, and he ducked his head. "Not really anything. I've been making collars since I was a child. I opened my shop a year ago, and I haven't had much time for much else. I live with my father, my stepmother, and my stepsister."

"What do they do?" Linford twirled Ash and dipped him before pulling him upright again in a fast move that made his head spin.

"My father is a woodweaver, and my stepmother a stringweaver. He makes furniture, and she designs clothes."

"A family of weavers! What about your stepsister?"

"Calla's still trying to find the right fit. She's tried mechweaving, string-weaving, swordweaving, and now she's currently interested in making jewelry without magic."

Linford grinned. "I bet you're helping her."

"How did you know?" He gave her all the gems she coveted even when his purchases had originally been for his shop and collars.

"You seem like that kind of person."

"And you?" Ash asked. "Who are you?"

"Beyond what's said in the gossip rags, you mean? I'm sad to say I'm not as talented as anyone in your family. I'm a pilot for the imperial magistracy."

Ash's eyes widened. "You fly dragons?"

"It's not as impressive as it sounds. They're mostly overgrown puppies, and they'll slobber all over you if you stay away too long because they miss you." A pause. "Though some of them are more cat-like, I suppose."

"Can I see them?"

"Come with me." Linford led Ash out of the ballroom, ducking into one of the servant halls. They walked through silent corridors and exited into a garden. Night flowers were in full bloom, the violet petals emitting soft yellow light. They passed a hedge maze entrance and a fountain, turned down a cobblestone path, and then, Ash heard it.

A growl. A sharp exhale. A puff of smoke. Instinct stilled Ash. He watched Linford walk forward without him. Linford lifted his hand and patted the air. Ash saw the glint of scales as an enormous animal *moved*. The dragon's eyelids opened. Large golden irises stared at them.

"I brought someone to meet you," Linford said, running his hand over the top of the dragon's head, scritching until the dragon let out a soft growl and pressed into the touch. "I like him, so don't scare him off." He looked up and turned to Ash. "Cinders, come here. He won't eat you."

Ash walked slowly until he was standing beside Linford. "What's his name?" For some reason, he was whispering, as though if he spoke too loudly, the dragon would open his mouth and swallow Ash whole.

"Brym," Linford said in the same tone. He took Ash's hand and brought it up to Brym's snout, resting their palms down gently together.

The scales were dry and warm under his hand. Brym huffed out a breath and shut his eyes again as if bored by the interaction, and Ash copied Linford's earlier movement, scratching him behind his ears. Brym nuzzled his hand, pressing hard enough to force Ash to dig his feet in to hold his ground. Something brushed against Ash's leg, and he jumped, backing off in a hurry until he met resistance.

"It's his tail," Linford said. "It's a sign that he likes you."

Ash looked at the tail slowly winding around his leg and patted Brym again. Suddenly, he realized he was pressed against Linford, who had a hand on his hip. "Sorry," he murmured, pulling away—or, at least, trying to. Brym held him in place.

"Here." Linford bent down and tapped Brym's tail until it relaxed, freeing Ash. "Do you want to stay out here or go back in?"

Ash shivered a little, the night air cold. "Can we stay a little longer?" He didn't want to leave his first dragon—a dragon here!—until he absolutely had to.

"Of course." Linford kept his hand on Ash, and Ash told himself that was just to keep the cold air from freezing them both.

He ran his hands over Brym, earning growled purrs, and the tail returned to hold him and Linford tightly. Unfortunately, neither of them were dressed for the cold summer night, and too soon, Ash had to admit that his teeth were chattering. "Is it okay if we go back in?" he asked.

Linford held him tighter as he shifted to block a cold breeze. "Certainly. This way."

Ash left Brym with one more pat and followed Linford through a small side door that he would never have seen on his own.

"Did you get a chance to eat at the party?" Linford asked as they crossed the empty halls. "I noticed you didn't leave your table."

Gods, his collars. He had left Calla there. "I have to go back," Ash blurted out. "Calla, she—"

"The ballroom is down this hall." Linford walked with fast steps, passing by the occasional server. Ash hurried after him. They returned to the extravagant masquerade, and he rushed to the back to see that Calla was sitting on a stool behind his empty table.

"Everyone loved your collars!" Calla beamed. "I managed to sell *everything*. Can you believe it? How was your dance with Linford? Do you like him?"

"I don't even know him," Ash said.

"Well, I hope you'll give me a chance," Linford said behind him.

Ash winced and ducked his head, pressing a hand against his hot cheeks. "Sorry, sir, I didn't realize you were standing here."

"I see. You'd badmouth me only when I can't hear!" Linford gasped, and Ash glanced up to see amusement dancing in his eyes, no traces of anger.

"Sir, never!" Ash protested. "I'd say everything right to your face."

"Actually, he'd never say anything bad at all," Calla whispered conspiratorially. "You'll have to encourage him to be a little brattier."

Linford laughed. "I think I'll take him how he is. Do either of you need to stay at the table?"

Ash shook his head. "I didn't bring any more collars. Thanks, Calla." Without her bubbly personality, he definitely would still have half a table left. Calla was so sweet that she drew in people naturally, then ambushed them with marketing. At sixteen, she had single-handedly found enough customers for Ash to keep his business going when he first opened up.

She stood on her tiptoes and brushed a kiss against his cheek. "Have fun," she whispered. "Don't do anything I wouldn't do."

"I don't think that's a whole lot."

Unoffended, she laughed and danced off into the crowd.

"What do you say about getting something to eat together?" Linford asked. "Remember, don't agree to anything you don't want to, no matter what your sister says."

Ash couldn't stop his smile from spreading across his face. "I know my limits, and I think I'd like that, sir."

There were large plates of dishes set up on the back, each an elaborate design of plants and animals made up of individual foods small enough to be eaten in a few bites. "What do you like?" Linford asked.

Ash faltered. He didn't know what any of those even were. "Will you choose for me?"

"Hmm, let's see. What kind of flavors do you like? Sweet? Savory?"

"Both."

"Any foods you dislike?"

Ash shook his head. "I'm not picky." He watched Linford pick up intricate red carnations with petals made of little red balls, ferns of green vegetables woven together, some kind of sunflower that he thought were meat cakes, and brown dragons breathing little fires. They went to an empty table. Once they were sitting, Linford used a tiny fork to break off part of a carnation and hold it to Ash's lips.

"Taste," Linford said, and Ash could only obey.

The sweet taste of berries burst in his mouth, and he licked the fork clean. The intimacy of a traditional hand-feeding ritual, one he hadn't experienced since his first Zenith, was even sweeter.

"Good?"

He nodded and Linford smiled, feeding him another forkful. The vegetables were spiced with unfamiliar flavors, and the meat cakes were light and fluffy with a sweet sauce drizzled on top. Each bite had Ash pressing closer and closer until he was snuggled up against Linford's side.

"Ready for dessert?" Linford asked after he swallowed a sunflower of his own.

Ash nodded and watched Linford break off the wing of a dragon. He bit down, tasting a delicious, sweet flavor. "What is it?"

"Chocolate. Hard to get but a favorite treat of mine. More?"

"Yes, sir."

They finished off the chocolate dragon together and Linford pushed the plate away. He wrapped an arm around Ash, holding him tightly across the chest. "This okay?" he asked.

"Better than." Ash sighed and rested his head against Linford, snuggling close. He wondered if Linford would ask about his limits, one of the first steps in a new relationship, but he dared not hope for more. They didn't need to talk, not now. Sitting here with the Zenith of his dreams, a man better than Ash could have ever imagined, was perfect.

Until another Zenith dressed in the dark crimson of dried blood came by. "Slumming it, Lin?" he drawled.

Ash's cheeks burned, and he pushed away from Linford, standing up abruptly.

"Yarrow," Linford said coolly, "I didn't realize you were around."

"Well, thank the gods I was, or who knows how far you'd have fallen. Really? Imagine being seen with a nadir who can't even get a proper fitting."

He didn't bother waiting for Linford's response, just kept his head lowered and eyes focused on the ground. Ash pushed through the crowd, trying to ignore the humiliation burning in his chest and the blood rushing to his cheeks. Someone shouted his play name behind him, but he didn't stop or look back.

A hand grabbed his wrist, and Ash moved to shake it off, just to see Calla's concerned eyes staring at him. "Ash? What's wrong?"

"This was a mistake," Ash said bitterly, hurt making his words come out harshly. "I'm leaving."

"All right. Let's pick up your crowns and go."

"No, you're having a good time," he protested. Calla fit in here, had a good chance of finding a Zenith she wanted, and he didn't want to take that away from her.

"If you're not having a good time, I'm not having a good time. Wait for me outside. I'll get the coins from the holders."

Too miserable to argue, Ash hurried out the front doors of the au Nari manor and left prying eyes behind him. He found the mechanical al Sena carriage and climbed into the back, shutting himself in the dark. A moment later, Calla joined him, a hefty bag in hand.

"Here," she said, placing it in his lap, but even successful sales couldn't brighten Ash's mood. "Do you want to ride up front with me?"

He shook his head.

"All right. Get some rest. I'll get us home in one piece, promise!" She gave him a tentative smile and opened the small door to the driver's seat, wiggling through. The carriage started moving, speeding up until they were rolling across the cobblestone paths back to the outer court where Ash belonged with his outer-court clothes and his outer-court manners.

Coming here was a mistake. He was going back to the safety of his shop, his Zenith-free life, and his comfortable clothes, and he would never, ever see Linford again.

* * *

Ash growled when the collar snapped in his hands. Two broken collars in a day. His failure rate hadn't been this high since he had opened the shop.

He tossed the scraps to the side to be repurposed later and flung his stringwoven gloves onto the dirty bench. The pair had been a present from Silene al Sena, his stepmother, and normally, he took exquisite care of the gloves that protected his hands from the heat generated by his magic. Not today.

Gods, it was *ridiculous* of him to still feel hurt even after three days. He had known that his clothes marked him as someone from the outer court. He had known the elite at the party had been judging his money, his attire, his manners. And now, he knew that no matter how good he had felt when he had been alone with Linford, they didn't fit.

It would never have worked out.

But, a voice in his head whispered, *what if it could?*

"Shut up," Ash muttered and threw himself back into work.

* * *

"Ash, I'm worried about you."

Ash looked up from the—thankfully unbroken—silver links embedded with small rubies to see Silene staring at him with a gentle look in her eyes. "I'm fine," he said. *He was.*

"You've been working nonstop for the last two weeks."

"I sold a lot of my stock, and I need to replenish my shelves and pay for rent and supplies." He ignored the voice in the back of his head telling him he had *just* paid all his bills and his storeroom was bursting with trinkets.

"So it has nothing to do with a certain Zenith you met?"

He scowled. "Calla needs to learn when to stop talking."

Silene grinned. "But then how will I know anything about my beloved son?" She reached out and rested a hand on his arm, stilling his movements. "She didn't tell me the specifics of what happened. Do you want to talk about it?"

Ash sighed. "Do you want tea?"

"Why don't you clean up here, and I'll go make it."

All Zeniths were pushy even when it was gentle and out of maternal love. Ash put the half-finished ruby collar in his drawer, wiped down his counter, and went to the break room in the back. There, he saw two perfectly steaming cups of tea and a blue porcelain pot in the middle of the small, glossy wooden table with blue flower prints along the edges. Silene and Nerium, his father, had purchased the tea set and designed the matching furniture for him when he first opened his shop last year.

Silene sat in one of the chairs and gestured for him to take the one across from her. Her fingers traced the rim of the cup as they sat in silence for a few minutes. Finally, she gave in when it was clear Ash wasn't about to talk. "Is Linford au Nari the reason why you've been locking yourself in here for the last two weeks? If he is, I look forward to having a long conversation with him."

Ash winced, not because he doubted Silene but because he didn't; on their first meeting, Silene had sworn to always tell him the truth, and she had kept that promise throughout the years. "No, he was fine. It's just…we don't fit. It would never have worked out anyway."

"Why not?"

Because he was an el Cin and Linford was an au Nari. They were just too different, the inherent power structure too wide in a way that would scare even someone interested in a total power exchange. And Ash was most decidedly *not*.

But then he remembered that Silene and his father had gotten together, two people with such a large social divide that they never would have met for infinite reasons. However, out of pure chance, they had, and their love for each other had given Ash hope for second chances and happy endings. "How did you and Dad do it?" he asked. "Why did you decide to collar each other?" Not every Zenith/Zenith relationship had a collaring ceremony since collars were traditionally meant to be gifted to a nadir, but Silene and Nerium had decided to gift each other a fragile bracelet as a symbol of their commitment.

"Because we make each other happy. Because we love each other. Most of all, because we decided we wanted to put in the work to make *us* work. A relationship doesn't flourish just because you love someone. You need time, commitment, and respect, and sometimes, it's not going to be fun. But when you find the person who fits you and you put in the effort, you get something beautiful, and it's worth it."

"How do you know who's the right person?"

"Despite what stories say, there's no such thing as soulmates. You can't look at someone and instantly know they're the person you're meant to sign a lifetime contract with. Instead, you try. You explore. You follow your instincts.

What do your instincts tell you about Linford?"

"I like him. But I don't know if he likes me. And even if he does, I don't know if his family will approve. Furthermore, I don't even know *how* to find Linford even if I wanted to." Aside from going to the manor, which Ash was never going to visit again.

Silene gave Ash a secretive smile and pulled out a piece of paper, pushing it towards him.

Ash looked down and saw a flyer for a tournament of metalweavers to make a collar. The metalweaver would submit a collar, and, if one of the forty chosen, compete to be the best in Rosenia. The winner would get a thousand crowns. It, too, was hosted by the au Nari family, to take place two weeks hence. "What's this?"

"Rumor has it that a certain au Nari has been going to metalweaver shops looking for someone," Silene said.

Ash's heart thudded in his chest. It couldn't be. "Maybe he just wants a collar," he said, voice coming out rough.

"Maybe. But if he does, he's looking for something very specific because he's left behind a lot of very disappointed shops. Are you interested?"

"I don't...if this is a ploy to judge the nadirs in the competition for worthiness..." Ash shook his head. There were always some Zeniths who thought they had the right to pit nadirs against one another, while they sat back and watched the commotion. They were also the ones who toyed with emotions and complained when no nadir wanted them. They were, in general, complete assholes.

"If it is, you walk away," Silene said simply. "You know the red flags. If Linford displays any of them, you leave immediately. But even if he doesn't, the power difference inherent in your names will always remain. Can you live with that?"

"I don't know. Even if I can, I don't know if he's aware of just how different we are."

"Maybe not, but you won't know until you talk to him. Now, looking at only the tournament itself, are you interested?"

"A thousand crowns," Ash murmured. It was enough to tempt even one of the elite families.

"Minus the entry fee of a collar."

"And assuming I pass the initial selection." He hesitated. "Will you leave the flyer here? Just in case?"

Silene smiled warmly. "Of course. Now, will you finally take a break and come to dinner so your sister and father can reassure themselves that you're still alive?"

He blushed and nodded.

* * *

Ash el Cin contestant 32 was printed in neat calligraphy on the name tag, and Ash couldn't breathe. He was doing this. He was really, really doing this. Gods, he was going to be sick.

"Let me help you with that," Calla said cheerfully. She hooked the yarn through the holes, knotted off the ends, and tiptoed to hang it over his neck. The yarn brushed against his nape, giving off almost the sensation of a collar. "This is so exciting! There are so many people."

"Don't remind me," Ash gritted out and forced himself to take a deep breath before he threw up or fainted. He could see vendors and long lines at food stations, children running around, and people filling up the stands that stretched up towards the skies. So many people. All here to watch the many tournaments.

It wasn't just a metalweaver tournament like he had thought at first. All kinds of Zenith, nadir, Meridian, and Horizon weavers were competing. Hosted by au Nari and a few other families, the weaver tournament would take place over two days. This was one of the best opportunities to demonstrate skills, impress a potential contract partner, or develop a name and recognition across Rosenia, and it had brought in the best of the best. His competition.

"Maybe this was a mistake," Ash said desperately. "Is it too late to go home?"

"Yes," Calla said. "Now go set up. Think of the customers you'll get. Financial security, delicious." She smacked her lips together exaggeratedly.

Lead replaced leather, and every step felt impossible. Ash somehow made it to his table. Every metalweaving contestant had two blocks of silver, a cup of bright beads, and a magnetic lock. When the timer started, they would have one hour, counted down by floating numbers in the air, to make a collar from their given materials.

Ash glanced to the sides at his competition, heart sinking at the silver succulent insignia embroidered on their stringwoven gloves. The School of Echeveria produced the best metalweavers, people who would go on to make collars that would be kept for a lifetime. When the wearer passed on to the stars, the collar would be sent with them.

Humiliating himself at the au Nari's masquerade under a play name had been horrible, but he could recover from that. Here? Under his official name? And his chosen profession? There would be no way to recover. Even if he walked out now, it was too late. Why couldn't he have been content with his shop as it was? Oh right, because he was still an unknown metalweaver, and even the profits from the masquerade would only hold him over for a month.

A nadir announcer walked onto the stage, her blond hair pulled back in an elegant braid that revealed the collar of roses around her neck. Her magically amplified voice could be heard across the entire enclosure. "People of Rosenia, welcome to the metalweaver challenge! For the first round, we have forty spectacular contestants who have traveled far and wide to show you what they can do! Only twenty will proceed to the next round! Gather here and see mystical abilities up close. Contestants, prepare yourself! Three! Two! One! Begin!"

Choosing to rely on a familiar design, Ash picked up the first silver bar and set it in the center of the table. He extended his magic, and the silver turned to liquid in his hands, spreading into hundreds of tiny, thin braids in front of him. He pulled them into tiny links shaped like butterflies. Ash shook out the beads, attaching each one to a butterfly, forming colorful heads on silver bodies. With the second block, he created a fine thread to weave through the butterflies as a vine, linking them all together into a delicate collar. The magnetic lock went on last, melded in with the butterfly ends.

He shook from the magical exertion and flexed his stiff fingers beneath worn leather gloves. Carefully, Ash picked up his collar and watched the butterflies twist and turn, giving off the illusion they were alive. This was always the final test, to see whether his product would hold together after his magic faded.

"Stop! Set your collar down and step back. Judges will now come around to collect your final product, and the contestants who will advance to the next stage will be announced in ten minutes!"

Ash obeyed and watched a tournament moderator hook a 32 to his collar and take it away, holding his breath and praying it didn't break from too-rough handling. The fragility of collars was always a balance, to be able to break it at will but not accidentally snap off a chain.

From the section in the stands where contestant assistants waited, Calla ran down in a flurry of movement, coming up to his side. "So? What do you think? I saw your collar while they were showing off each contestant, and yours is so much better than everything else!"

"I think you're obligated to say that as my sister," Ash said dryly.

"Maybe, but I still mean it." She nudged his side and laced her fingers with his. "I saw a certain Zenith in the stands, by the way."

He stiffened, hand clenching down on hers. "And?"

"He didn't try to talk to me, though maybe that's because I kicked him out last time."

"Last time? What?" How had he not known about this?

"He was looking for you. I guess he didn't know your official name, but he knew mine, so he found me instead." Calla rolled her eyes. "It was three days after the masquerade, and he showed up on our doorstep. You were working yourself to the bone, and I wasn't going to make your life worse by surprising you with him. We're nadirs, Ash, and not pushovers, and we don't surrender our time whenever some Zenith off the streets demands it, right?"

Ash swallowed and nodded. Linford had been looking for him. His heart pounded, and his palms sweated beneath the cooling spells woven into the leather. A month ago, he hadn't been in the right state of mind to meet Linford again as himself, too frustrated with a power difference beyond Zenith and nadir. Between then and now, nothing had changed except for repeated conversations with Silene and Nerium. Was that enough?

"Are you mad? It's okay if you're mad."

156

"Thanks for your permission," he deadpanned.

"Any time. As long as you're not sad." Calla leaned against his side, affection clear on her face. "I think he might know who you are now though, so if you need someone to safeword for you, I'm here."

Ash snorted and opened his mouth to reply, but the announcer's voice broke out over them. "Contestants, your judges have deliberated, and twenty have been chosen! Moving on to round two are one, three, six..."

He thought he misheard when the announcer said, "Thirty-two!" except Calla's scream almost deafened him as she slammed into him with a hug that squeezed his ribs.

"You're moving on!" she shouted.

He had made the first cut. In the stands, Linford stood up, clearly recognizable even in the distance, a smile on his face as he raised a hand in greeting. Their eyes met, and Ash knew that, despite his fear, he wanted to have this conversation even more than he wanted to win this tournament.

It was time to lay out all the facts and let Linford decide whether he wanted a relationship with an el Cin.

Though if this tournament was a way to decide whether Ash was "worthy," he'd slap Linford and walk out before anyone could stop him.

* * *

"Cinders," Linford said in a rush the moment Ash took a step out of the enclosure, "can we talk?"

Ash nodded wordlessly and followed Linford in silence as they turned away from the emerging crowd down to a more empty, private alley. He glanced back and saw Calla a few steps behind them. She sent him an encouraging look, and Ash braced himself for the conversation he had imagined every day for the last two weeks.

"I'm sorry. Yarrow is a pretentious creep, and the only person he speaks for is himself. I need you to know that I don't care about your clothes or your money...unless that's important to you. In which case, I will care, but if it doesn't matter to you, it doesn't matter to me." A pause as he took a deep breath. "Sorry, I'm rambling. What I mean to say is, if you never want to see me again, tell me now, and I'll walk away. However, if you see the potential

157

for something to work out between us, I do too. If you're willing to try a trial scene, I am too."

Ash swallowed. A trial scene allowed the people interested in a contract to see whether they were compatible. It was rare to ask for one before limits were shared. Most importantly, it was a declaration of intent. Almost all trial scenes led to a six-month preliminary contract.

They said all the power was in the hands of the nadir. He had heard the talk-limits-and-use-your-safeword speech from his mom first, then from Nerium, and again from Silene. Ash knew it by heart now, but for the first time, a Zenith stood vulnerable in front of him, waiting for him to pass judgment. The choice was his and only his to make. Did he want a contract with Linford?

Walking away was the safer option. He could protect himself, avoid the risk.

But no matter the outcome, Ash knew that if he didn't try, he'd regret it.

"I think," he said, "that I've never heard a Zenith apologize before, and I'm worried if you're okay." He smiled and tried to swallow his nerves, only to choke and start coughing violently.

Arms wrapped around him, holding him steady. "Are you okay?"

"Fine." Ash felt his cheeks burn and he looked up at Linford, who was pressed up against him. "Hi."

"Hi," Linford said. "You and me, yes or no?"

Pushy Zeniths. Couldn't live without them. "Will your family be okay with it? I'm not going to force you into something you regret."

"I think they'll be grateful that I've stopped flying all over Rosenia looking for metalweavers."

Ash couldn't stop himself from beaming. "You looked for me?" he asked, euphoric from Linford's confirmation, though Calla had already told him as much.

"Of course. If nothing else, you deserved an apology."

"I suppose if you tried so hard, you can get my official name."

Interest lit up his face. "Oh?"

Ash swallowed and took a breath. "Ash el Cin."

"Linford au Nari." They clasped hands, Linford's on top of his because he was the Zenith. "Do you want to get something to eat before the next match?"

Ash glanced back at Calla, but she waved him off. "All right."

They walked past the vendor stalls, still holding hands. Ash purchased a meat pie, grateful that Linford didn't offer to buy for him. Gods, he hoped Linford didn't think Ash was interested in him because of the money. He needed money for his shop, but he would earn it through his collars. If there was to be something between Linford and him, it would be based on mutual respect and interest, not wealth.

"So why the tournament?" Ash asked as he broke off a piece of the pie to share with Linford.

"Believe it or not, my family has been planning this for a long time. However, I admit that I may have spread more flyers for metalweavers during my search for you, and I decided to watch the metalweaver competition in hopes that you had heard and decided to enter."

Ash exhaled in relief and smiled at Linford. "You thought I'd be chosen as one of the forty?"

Linford frowned. "Of course. Your work is unparalleled."

He laughed. "Thank you for your faith. Will you stay for the next two rounds?"

"And wish you the best of luck. May I kiss you?"

"Not with the aftertaste of pie in my mouth," he said. Shyly, Ash pulled out a folded-up piece of paper and handed it to Linford. His handwriting was nowhere near as neat as the calligraphy on his name tag, but it was legible.

"What is this?" Linford asked as he unfolded the page.

"My limit list. If you want."

Linford froze, and then a smile turned his face from handsome to beautiful. "You've just been carrying this around on you?"

Ash shrugged, unwilling to admit he'd had this on his person for the last two weeks just in case Linford showed up.

"Thank you for your trust. Yes, I do want it. Unfortunately, I don't have my own on hand."

"That's fine. I think the next match is about to start soon anyway."

Ash couldn't contain the giddy feeling in his heart, and he walked back to the metalweaver challenge with a bounce in his step and a smile no competition could wipe from his face. He could feel the ghost of Linford's fingers tangled with his, and when he arrived at the table, Linford was already in the stands, looking at him from afar. Suddenly, as the announcer was counting down, Ash knew exactly what he wanted to make. It would be a risky collar, one he had never tried before.

The table held a large silver block, a roll of copper threads, and a white metallic lock. Ash reached for the lock first. Silver was the easiest for magic, but trying to change the lock felt as though he were lifting lead. He had to force his magic in. It resisted him, but he clenched his teeth and continued inserting tendrils until his power saturated the lock. He *pushed*, and slowly the white wood started to deform and reform into leathery wings.

Ash tried the lock to make sure it could still open and close and smiled when it snapped easily. Next, he reached for the silver. After the lock, this should have been easy, but Ash was drained, and it felt like he was trying to use magic on diamond. Beads of sweat rolled down his face. His shirt dampened.

Slowly, the silver turned into thin droplet-shaped scales. Ash arranged them in a circle that started at the base of the wings and melded the pieces together. He fused the copper threads, pulling at the pieces until he had two horns and a snout. Setting the pieces on the side opposite of the wings, Ash merged the edges. He stared critically at a dragon curled in a circle, tail wrapped around its neck, for a long moment and decided it would do. Last, Ash created four tiny legs in the collar. He grimaced at how disproportionate it felt, but before he could fix it, the announcer yelled, "Stop!"

Ash stumbled back, legs heavy and almost too weak to support his body. He listed to the side and forced himself to take deep breaths.

In a moment, Calla was down from the stands. She slid up beside him and wrapped an arm around his side. To an outsider, it looked like the hug of a sister, but he slumped into her arms, relying on her to hold him up.

"When are they going to announce?" she muttered.

"Soon, I hope," Ash said. His legs trembled. He shivered uncontrollably despite the hot summer afternoon. The magic burn was consuming him. There was no cure except time, food, and rest.

"A fierce competition, and so many impressive collars! Your judges have made their decisions, and these are the five who will move on to the final round: three, eight, thirteen, twenty-eight, and thirty-two! Final competitors, return tomorrow at eight bells to see who is the best metalweaver of Rosenia!"

"You did it!" Calla beamed.

Ash managed a weak grin, but he couldn't manage to raise more than a smidgeon of joy at progressing to the final round. "Can we go?" he rasped.

"Here, hold on to me." They walked out, the steps coming out slowly as Ash struggled to walk on his own. He wouldn't—couldn't—collapse here with so many eyes on him.

Linford met them at the exit. "Ash, are you well?"

"He's fine," Calla said.

Linford shot them both a look of disbelief, a Zenith command clear on his face that had Ash giving in immediately. He forced out, "Magic burn," and it was all the explanation that Linford needed.

"How can I help?" Linford asked, moving around to support Ash's other side.

"Carriage. This way." Together, the three of them managed to walk to the al Sena carriage parked in the distance and Ash collapsed on the velvet seat. He shivered uncontrollably, breaths coming in short and fast.

A warm coat was tucked around him. Ash blinked and saw Linford kneeling on the ground beside him, eyes worried. "I work with some weavers, but I've never seen magic burn this severe before," he said. "You shouldn't push yourself so hard."

"I wanted to impress you," Ash mumbled. He wasn't sure if he was speaking real words, but he hoped that he was coherent enough for Linford to understand. "Did you see it? It was for you."

"I did, and I'm honored," Linford said softly. "But I already think you're incredible. I don't need to see a testament to your skill or anything else to know that I want to get to know you. If I like you any more, my heart might just explode."

Ash grinned and snaked an arm out from under Linford's coat to hold his hand and pull it to his chest. Linford's fingers were long, his palms calloused.

"I don't think I've ever seen a Zenith kneel before."

"You'll be seeing it more; I do enjoy sucking my nadirs off."

Ash inhaled at the thought, but he was too tired to even think about getting aroused. The mental picture seared itself into his brain for future...use. A yawn stretched his jaw wide open, and by the time Ash remembered that he might want to cover his mouth, it had already passed. His eyelids felt heavy, and he was beginning to warm up under the coat. "I like this," he said, patting the fine leather with the hand that wasn't holding Linford captive.

Linford chuckled and leaned forward, pressing dry lips against Ash's forehead.

"I'm sweaty," Ash said, but he was smiling anyway. He gave in to the fight against his eyes and let them drift shut.

"You're perfect. Sleep, darling."

The carriage started moving, and the rocking motion sent Ash to a peaceful sleep.

* * *

The next time Ash opened his eyes, he was staring at the ceiling of his room. Someone had carried him to bed and tucked the soft handwoven blanket around him. He swung his legs off the bed, stood, and immediately sat down again. Gods, his legs ached. His fingers ached. His *hair* ached.

His stomach growled a loud complaint, and Ash groaned, forcing himself to stand again. He stumbled to the door, then cursed at the stairs between him and the kitchen.

"Need a hand?" Linford called up, and Ash nearly fell on his face.

"You're here," he blurted out. Linford au Nari. In his home. Ash rubbed the exhaustion out of his eyes and looked again. Linford was even closer, halfway up the stairs. Not a hallucination.

"Calla brought me to your home. I hope you don't mind." He gave Ash a bashful smile, and Ash could only shake his head.

They walked down the stairs together, and Ash tried to ignore the giddy feeling threatening to turn him into Calla at her bubbliest. Silene and Nerium were already in the kitchen, and Calla bounced up behind them.

"Ash, you're awake! Eat this!" She ran to the table and grabbed a pastry from the center plate, pushing it into his hands. "Did you know that Linford can cook? He made it just for you."

"For your entire family," Linford corrected. "As both a thank you and an apology for my intrusion. I swear I didn't intend to follow you home."

Ash remembered holding on to Linford and winced. "I don't think I gave you a choice," he said dryly.

"I think this is the first Zenith you brought home," Nerium remarked. "Must be special."

Thank the gods for Silene because his father and sister were apparently trying to kill him via humiliation. Ash stuffed the pastry in his mouth to avoid having to answer and moaned from the burst of sweetmeat filling. Gods, this was amazing. He devoured the pastry and grabbed another one before forcing himself to take a breath and pace himself. Magic burn always led to overeating, which then made him nauseous and bloated.

"Congratulations on your win," Linford said. "I don't think I mentioned that."

He blushed and ducked his head. "Thank you, sir," he said. Ash knew he was a talented metalweaver, but the praise from Linford made him giddier than Calla at the peak of her sugar consumption.

"Are you going back tomorrow?" Silene asked as she brought a large pot of stew over and started pouring out bowls for everyone.

"Yes," Ash said. He couldn't afford to back out now, not when he was only one of five contestants and his face no longer just one in the sea of metalweavers. If he dropped out, he'd lose his reputation, and with that, his career and shop.

"It normally takes you at least two days to recover from magic burn," Nerium pointed out.

"I'll go easy. Besides"—Ash snuck a look at Linford—"I think I've already won the real prize."

* * *

During the final competition, the stands were filled to the maximum, people packed closely together as the realm came out in full. Five tables were arranged in a pentagon facing outwards. Ash walked up to his table, a strange calmness settling over him. His lips tingled from the goodbye kiss. Ash knew Linford was up there, watching him, and he wasn't nervous, not today.

Then, he saw what awaited him, and he changed his mind.

Before him, the table held five blocks of silver, a copper lock, and a gods-cursed black diamond. Diamonds were inert, their ability to nullify magic legendary. Ash hated diamonds like any good weaver. He bit back a growl and resisted the urge to fling it to the ground and bury it too deep to ever be recovered.

When they began, Ash pushed the diamond to the edge of the table with a silver block and moved so that he was as far away as he could get. What was he supposed to do with a *diamond*? A glance around told him his competitors at the adjacent tables had already started when he'd been wasting time.

Ash grimaced and picked a design from a memory of when he was small and standing on a stool beside his mother, watching her mold silver in her hands. *For you*, he thought, wondering if she could see him from where the wasting sickness had taken her. Would she have liked Linford? He hoped so.

With the first silver bar, he sliced off slivers and curled tiny petals, forming the calla lilies that were his sister's namesake, and held them together with thin links. Ash set the finished piece down and picked up three more blocks of silver. Ash pulled out teardrops, fourteen large and fifteen small. He created more links and, below the calla lilies, added the teardrops in alternating size. When he held up the collar, he saw a conspicuous gap in the middle where a large tear should have been. With the last of his silver, Ash crafted little basins that hung off the teardrops. *I'll catch all your tears*, it said, Zenith to nadir.

The copper lock went on the back, and Ash turned to the last, and most despised, item. He gave the diamond a death glare, and it stared back, sucking the life out of him. Ash braced himself and peeled off his gloves, tucking them into his pocket to protect the stringwoven charms. He pinched the diamond with his left thumb and index finger, unwilling to risk his dominant hand. Ice seeped through his skin and stunned his fingers, spreading through his wrist and up his arm.

His body shook from the strain. Inch by inch, Ash dragged the diamond to the collar. He rested it in the empty center, its edges brushing the adjacent small tears. The moment the diamond hit the silver, the collar fully solidified as the diamond nullified the remnants of magic. Ash ripped his hand away, cradling it to his chest. His chest heaved from heavy breaths. Too late, he saw that the diamond was an inch off-center. It was too close to the silver for him to fix with magic, and Ash could only watch the timer count down.

"Stop!" the announcer yelled. "Contestants, step back and await your judges!"

The moderator came around, lifting each beautiful collar carefully. The first was a bouquet of roses, the second stars and planets, the third tiny birds in a cage with the door open that would then be closed when the lock was shut, and the fourth a diamond at the base of a tree with roots curled and intertwined.

He walked away from the tables and met Calla at the edge. "I can't believe they made you use a diamond," she said, scowling.

"Did you see how the others used it?"

"Most of them didn't use all the silver. They created pliers and used it to pick up the diamond in the end."

Ash hadn't even thought about using the materials they had given him for alternative purposes. Would he have known what to do had he attended the School of Echeveria? But it was a useless question to consider. Instead, Ash filed the idea away for the future in case he ever lost his mind and decided to work with diamonds again, and waited for the judges to deliberate on the winner.

"In third place, we have Iris au Vera!" The announcer held up the tree and roots for everyone to see. "In second place, Ash el Cin!" His design, the diamond sparkling brightly under the sun. "And in first place, Lucerne ar Maro!" The birds who stayed in their cage willingly. "Winners, please come up and collect your rewards!"

"Second! Can you believe it?" Calla beamed and pushed him forward. "Go!"

Ash tried not to fidget as he stepped forward to accept the second-place reward. He could see all the eyes on them, and he prayed that he wouldn't trip. Then, his eyes found Linford's, and the rest of the world grew a little quieter.

It wasn't the first-place reward he had entered for, but Ash wasn't disappointed. He came away with five hundred crowns and his name known by everyone present. Excitement bubbled inside him, but those reasons were only responsible for a small part of it. One more prize waited for him, one that he hadn't had to compete for, one that wouldn't foist diamonds on him, one that he had never expected but now refused to release.

Linford met him outside and pressed a chaste kiss against his cheek. "Congratulations! Do you want to celebrate with a lunch in the city nearby?"

Ash turned to Calla. She had a silly grin on her face. "Don't stay out too late! Or if you do, be sure to tell me all the details tomorrow." She winked.

"Here, will you take this too?" He handed off the bag of crowns, heart pounding as he watched her skip off with enough money for five months of rent and supplies.

"This is for you," Linford said when they were alone in the crowd. He handed Ash a thick envelope, and Ash opened it to find a handwritten list of hard and soft limits. He studied it and learned that their limits overlapped a lot. Like Ash, Linford didn't want a total power exchange or edgeplay. No blood or permanent or long-term damage. Nothing risky like breathplay. No surrendering his job. His safeword was dragons.

"Did you tailor this to me?" Ash asked, only half-joking because there was no way Linford and he could be this compatible. What were the chances?

"No. If you don't believe me, I have ten more of these at home," Linford said with a grin.

"Ten, wow. You must really get around."

"Or maybe I was prepared in case my nadir was clumsy and messy."

"I'll have you know that my workspace is *pristine*." Too late, Ash realized that he was already talking as though he were Linford's nadir without a contract. They hadn't even talked about it.

"You'll have to show me," Linford said, stepping closer to embrace him with loose arms.

"Tomorrow? If you want to come home with me again."

"It's a date. Do you have any food preferences?"

"Choose for me."

Linford smiled. "Are you well? Can you walk?" At Ash's nod, he led them away from the tournament, leaving the crowd behind them for the twists and turns of small cobblestone alleys lit by expensive glassweaver lights. At the end of the street, they stopped at a nondescript door with a small sign overhead that read Auspicious Aroma. Linford opened the door for Ash, gesturing for him to enter.

"Where are we?" Ash asked as he looked around. It appeared to be a small restaurant with a bar on the side. Lights hung from the ceiling, over each setting, giving the place a warm glow. The tables were large, each side able to fit a chair on the left and a cushion on the right. There were large metal rings on the tables and floor for binding nadirs, with slits built into the wood so they could be pulled out and pushed back to avoid becoming hazards.

A few people were present. In the corner sat two Zeniths with a nadir kneeling beside them. At a table closer to the door, two nadirs were having lunch together and laughing.

Without a contract or even a negotiation, no nadir would kneel for a Zenith. Ash didn't think he would mind settling at Linford's side, but he took the chair across from Linford, meeting him as a nadir who hadn't surrendered any power.

"Welcome to Auspicious Aroma," Linford said. "This is owned by a cousin of mine and his Zenith. Oliver and Flora don't have a staff, so it's a pretty small place, but they're both incredible. The food is delicious, and they did the catering for the masquerade."

A pretty young Zenith came up to them. "Good afternoon, lovelies. Can I get you something to drink?"

"Hot tea for both of us and two of the house special, Flora. Thanks," Linford said.

"Twenty minutes." They gave Ash a wink. "This is the first time he's brought someone here," they said. "You must be really special."

"Shoo. Let me court him in peace." Linford sighed and gave Ash a wry smile. "As you can see, you're not the only one with nosy family members. If you were worried about them meeting, trust me, they'll get along great."

Ash was more worried about Linford's family meeting *him*. What if they decided they didn't like him and Linford deserved better?

"Tell me about yourself," Linford said. "What do you like? What are your goals?"

Ash started with the easy part first. "My professional goals are to get my shop sufficient, maybe expand a little. I've only been open for a year, and it's been hard to reach customers, but Calla helps with that."

"And your win will help secure your shop."

"Second place," Ash corrected automatically.

"Do you think you'd try again if it became an annual tournament?"

He shook his head. "I did it for my shop, to hopefully get enough attention to fully support myself without having to rely on my parents. I don't miss the magic burn, and if I never see a diamond again, that will be too soon."

"How badly does it affect you?" Linford asked. "If I had known, I'd have pushed against its inclusion."

"I hate it," Ash said honestly. "I don't know if formal schooling teaches you how to handle it better or if it gets better with repeated exposure, but it feels like magic burn at its worst. I think I was lucky that I wasn't fully recovered, or I would feel even more drained right now."

Linford paled, and his lips tightened to a fine line. "I can't change the tournament now, but it won't happen again in the future."

Ash couldn't find it in him to object, and he smiled at his hands. "Why all this talk of the future? Is it going to become something annual?"

He shrugged. "I'm not one of the planners behind the event, but from what I hear, yes. It turns out good revenue for a lot of people, and several weaver groups want the chance to reach a wider audience."

"If you don't plan tournaments, what else do you do besides fly dragons?"

"I also feed them, pet them, and scratch them when they're peeling and grumpy." Linford grinned. "There are other duties, but"—he shrugged—"I can't talk about those."

"Is it a security problem?" Ash asked. He hadn't even considered that, his focus on their inherent social differences.

"Yes. Some days are worse than others, and I won't be able to tell you why. The other reason I've struggled to hold down a contract in the past is that I travel for my job, so I have odd hours. " Linford's dark eyes met his. "I won't lie or tell you that my schedule will change."

"It would be hypocritical of me to expect you to change your job when I refuse to give up mine. I get distracted by all things shiny and bring home lots of trinkets that others would describe as junk. If you ever bring me to a metal or jewel market, you'll lose hours waiting for me."

"When my dragons get sick, sometimes I bring them home to isolate them from the rest of the team. You'll have to deal with grumpy lizards, burnt vomit, and sleepless nights."

"Some days I forget to go home because I get invested in a project. Then, I use too much magic and suffer from magic burn for the rest of the week. I'm demanding and I get cold easily, so I'll be raiding the blankets and turning into a ball by the fireplace."

Linford let out a thoughtful hum. "I have experience with dragon nesting. Human nesting can't be that much different."

Ash grinned. "Is it settled then? Is this our kink negotiation?"

"Did you have anything specific you wanted to ask about my limits?" Linford asked. "Or clarify about yours?"

He shook his head.

"Then, let's talk about a trial scene. Thoughts on sex?" Linford asked just as Flora came with two plates and a porcelain tea set.

Ash's face turned bright red and froze as Flora poured the tea into cups dotted by rings of green. Thankfully, they didn't say anything, and he immediately reached for the tea when Flora left, taking long sips as he waited for them to go through the door behind the bar where they surely couldn't hear. "It's—um—I'm not against it," he said. "With you."

Linford's lips crept up in a smile, and Ash felt a boot nudge against his foot. "I'm not against it with you either. Bondage? Blindfolds? You should try the food. Flora's a walking miracle."

He squirmed in his seat, trying to juggle the abrupt changes in subject. A bite down on the chicken had spices and flavors bursting in his mouth. Ash chewed, trying to figure out how to respond without spontaneously combusting. "I like both," he said simply.

"I think we're going to have some fun together, darling."

* * *

Ash paid a runner to deliver a message home so his family wouldn't worry, and Linford draped his arm around Ash's side, an easy hold that declared to the world that they were together. They walked, not to the au Nari manor that had hosted the masquerade, but to Linford's house in the city. Ash hated that Linford was taking his time. If his cock got any harder, it would break off. Thank the gods for loose pants.

"Having trouble walking?" Linford asked, a knowing glint in his eye.

"Not at all," he choked out.

"Good. I'd kiss you but I know you said exhibitionism was a soft limit."

Ash grinned and thought he wouldn't mind if it was Linford. Slowly, his arousal died to something more manageable, and they walked peacefully through the streets. When they reached their destination, Ash thought Linford had vastly understated his dwelling.

There was no way something that big could be accurately described as a house. It stood at three stories, multiple windows across that meant each story had at least three rooms. Behind the estate was a large patch of greenery, and Brym flew freely overhead.

"Intimidating, I know," Linford said with a grimace as he unlocked the door. "It's because I occasionally host events and people for work and I need the space."

"I'm not intimidated at all," Ash lied and shut his gaping mouth.

They walked in to see two people sitting and talking in the living room. Linford froze. "Mother. Father. What are you doing here?"

Ash stiffened and stepped slightly behind Linford before halting. He didn't want to look like he was hiding even though that was exactly what he was doing.

"We thought we'd stop by for some tea," the woman said. "Meet your new nadir while we were at it."

"He hasn't signed, Mother," Linford said with a sigh.

The woman ignored him and came up to Ash. "I'm so glad to meet you. Would you do an old nadir a favor and sit with me, tell me about yourself, and

170

reassure me that my son is the Zenith I raised him to be?"

There was only one answer to that. "Of course," Ash said and let the woman lead him away by the hand. He looked behind and saw Linford following him with a fond look on his face.

"You should know that I've spoken to Yarrow," she said primly. "He seems to have forgotten that you're not the first person with a modest upbringing he's met."

"Pardon?"

She stretched out her arm for him to clasp hands with, side to side as two nadirs. "I'm his aunt. Jessamine en Zen."

"Ash el Cin."

* * *

"Well, that was unexpected," Linford said, exhaling loudly as he shut the door to the bedroom. "I wasn't going to introduce you to my family so soon, but what do you think? Did they scare you away?"

"They're lovely," Ash said honestly.

"Fantastic. That's all I want to know because for the next few hours, we're not going to think about your family or mine." Linford pressed Ash against the door and kissed him first chastely before deepening it so that Ash was grasping at Linford's shoulders, trying to hold himself up because his legs weren't working.

They undressed each other, clumsy hands tugging at buttons and shucking off pants. It was a mess, neither one of them willing to let the other go. Ash fell backward, landing on a soft cloud, and he stared up at Linford's muscular shoulders.

Linford pulled his arms over his shoulders and, with a coil of rope from the bedside drawer, secured Ash's wrists to the bars of the wooden headboard. "Say your safeword for me," he said.

"Silver," Ash breathed. "But I don't want you to stop."

He didn't stop. Instead, he pressed down on Ash, kissing him once again quickly. Linford reached to the side drawer again and pulled out a long dark blue cloth. "Lift your head."

Ash arched up enough for Linford to tie it around his eyes, knotting it at the side so he could lie back comfortably. The cloth was soft and thick, blocking out all the light in the room. He couldn't see Linford, couldn't touch him. He could only wait.

"You're so pretty," Linford said. "Here, in my bed." A calloused hand wrapped around his cock. "Hard for me."

He gasped and pushed his hips up into the touch. It had been too long since it had been anyone's hand but his, too long since he'd even bothered to get himself off, and it was almost too much to bear. Ash bit his lip, trying to hold back pleas for more.

A fast kiss against his mouth. "I want to hear you," Linford said, lips brushing against his.

"Sir, please," Ash moaned.

"You want more?" Linford stroked him once. And only once.

"You're a sadist," Ash gritted out when the hand disappeared from his cock

"Just a little. And you're a bit of a masochist." Linford pulled Ash's hips up, placing a pillow under him for comfort. A slick finger brushed against his entrance. "Looser than I expected," Linford murmured, sliding a finger in smoothly.

His face burned. "I cleaned. Just in case."

"I did too, just in case you wanted to top."

The thought hadn't even occurred to him, but now, arousal flooded Ash. Bottoming hadn't been one of Linford's limits, but Ash had just assumed. "Would you really?"

"Of course. It feels good, doesn't it?" Linford rocked against him, their cocks brushing against each other. "So? What are your thoughts on being tied to my bed and letting me use you to get myself off?"

"Next time?" Ash gasped out. Because gods willing, there would be a next and a next and a next. He still couldn't believe it.

Linford pushed a second finger in, the stretch burning a little. The pain went right to Ash's cock, and a whimper escaped. Linford stretched Ash slowly and made sure *not* to brush up against his prostate. His Zenith was a tease, and actually, there wouldn't be a next time because this time was going to kill him.

"Please, sir," Ash gasped out again. "More."

"Since you beg so nicely," Linford said, and finally, he began getting Ash off properly.

A hand on his cock, two fingers pressed against his prostate, Ash could only moan and choke out curses and pleas as Linford pushed him to the edge. Right as Ash thought he was about to come, Linford stopped.

"You're more than just a little sadistic," Ash accused in between heaving breaths.

Linford laughed and trailed a finger down his hard cock. "I think you like it," he mused, and he wasn't wrong.

But nadirs had weapons of their own too. "Sir, I need you in me," Ash pleaded, need infused in every syllable. "Please?"

Linford groaned and pushed up, body disappearing briefly. Ash heard the rasp of a package tearing, and then Linford was back, a heavy weight that settled over Ash. He pushed inside Ash with a single, smooth move, and it was almost too much. The sensation made Ash thump his head back against the pillow, and he pulled against the ropes holding him down, wishing he could touch.

But still, Linford didn't do enough to make either of them come. He moved slowly, stopping for long moments of time that made Ash want to curse him out again.

"I had no idea," he said, "that it was possible to be both masochistic and sadistic at the same time."

Linford laughed and pulled out, before pushing back in, striking his prostate directly. "You're a bit of a brat, aren't you, darling?"

"Was"—a moan from another hard thrust—"was that not clear?"

"You're sweet too. I think I like the combination." And then there was no more talking as Linford *finally* stopped teasing them both.

Ash came in a burst of pleasure and saw stars in the dark. Linford followed him over the edge soon after. They rested, breaths coming in hard and Linford a comforting weight pinning Ash down. With a groan, Linford slid out of Ash. He freed Ash's hands and undid the blindfold with deft fingers.

"I love your fingers," Ash mumbled.

Linford grinned and kissed him. "Let me clean up. I'll be right back."

He rubbed the blurriness out of his eyes and watched Linford pull off the sleeve for his cock that made clean up easier, disposing of it in the trash. Linford disappeared into the bathroom and came back with a warm washcloth, settling in beside Ash to wipe them both clean.

Ash had allowed his eyes to drift shut as he enjoyed the aftercare when he heard a rumble. He opened his eyes and met a large golden eye staring back at them through the window. Ash yelled and scrambled to the side, nearly pushing both of them off the bed.

"What?" Linford demanded, and then he groaned. "See? This is why I can't hold down a relationship." Laughter broke out of both of them, and Linford set the washcloth to the side, pulling the duvet over Ash as he stood and grabbed a few things from the corner. Dressing with one hand, Linford placed a file on the side table. "Let me see what Brym wants. Here. For you to look over if you think you want a life regularly interrupted by needy dragons."

Ash lifted the folder and opened it to see the beginnings of the contract. Six-month preliminary period, with the option to renew afterward if they both wanted this relationship.

He couldn't sign now, not when he was sex-dazed and flooded by endorphins. However, Ash was pretty sure that when morning came and the trial scene officially ended, he'd scrawl his name in the free space.

A life of silver and dragons?

He couldn't wait.

7

The Diamond Chalice by Zelena Hope

Princess Cascadia squeezed her twin sister's hand tightly as her heart pounded in her chest. White noise buzzed in her ears. She felt as though she were underwater, the world around her distant and insubstantial. Only her twin's hand kept her anchored to the shore.

"Simply put," Laine said as she turned away to address the Healer that had been speaking for the last ten or so minutes, "our Father has been put into an enchanted sleep?"

The Healer bowed. "Yes, Your Highness. This particular enchantment, however, is quite rare and its cure near impossible to find."

"Impossible?" Cascadia stopped staring at her sister's hand and looked up to stare at the Healer. "What's the cure?"

The Healer looked between the two princesses, taking in their stern looks, and spoke hesitantly. "Legend speaks of a Diamond Chalice, hidden somewhere inside the Great Forest. The Chalice, once filled with water and drunk by the person most in need of it, will end any enchantment."

"Then, we need to go get it," Laine said matter-of-factly.

"Wait." The Healer held up a large hand. "The Forest only allows those whom it deems worthy to find the Chalice. Three—and only three—attempts are allowed. Should anyone fail all three chances, the Chalice will be forever hidden from them. Without it, your father will surely die."

"*Die?*" Cascadia took a step back, horrified. "Father will die if we can't find this Chalice?"

The Healer looked at her. "Yes. The enchantment is robbing him of life even now. I believe he has a month at most."

Laine and Cascadia looked at each other, their expressions saying more than words ever could.

"Well then," Laine spoke at last, "we need to start looking straight away."

* * *

Retiring to their shared living area, Laine moved around with a speed Cascadia found nauseating.

The room was decorated in warm earthy browns and greens that beautifully completed the exposed oak beams and stone walls. Cascadia sat curled up in a dark, hardwood chair, softened with leather cushions.

"Laine, are you sure about this?" Cascadia asked gently. "You don't know the Forest as I do."

"I may not be the hunter you are, but I know my way around a forest. Have some faith."

"I do," Cascadia insisted, "but this is going to test us and I'm not sure if we really know what we're getting ourselves into." Cascadia ran her hands over the arms of the chair. "I wish I could go with you."

Laine chuckled. "Sorry, but you know as well I do that, as the older one, you have to stay behind."

"I know," Cascadia huffed, "but that doesn't mean I have to like it. There has to be another way to save Father."

Laine paused in her packing to gaze at her sister. "Cas, did you listen to a word the Healer said?"

"I tried. Nothing feels real. It was a bit a blur." Cascadia turned her head away. A world without her father to guide her—Cascadia didn't want to imagine it. "This is scarier than riding headfirst into danger and taking stupid risks with my life."

Laine looked at her kindly. "Trust me, this is the only way—the only chance—we have at saving Father."

Uncurling herself from her seat, Cascadia rose and walked over to where her sister stood, eyes flicking over Laine's figure, needing to commit every inch to memory. She was so scared that she would lose not only her father but her sister as well.

Laine was a few inches taller than Cascadia and preferred to keep her kinky hair natural, a cloud of obsidian curls floating around her head. Unlike Laine, Cascadia kept her own kinky hair in thick braids, entwined with gold rings and blue topaz gemstones.

Both as dark as the raven, the sisters looked more like their father than their mother, with sharp cheekbones and strong jaws. Or so they had been told. Their mother had passed away during childbirth and neither twin had ever seen so much as a picture of her.

"Please," Cascadia said, taking Laine's hands in her own, "come home safe."

"I will." Laine pressed a fond kiss to her sister's forehead. "I promise."

* * *

As the golden rays of dawn touched the kingdom, Laine had begun her journey to the Great Forest. From past trips, Laine knew it should take Vidal, her dark grey thoroughbred, only a few days to reach the Forest.

Laine had never been inside the Forest alone before. Cascadia was the natural huntress between them. Much to everyone's bemusement, Cascadia had become an unofficial Huntsman and would often leave for days, returning with blood-stained jerkins and boots, and a satisfied grin on her lips.

Laine had dressed practically. Instead of her typical billowy, long-sleeved dresses, she had opted for a long dark green skirt and a matching dark green bodice with fine silver beading.

Laine had also tucked a small dagger into her soft brown leather boots. It never hurt to be prepared.

After two days in the saddle, Laine finally reached the edge of the Great Forest. The Forest was the largest in the known kingdoms and bordered several of them. As deep as it was wide, the Forest was a challenge for even the best Huntsmen.

Turning her head towards the sky, Laine decided that the practical thing to do would be to make camp and begin the search for the Chalice in earnest tomorrow—the night was setting in fast.

Dismounting her horse, Laine chose where to step carefully. Underfoot were small stones that littered the first several hundred yards of the forest. It would be easy to twist an ankle.

Eventually, Laine found firmer ground, tied her horse to a redwood tree, and set about collecting dry wood to build a fire. Busying herself with making camp, Laine could easily forget her loneliness. Laine had brushed away offers of help from the Huntsmen. The King was her father. It was her responsibility to find the cure and save him.

Still, she mused as she filled the small cooking pot with water, it would have been nice to have some company.

* * *

"Hold, Princess."

Laine had been riding for the better part of the day when she first heard the voice of whoever had spoken. Looking quickly around her, Laine could not spot the speaker...

"Hello?"

"What troubles you to travel so far from home, Princess?" A branch shook in front of her, revealing the face of an Imp through the rich green leaves.

Laine blinked in shock. Never before had she seen a creature like this. It was one thing to know they existed, quite another to come face to face with one.

"My father has been put into a deadly enchanted sleep," Laine explained. "I am here searching for the Chalice that can save him."

"Ah." The Imp leaned forwards, revealing a soft golden face with amber eyes. "A noble reason indeed."

The way the Imp looked at her unnerved Laine, and she twisted the reins of her horse around in her hands as she fixed a smile on her face. "Well, if that's all, I had best be off."

"Two paths lie ahead of you," the Imp informed her, a sly smile on its face. "Choose the right one and it will take you straight to the Chalice. Choose the wrong one and you will spend your days riding through the Forest for the rest of time."

"Thank you," Laine said with a smile, "but your advice is not needed. I know the way."

The Imp threw back its head and laughed. "Good luck, Princess."

Laine pushed down the sudden fear that she had just made a terrible mistake as the Imp winked at her and then vanished from sight. She could *do* this, Laine told herself firmly. No matter what happened, she could—would find the Chalice.

* * *

A day later and Laine was growing frustrated. The Forest was just so *huge*. Hidden dips, large tree roots, caves—there were so many places one could hide a Chalice. Laine wanted to scream about how unfair this all was. Every day she was away from home was a day less for her father to live. Not to mention Cascadia, who was still at home. What would her sister do if she were left all alone in the world?

No, she would return home at any cost. Laine vowed to herself that she would return to her twin and save their father.

Laine straightened her shoulders as she guided her horse into a trot. The sun was sinking low in the sky, casting long shadows through the trees, when Laine saw it: *a path*. Approaching cautiously, Laine weighed her options.

At first glance, the way looked like any other well-made dirt path. Laine dismounted, her legs aching from riding for so long. Once again, she marvelled at how Cascadia could do it so easily.

Stepping onto the path, Laine frowned. It felt firm. Suspiciously so. Kneeling down, Laine wiped away the first layer of dirt. *Gold.* Underneath the first layer of dirt, the path was made of large slabs of gold. Enough gold to enrich her kingdom for generations. There were enough gold slabs that she would not even have to give them all to the kingdom. Not only that, with gold came jewels. The ability to buy whatever she wanted. Standing, Laine thought hard. If she rode over the path, she could damage the gold, lowering its value. Would that matter though if she were trapped inside the infernal Forest forever?

Staring down the path, Laine tried to imagine herself riding over the gold. She couldn't risk devaluing it. "We'll find another path." Laine quickly remounted her horse and, with one final look at the golden slabs, turned away and rode deeper into the Forest.

In a nearby oak tree, the Imp shook its head sadly.

* * *

"A week has passed and there has been no sign of Laine returning." Cascadia's voice didn't waver as she strode around her bed-chamber, packing the items she would need for her trip into the Forest.

"Princess," Boone, Cascadia's most trusted Huntsman, said as he rubbed a large, calloused hand over his face, "if you leave, the kingdom will be without a leader."

"Nonsense." Cascadia swept her long braided hair over her shoulder as she paused mid-stride to gaze at Boone. "You and Advisor Laken will take over doing the day-to-day duties with the other advisors assisting when necessary."

Boone frowned, his features taking on a quizzical look that she knew so well. "With all due respect—"

"You're going to be fine," Cascadia assured him, returning to her packing. "I wouldn't have put you up for the job if I didn't believe you could do it."

"I think your confidence has been misplaced, I'm a Huntsman, not a ruler."

Cascadia smiled ruefully. "Words in which I have often described myself and yet..." She paused, holding a pair of thick leather boots close to her chest. "Yet, this past week has been an *experience*. I have found myself equal to the task of leading this kingdom and enjoyed it."

Boone smiled softly at her. "You were always more than what you claimed to be."

"So are you." She placed the boots into the bag with a hand and made shooing motions with the other hand. "Go," she said, the hint of a smile on her lips. "I need to change."

"As you wish, my princess." Boone bowed deeply, closing the door firmly behind him.

* * *

The thundering of hooves rang out through the stone covered palace courtyard as Cascadia galloped away.

Pal, Cascadia's dark bay draught horse, ate up the leagues between the palace and the Forest, enjoying a chance to stretch his powerful legs. Cascadia patted Pal's neck lovingly as they rode together. This was what Cascadia loved the most: the feel of the wind rushing past her and the unknown ahead of her. The world made sense when she was in the saddle.

Cascadia stopped at her usual camping spots on her way to the Forest and noted with pride the signs that Laine had stopped in the same spots. Laine had listened to her advice after all.

As much as Cascadia enjoyed being on the road again, the twin fears of losing her father and her sister plagued her thoughts. No matter how hard she rode Pal, her mind never stopped buzzing with the heart-stopping fear that she could, in all likelihood, lose her entire family.

Without her family, Cascadia wasn't quite sure she knew who she was. Sitting cross-legged in front of the fire she had built, Cascadia swore to herself that she would not leave the Forest until she had her sister *and* the Chalice.

* * *

"Hold, Princess!"

Cascadia raised her hand to her eyes, squinting in the early afternoon sun. Searching for the location of the voice, Cascadia replied, "Hello and well met."

Between the branches of a large redwood tree in front of her, a set of amber eyes appeared. "Why is such a lovely princess so far from home?"

"Noble Imp, before I tell you my tale, may I ask for your name? I am Princess Cascadia of—"

The Imp cocked its head, considering her before cutting her off. "I know how you are." The Imp gazed at Cascadia a moment longer. "I am known by many names. Some are true and others are false. You, however, may call me Holokai."

"I'm honoured to meet you."

Holokai looked amused, a thin mouth appearing through the leaves, its face becoming more solid. Its skin was a light, earthy green, its hair seemingly made out of leaves.

Clutching at her heart, Cascadia gasped. She was not looking at an Imp but at the Spirit of the Forest. "Noble Holokai, I am here searching for a Chalice to save my Father. I am also searching for my sister, whom I fear has become lost in the Forest."

"Princess Laine."

"Yes! Have you seen her?"

"I have and she is safe," Holokai informed her. "As for the Chalice, that is not so easily found."

"I'm prepared to do whatever it takes to save my father's life." Cascadia squared her shoulders, her mouth going taut. "I will lay down my life if it means saving my Father."

"Brave words," Holokai noted with some mirth, "but words are not actions."

Cascadia opened her mouth to protest, but Holokai had vanished. "Come on, Pal." Cascadia patted Pal's strong shoulder. "Let's get moving."

Find Laine. Save Father.

The words repeated around her head, inescapable, unrelenting. By nightfall, Cascadia had made camp by one of the smaller rivers that flowed through the Forest. She struggled to find sleep that night.

The following morning dawned cold, the grass underfoot heavy with dew. Cascadia sullenly cleaned up after herself, her mood souring with the dawn of a new day.

Find Laine. Save Father.

By the time Cascadia was ready to mount Pal and begin the day's searching, the cold had turned into a summer thunderstorm. Rain poured down from the heavens and the already soft dirt began to turn into mud.

With the conditions worsening by the hour, Pal was unable to move faster than a walk. Mudslides were becoming common. Twice, Cascadia was forced out of the saddle to guide Pal safely away from danger.

Cascadia's hunter instincts screamed at her to find shelter, wait out the storm. She was risking her life as well as Pal's by continuing to struggle through the Forest.

Find Laine. Save Father.

There had been no obvious sign of Laine. No fires or campsites. No tracks. The thunderstorm wasn't helping. Any signs Laine could have left were being washed away.

Gritting her teeth, Cascadia encouraged Pal to jump a fallen tree. He landed heavily on his front legs, his hooves scrambling to find purchase.

"We can do this!" Cascadia tried to sound upbeat but knew she was pushing Pal close to his limits. "Come on." Squeezing her knees together, she managed to get a disgruntled Pal to move up to a careful canter.

Shielding her face with her arm, Cascadia was forced to duck to miss tree branches that seemed to appear from nowhere. Mud splattered her thighs and Pal's neck and still, Cascadia urged Pal on. The rain came down harder until all that could be seen was a solid wall of rain.

Cascadia screamed with frustration. Tears born from anger and hopelessness pricked at her eyes. She couldn't fail. Laine was still missing. Her Father was still dying.

Breaking into a sob, Cascadia buried her face in Pal's neck. She wrapped her arms around her oldest friend and gave in to her tears. Pal nickered, his ears flattening as Cascadia wept.

Several long moments passed while it seemed the only sounds in the Forest were Cascadia's tears and the drumming of the rain pounding into the ground.

As Cascadia collected herself, wiping her eyes harshly with the back of her hands, Holokai watched, saddened.

"Come on, Pal." Cascadia had dismounted, lost and forlorn—a lone figure encased in mud, "Let's find shelter."

* * *

Laine was trapped in a nightmare. Every path she rode down led back to the path with golden slabs. She was sure that days had passed since she had first made her choice and yet nothing around her had changed. The same gnarled tree with twisted branches appeared every time she turned away from the gold. In less than half a day, Laine found her back at the start.

Over and over again, the same path. The same choice. Laine knew, outside of her bubble, Cascadia would soon begin to worry, that her Father could already be dead.

The path came back into view again. Laine swore under her breath. Curling her fists at her side, Laine tried again, taking the dirt road to the left of the path. Vidal whinnied in protest, his strength the only thing that had remained constant.

"We have to keep trying," Laine insisted. "We have to." Vidal snorted but broke into a canter, following the path that led them, once more, back to the golden path. Cascadia would've chided her for being so stubborn. Not that her twin had much of a leg to stand on; Cas could be just as stubborn—if not more so.

"OK," Laine said, growing tired of this game, "two more times." Vidal shook his head and pawed at the ground. "Twice more and then we'll go the other way."

* * *

Cascadia stared out at the rain. She had found shelter in a nearby cave. Her first concern was to make sure Pal kept warm, and so had wrapped him in a blanket as soon as she could. Crossing her arms over her chest, she paced the small cave. Pal watched with one open eye, pretending to sleep.

"I'm sorry," Cascadia knelt beside him, bowing her head. "I pushed you too hard. I risked our lives and that was a mistake." She ran her hands over his flank. "I'm so sorry."

Pal twisted his neck, resting his head on Cascadia's shoulder. His breath tickling her ear.

"We'll leave in the morning," Cascadia decided. "The rain can't last forever, and we'll be careful. I promise."

* * *

Laine pursed her lips, head raised towards the sky. "Alright," she said, her voice resigned. "Alright, who needs a wealthy kingdom anyway?"

She gripped Vidal's reins tightly as she stared down the gold path. "Let's go."

Finally agreeing with Laine's actions, Vidal raced eagerly across the path at a gallop.

"You're smarter than I am, huh?" Laine laughed. Vidal let out a soft nicker.

New parts of the Forest sprang up as Laine and Vidal reached the end of the golden slabs. Taking a left, Laine felt her confidence return. She was going to find the Chalice and save her father.

She *knew* it.

* * *

The rain had eased somewhat, much to Cascadia's relief. Walking Pal out of the cave, Cascadia stretched her back. Her pride and recklessness had cost her precious time in searching for the Chalice and her sister. She needed to make up for it somehow without falling back into bad habits.

The rain had made the ground treacherous. Fallen branches and broken roots covered the ground.

"Let's walk," Cascadia decided, dismounting Pal. "I'll guide you."

* * *

Laine crested a grassy hill, and paused, scanning for anything that could help her find the Chalice when she spotted a familiar sight.

"Cascadia!" Her sister did not look up. Instead, she carried on walking her horse, Pal, each step slow and laboured. Cas looked rough and Laine itched to know why.

"Well, if she won't come to me..." Laine muttered. Vidal snorted in agreement and took off at a trot, following the hill down and towards the plain.

* * *

The rain continued to ease as Cascadia guided Pal through the Forest. "When I get home, and Father is well again, I am not leaving the palace for a *month*."

Pal bumped her shoulder with his nose.

"You agree, huh?" Cascadia carefully hopped over a tree trunk. "Come around the side, no jumping."

Cascadia chose to imagine the sarcastic look that crossed Pal's face. "I should have done this from the beginning. I should have taken better care of you."

"My wayward sister being reckless and headstrong. Gee, that sounds strange."

"Laine!" Cascadia dropped Pal's reins and spun on her heel, throwing her arms around her sister. "How did you survive the storm? Where have you been?"

"What storm?" Laine pulled back, puzzled.

"The thunderstorm." Cascadia's brows knitted together. "Oh."

"Oh?"

"Did you find yourself trapped?"

"I—yes. How did you know?"

"The Forest." Cascadia stepped back and let out a laugh. "It's the *Forest*."

"Shall we trade stories while we search for the Chalice?"

"I have a better idea. It's time we started asking the Forest for help."

Laine wrinkled her nose. "I've never liked asking for help." Laine took Cascadia's hand gently. She had been reunited with her sister. Anything was possible, even finding the Chalice.

"Don't I know it," Cascadia teased, "but this is for Father, and it's time we both shelved our pride. For him."

Laine sighed. "What's your plan?"

Cascadia grinned. "This." Cascadia stepped away from her sister, noticing for the first time that the rain that had been plaguing her had vanished.

"Noble Imp, Holokai, Spirit of the Forest, we humbly ask for your help."

"The Imp?" Laine's surprise was clear on her face, then, "Oh." Laine chewed on her bottom lip thoughtfully. "If we ever escape this Forest, we have to promise to do better."

"I don't have to wait until then—Laine, I'm so sorry."

"I am too."

The sisters embraced, resting heads on each other's shoulders. After a moment, they pulled back.

"Ready to try again?" Laine asked.

"Yes."

A wind picked up around them, forcing them to stagger back, arms raised to shield their faces. Once the wind had died down, they lowered their arms.

"Holokai," Cascadia breathed, delighted. "You honour us." The two women bowed at the Imp.

"You asked for me by name and so here I am." Holokai sat on Vidal, hands locked together. Holokai smiled at the two women. "Your search is nearly over. The Chalice awaits, though I hasten to warn you both: never forget what you learned in this Forest."

"We won't," Laine spoke up. "Gold isn't everything. There is more than

186

one way to make a kingdom prosper." She gazed at Cascadia. "I risked losing my sister and my Father, all because I wouldn't ride over gold."

"Oh, Laine." Cascadia shook her head. "The kingdom is fine. We're going to be fine."

"I see that now."

"Good." Holokai pointed north. "Find the plinth by the brook and you shall find the Chalice."

"Thank you," Cascadia said, "for everything."

* * *

"There it is." Laine leaned forward in the saddle. "I pray Father is still holding on."

"He has to be," Cascadia said, dismounting. "Come on, together."

The Diamond Chalice sat upon a plinth made of black marble. The brook itself was hidden by a thicket, one they would have easily passed had Holokai not told them to be on the lookout for it.

For such an incredible and powerful item, the Chalice was remarkably small. The stem was embedded with rare jewels that sparkled and glinted in the afternoon sun.

Picking up the Chalice with shaking fingers, the sisters gazed in amazement at each other. At last, they held between them the cure for their father.

* * *

Arms wrapped around each other, Cascadia and Laine watched as the Healer filled the Chalice with water and pressed it to the King's open mouth. The King's breathing had been heavily laboured and Cascadia had found herself counting every one.

The Healer stepped back and silence descended over the room. The King shuddered and gasped.

Fingers dug tightly into arms as the sisters' grip on each other tightened painfully, though neither complained.

The King coughed before finally opening his eyes. Seeing her father blink, Cascadia felt as though she had come up for air after swimming too long underwater. Her face felt wet and with a jolt, she realised Laine was silently crying, her tears falling on Cascadia's face and mixing with her own. The

NOT SO GRIMM: NEW TAKES ON OLD TALES

relief they both felt was unmistakable.

They were moving before they even knew it, kneeling by the King's side and basking in the fact that he was *alive*.

"What," the King said in between coughs, his voice rough, "is all this fuss for?"

Years later, when their father had passed of natural causes, the twins made good on their vow to do better. Cascadia and Laine ruled together, ensuring that they both ruled justly and fairly. Each kept the other's flaws in check. Under them, the kingdom entered a new golden age of joy and prosperity.

Author's Note by Zelena Hope

Over the last two days, I've written and rewritten this author's note. I wanted to keep it small, so it wouldn't distract from the story too much. That is part of the problem—Black voices keeping quiet through fear of not wanting to upset the apple cart.

It's time to not only upset the cart but to throw it over.

If you haven't been able to tell by the list of author names, some of us are white. Some of us are Asian. Quite a few of us are non-white in the same way. Most of us identify as female, but not all. We're a diverse group of writers coming together to share stories with the world.

I'm lucky. I was born to a black father and white mother. My privilege is the protection my white genes afford me. I have never and will never have to go through the kind of racist nonsense my father has in his lifetime.

It's time that changed.

By reading this book you are supporting LGBTQIA+ authors and non-white authors. Our lives matter. My life matters. Black lives matter.

If for some reason, you are someone who says, "All Lives Matter" or "Blue Lives Matter", then, my love, you are part of the problem.

Below is a list of names. Writing this out was the hardest part of this note. I cried more than once.

Not all these people were killed by the police. Some were killed because they were black women. Some died because they were black and trans. Heartbreakingly, one of these people was not only killed but violated. A gruesome murder, just because they were different.

I'm tired of seeing lists like this. Aren't you? If a person is killed, then justice should follow. Everyone, no matter their skin colour or gender, should feel safe to go to the police. Everyone should feel protected by those meant to protect and serve.

All the people listed below have died, too young. Too soon. Right now, there are people dying. This is just a handful of names. Look them up. Remember them. They were sons and daughters, brothers and sisters, aunts and uncles, mothers and fathers.

Say their names. Say her name. Say it loud and with pride. Their lives mattered. **Black** Lives Matter.

Merci Mack. Riah Milton. Dominique Fells. Brayla Stone. Vanessa Guillen. George Floyd. Breonna Taylor. Kevan Ruffin. Rayshard Brooks. Michael Thomas. Kamal Flowers. David McAtee. Ruben Smith. Dion Johnson. Willie Quarles. Finan Berhe. Nia Wilson. Bree Black. Lavena Johnson. Sophia King. Keisha Williams. Charmene Pickering. Eloise Spellman. Shantel Davis. McHale Rose. Toby Wiggins.

Content Warnings

The Golden One and the Miller's Son: none

Breath of Roses: none

The Fisherman's Catch: none

Meadowsweet, Woodbine, and Lavender: This story contains partner-sharing between siblings (but no incest).

The Tower Girls: none

Of Silver and Dragons: This story contains elements of BDSM and explicit sex.

The Diamond Chalice: none

CPSIA information can be obtained
at www.ICGtesting.com
Printed in the USA
BVHW070719080920
588294BV00001B/37

9 781735 443058